FEAR THE DARK

FEAR THE DARK

KAY HOOPER

BERKLEY BOOKS, NEW YORK

BERKLEY

An imprint of Penguin Random House LLC
375 Hudson Street, New York, New York 10014

This book is an original publication of Penguin Random House LLC.

Library of Congress Cataloging-in-Publication Data

Hooper, Kay.
Fear the dark / Kay Hooper. — First edition.
p. cm.
ISBN 978-0-425-28072-0
1. Paranormal fiction. I. Title.
PS3558.O587F43 2015
813'.54—dc23
2015026605

FIRST EDITION: October 2015

PRINTED IN THE UNITED STATES OF AMERICA

10 9 8 7 6 5 4 3 2 1

Cover photo © Paul Knight / Trevillion Images.
Cover design by Rita Frangie.
Text design by Kristin del Rosario.

Penguin
Random
House

AUTHOR'S NOTE

Once again, and at the request of many readers, I have chosen to place this note at the beginning of the book rather than after the story, so as to better inform you of the additional material I am providing for both new readers and those who have been with the series from the beginning. You'll find some brief character bios, as well as standard SCU definitions of various psychic abilities, at the end of the book, plus a Special Crimes Unit "timeline," information that will hopefully enhance your enjoyment of this story and of the series. I hope you enjoy *Fear the Dark*.

FEAR THE DARK

PROLOGUE

Amy Grimes was bored with her life. She was bored with school, bored with her parents, bored with most of her friends, and had been well on the way to being bored with her boyfriend, Simon Church (of all things!), until he suggested that they just pack up and leave this very boring little town.

Amy was sensible enough even at seventeen to know that the suggestion had been prompted more by his failing grades in school and the six-pack of beer he'd polished off that night than any seriously deep feelings for her, but she discovered that she didn't really care what had prompted the suggestion.

It suited her just fine.

Simon had worked construction since his midteens, and Amy was only one credit away from earning her certificate as a beautician at the nearby community college, so she was confident they could support themselves. She had her college savings (fairly pitiful, which was why beauty school) and Simon had two weeks' pay in his pocket, and they decided that was enough to get started on.

Even after he'd sobered up, Simon was ready to leave Serenity and take Amy with him, even to the point of being willing to go along with her plans for a mysteriously secret buildup to their departure. She didn't confide even in her girlfriends, because she knew all too well that one of them was bound to blab to her older brother or one of theirs, and before you could say *scat* everybody in town would know.

Since Simon was eighteen and had a decent car in his name— courtesy of his parents—all paid off and insured and everything, they decided to take that. And for nearly a week, they had a lot of fun in gradually sneaking into his car those items they felt unable to leave without. There was a brief argument about Simon's flat-screen, but in the end he managed to make room and Amy agreed that they'd certainly need a TV wherever they landed.

Because that was the fun part, as far as she was concerned. No real plans. They'd just leave, and drive, and decide somewhere along the way where to settle—at least for a time.

"We'll stop in Pigeon Forge or Gatlinburg," she'd suggested to Simon, "and both write postcards to our families."

"Then just keep going," he said with some relish.

Amy nodded. "Then just keep going. We could head west, or north—wherever."

"And our parents probably won't even know we're gone until they get the postcards," Simon said.

Amy wasn't so sure about that, given her father's watchful eye, but she was still certain she could sneak out once her parents were in bed, and by morning she and Simon would be out of the reach of both sets of parents.

She was certain of that.

She just loved the idea that people would wake to find the two of them mysteriously vanished. She did spare a pang for the worry that would undoubtedly seize her parents but was certain a reassuring postcard in a couple of days would be enough to allay worry.

The plan was perfect. And over the course of just three days, they were somehow able to sneak their things from their respective houses and get everything in Simon's car without anyone the wiser. Three days, and they were ready to leave, Simon telling his parents casually that he was spending that Friday night with a friend because they'd planned a very early fishing trip in the morning, and Amy all set to just wait until her parents were in bed to sneak out and join her boyfriend at the appointed meeting place just down the block.

It wasn't until then that it crossed her mind that Simon hadn't said anything at all about getting married, but she shrugged that thought off with careless ease.

It would all work out just fine, she was sure of that. And their departure would certainly give everyone something to talk about for quite a while. A mystery to brighten their dull lives.

She had no trouble sneaking out of the house, and it was just after midnight that Friday night when she slid into the passenger side of Simon's Jeep.

"Ready?" he asked.

"Am I ever. Let's get out of here." Amy was looking forward to being, however briefly, a mystery in a town where nothing mysterious ever happened.

EVEN BARELY AWAKE, Jonah Riggs groaned as the phone on his nightstand shrilled a demand. He was tangled in the covers as usual but managed to maneuver himself over far enough to grab the phone and shut it up.

Lying back with his eyes closed, he muttered, "It better be good." He had gotten to bed somewhere near dawn after winning enormous imaginary sums at the monthly poker game the city fathers would have frowned upon—had they not been his opponents.

He didn't know what time it was, but his aching head and scratchy eyes said it was too damned early.

"Sorry, Chief, but there's something you need to see." Sarah Waters didn't sound all that sorry, but she was his lead detective, his second in command, and since she and his younger sister had played together in the sandbox, he was only mildly surprised she didn't offer a more colorful and less apologetic awakening.

"It's Saturday, Sarah. My day off. My first day off in three damned weeks. Can't you handle it?"

"No," she said simply.

That woke him up, because in her whole life, he'd never seen anything Sarah couldn't handle.

He fought free of the covers and sat on the edge of his bed, running his fingers through his hair. He needed a haircut. "What's going on?" he asked her.

She hesitated, then said, "It'll be easier if you just come see for yourself. Honest, Jonah, I wouldn't call you out here if I didn't think it was important."

He knew that. "Out where?"

"North side of town, off Main and about a hundred yards down Street."

That was actually the name of the street. Street. Jonah had wondered more than once if they'd just run out of names, or if somebody had been having fun and it just stuck.

"Okay," he said. "I'll be there in fifteen. Oh—Sarah? Are we talking about an actual crime?"

"I'm not quite sure," she replied.

He found that somewhat baffling but didn't waste time with more questions. "Okay, you know the drill. Keep everybody back away from whatever it is until I get there."

"Copy that."

Jonah hung up the phone, frowning, and headed for the shower, hoping enough hot water would clear his head. Because so far, this was hardly a normal Saturday morning.

It got stranger.

Jonah seldom wore a uniform, virtually always in jeans, clipping his badge to his belt near the front, wearing his gun on his right hip, and depending on the weather, either a T-shirt or sweatshirt or else a light Windbreaker over a button-up shirt.

This Saturday morning in May was cool but comfortable, the middle-of-the-night rainstorm hours past. But it was also supposed to be an off day for Jonah, so he wore a sweatshirt with the faded letters of Duke University across his chest.

He had stopped at a coffee shop in town *and* swallowed some aspirin, but his head didn't feel any better when he stopped his Jeep behind Sarah's cruiser and got out to join her.

She was leaning against the front of her cruiser, frowning at another Jeep, this one pulled more or less off the road, with both front doors standing open.

Jonah didn't see another soul about. Clearly, Sarah had decided against calling the station, for whatever reason. It wasn't a large police station or police force, and it was rare to see more than one officer or detective out on patrol.

"Isn't that Simon Church's Jeep?" he asked as he reached her.

"Yeah. I checked the registration and tag to be sure."

"So where is he?"

"The question of the day." Sarah eyed him. "You up for this?"

He grunted. "Depends on what *this* is. You gonna tell me, or shall I figure it out for myself?"

Unsmiling, she said, "Take a look inside the Jeep."

Jonah didn't argue, just moved forward, sticking to the paved-road side of the Jeep. He had already noted that there were no skid marks, and no sign that the vehicle had been forced off the road. No body damage he could see, and all four tires seemed fine.

He looked in the front passenger door, and a nameless dread began to crawl up his spine. The vehicle was packed with stuff. Not stuff one would expect if a robbery had been committed—despite the flat-screen TV. Packed in tight in the back were clothes, shoes, luggage presumably holding more of the same and . . . things.

A stuffed bear sat atop a stack of books, squeezed in beside a golf bag. There was a basket holding an odd assortment of things that included a dog's collar and leash, a can of WD-40, a laptop and tangle of cords and cables, a case holding CDs or DVDs, and a teapot.

Shirts and dresses and sweaters still on hangers were laid across luggage probably filled with the same sort of thing. There was what looked like a little sewing kit sitting atop a tackle box. There was a cooler of the sort most people used to transport adult beverages. There was another stuffed animal, this one a puffy cat, sitting atop a goldfish bowl where one lone fish swam rather desperately around in his shallow world.

Still bent forward and still without touching the car, Jonah turned his gaze to the front seat. Not much on the driver's side. A little open change niche filled with coins and gum wrappers and at least two petrified French fries.

On the passenger seat, very neatly in the center, sat a purse decorated all over with beads and fake gems. It was very colorful.

Jonah straightened and looked back at Sarah. "You checked the purse?"

"Yeah. Amy Grimes. Her driver's license is in a wallet that contains, I'm guessing, a few thousand dollars. I didn't want to disturb anything even with gloves, until you saw it all."

Jonah frowned at the Jeep another moment, then returned his gaze to Sarah. "All the earmarks of an elopement."

"Yeah, that's what I thought."

"But?"

"Well, they didn't get very far, that's one thing. I'm guessing Amy sneaked out of her house sometime after midnight; even at a crawl, they should have reached the highway before dawn."

Jonah glanced back toward town and silently agreed with her. Hell, even if they'd left at dawn, they should have gotten farther.

"Gas? They broke down?"

"Key's in the ignition, as you see. I cranked it up. Tank's full, and the engine seemed to be running fine."

Jonah looked over the inside once again, then walked back along the Jeep until he reached the bumper. He lifted his brows at his lead detective. "Both doors found open." It wasn't a question. "Pulled mostly off the road. A purse with money. Valuables in the back. And the key in the ignition, making it easy for somebody to steal the whole shebang."

Sarah nodded. "Now we come to the very weird part."

"*Now* we come to it?"

"Yeah." She stepped over onto the grassy verge and led the way just as far as the open driver's-side door. "Look down there."

There was no guardrail here, and the bank on the side of the road sloped gradually down to a flat area; from that, a vague path led toward a stand of trees while another vague path led off to the left, toward a distant creek. Neither of the paths was well traveled, just handy short-cuts, mostly for kids.

But right now both the bank and the flat area were more dirt than grass. Mud, since the rainstorm hours before.

Very clearly, two sets of footprints were visible going down the bank and to the flat area. One larger set, probably boots; one much smaller set, undoubtedly a woman or girl.

The prints were absolutely perfect, showing no slipping or sliding. The bootprints and shoeprints were side by side down the bank, to the flat. Where they stopped.

Where they just . . . stopped.

That wordless dread was growing in Jonah. "You've been down there?"

"Yeah. I stayed away from the prints, circled. There's nothing, Jonah. And there *should* be. All around the place where the prints stop, there would have been prints if they'd gone on. There's no way they could have jumped far enough, and no sign at all they did. No sign of a vehicle, no sign of a horse. No sign of a third person. I'd dare anybody to back up that bank, putting their feet in exactly the same spots as when they went down; it's slippery as hell and there's nothing to hold on to." She drew a breath and let it out slowly. "If this is a prank, it's a damned good one. But I don't think it's a prank. I think those two kids walked down that bank to the flat area—and something happened."

"Something took them," he said slowly.

Sarah nodded. "That's the only thing I could think of. It's like something just swooped down and carried them away. And judging by the footprints, they had to be lifted cleanly, straight up. No sign of a struggle. No sign of a fight. There are houses close enough to hear if someone had screamed. Even in the middle of the night." Without turning, she jerked her head back and toward the other side of the road. "Mildred Bates is watching us from her front porch now; she sleeps with her windows open and the slightest sound wakes her. Her bedroom windows face this way. Less than fifty yards from here to there. If there had been any kind of a commotion, she would have heard—and called us. She didn't."

"So, where are those kids?" Jonah said slowly. "And how the hell did they just . . . vanish?"

Jonah didn't voice what he felt, that what they were looking at was not exactly an ending—but the beginning of something. The beginning of something bad. The beginning of something that was going to shake his town to its foundations.

ONE

There was no hope at all of keeping the disappearance of Amy Grimes and Simon Church quiet, Jonah knew that. In fact, he expected to find both sets of parents in his office when he returned to the station. But that didn't mean he couldn't do whatever was possible to minimize the . . . strangeness of all this while he tried to figure it out.

"Okay," he said, after considering the matter. "Roust Tim out of bed and get the station's tow truck out here. I don't much like moving the car, but I sure as hell don't want to leave it just sitting, and we don't have the manpower to guard it."

"I'll tell him to hurry," Sarah said calmly.

Jonah eyed her. "Left him in bed sleeping, did you?"

"Not that it's any of your business—Chief—but, yes, I did. It's his day off too."

Jonah didn't forbid his people to get involved romantically; he was a realist. And he preferred openness to sneaking around. Not that Sarah or Tim, both sensible professionals, had made it obvious, but Jonah knew, and he figured if he knew then everyone else did too.

"Well, tell him I'm sorry, but it can't be helped. We need to get this car into the police garage, pronto."

"Copy. Want to call Sully and get his dogs out here?"

"I doubt there'll be time before we get a downpour. We'll just have to wait and hope we get a lead. Maybe the dogs will come in useful then."

"What'll you tell their parents?"

"Damned if I know. Lie through my teeth, probably. Or just say what little we're reasonably sure of. Say the kids were clearly eloping, must have had car trouble—and we're investigating the rest."

"And how are we investigating the rest?"

"Get the good camera out of the back of my Jeep and start taking pictures. The car, the way it was left, that bank. The footprints. You know the drill, Sarah."

"Copy that. I take it you'd rather no one else saw the scene as we found it."

"I'd rather, yeah. Call Tim, and wait till he gets here. He won't have to be told, but remind him nobody but the three of us will know about how the car was left and the footprints until I say different. Once you have the pictures and he has the car, both of you get back to the station. I'd also rather nobody too nosy just wandered out here to see what was going on."

"Mildred Bates has been watching."

"Yeah, I can feel her eyes boring into my back. But she can't see over the edge of the bank even with binoculars, she's virtually immobile with that cast since she wrenched her knee, and I don't expect even her to come out here, especially once the car is moved. With a little luck, once the car is moved she won't wonder if there's anything else *to* see out here."

"Like the footprints?"

"Exactly."

A rumble of thunder made them both look up at dark clouds rolling in.

"Shit," Jonah said. "Weather's coming in faster than the forecast. Get those pictures, Sarah. Close the car doors. And when Tim heads back to the station with the car, you follow. If there's a little more luck for me today, the rain will wash away those footprints before anybody else sees them, and nobody will realize something very weird happened here."

"Hope you got a lot of luck stored up," Sarah said as she headed for the back of Jonah's Jeep. "I've got an awful hunch we're going to need every bit of it."

Since it wasn't raining yet, Jonah walked farther up the road a stretch, just to see if anything else looked odd, but found nothing. And no sign that a car had pulled off the road. In this area, the weeds pretty much ran right up to the road, trimmed back later in the year; in May even the hardiest of weed was hardly more than a foot tall.

Giving that up, Jonah returned to the abandoned car. Thunder rumbled again. "Hurry," he called out to Sarah, who was near the bottom of the bank, placing a ruler beside each footprint before she photographed it.

"Yeah." She didn't look up. "Meet you back at the station."

Jonah wanted more hot coffee, lots of it, and he wanted breakfast. He had a feeling he'd need to be fortified. He got in his Jeep and headed for town, pretending not to see Mildred Bates beckoning imperiously to him. Sarah must have used her cell while he'd been checking out the road to call Tim, and lit a fire under him to get here in a hurry, because Jonah passed the police tow truck, lifting a hand to Tim as they came abreast but not slowing.

The small downtown diner, simply named the Diner, hadn't been open long this morning; Jonah was the first one to take a seat on a stool at the counter, and the booths were all empty. The coffee was just beginning to percolate.

He wished it would hurry.

He didn't waste time calling out his usual breakfast order, hearing an acknowledgment yelled from the back. A glance at his watch told him he still had time before the usual breakfast crowd arrived. The waitresses hadn't even arrived yet. But then he noticed something odd.

"Hey, Clyde? Is your clock right?"

The owner/operator, who usually cooked and was fixing Jonah's eggs and bacon in the kitchen, popped his head into the opening where the waitresses picked up orders. "What? Loud back here, Jonah."

Loud because he played country music on an old CD player. He favored Johnny Cash and Waylon Jennings.

"Your clock." Jonah raised his voice and nodded toward the clock that hung in a place of prominence on the wall behind the cash register. Clyde had gotten it on his honeymoon, apparently having stopped at some point at one of those touristy places along the side of the road that sold novelty items.

The big clock boasted an eagle, its gradually unfolding left and right wings showing the time. Most thought but never said that it was a peculiar-looking bird, especially at certain times when the wings were sort of cockeyed.

Clyde was very proud of it.

"My clock? What about it?"

"Time right?"

"Yeah, I set it when I came in this morning. Used my cell phone." He vanished back into the kitchen before Jonah's bacon burned and before Waylon could get to the chorus.

Jonah looked at the big watch on his wrist for a moment. It had stopped. It never stopped, warning him when new batteries were needed, and he'd just put in fresh ones barely two weeks ago. It was more of a sportsman's watch, with more than one dial so he knew his current elevation, and the time in another country if he wished, and he could also use the device as a stopwatch.

Not digital.

Staring at the still face and keeping the time on Clyde's clock in mind, then as far as he could remember the time it showed would have been just about when he'd reached the abandoned car and the mysteries surrounding it. It was also showing zero elevation when the town was several thousand feet above sea level.

He stared at it for a moment, then fished for his cell phone and checked the time. It appeared to be still working normally, showing the correct date. But . . .

The time on the cell was off by more than half an hour. Pretty close to the amount of time he'd spent out at Simon Church's abandoned car.

"Well, shit," he said under his breath.

———————

"WHERE COULD THEY have gone?" Monica Church twisted a hand-kerchief in her hands anxiously. Long married to a man who, if he had deep feelings about anything, never showed them, she tended to be emotional enough for both of them. She also tended to dress in simple, elegant outfits that usually stood out in Serenity, which was more of a jeans-and-sweatshirt sort of town.

The pretty spring dress she wore now, colorful and a bit filmy, would have looked more in place in a larger town and warmer weather. But neither ever seemed to dictate Monica's choices. Gossip said she had found a man who showed her more attention than her husband, but if said lover had been identified, Jonah hadn't heard about it.

"Told you they were going to elope," Ed Church said, taciturn as always, and casual as always in jeans and a black T-shirt. "Been obvious for weeks. No sense in trying to stop them."

"But something *did* stop them." Monica's reddened eyes turned to Jonah's face. "Mildred Bates called me and told me she saw the police tow truck taking Simon's car toward town."

Of course she did.

"Where is my son, Chief?"

Jonah sighed as he leaned forward in his chair, elbows on his cluttered blotter. He was expecting the second set of parents any minute now. "I'll tell you what I can, but let's wait for Stuart and Sue Grimes; they called they were on their way."

Five loudly silent minutes later, the other set of parents burst in. Sue Grimes was every bit as emotional as Monica, but not crying and not neat; she was wearing pale slacks and a bright pink blouse that was buttoned wrong and *almost* matched her almost neon lipstick. Which had clearly been applied in haste. One eyebrow was darker than the other as well, and her blond hair didn't look as if it had seen a comb since at least the night before.

Jonah wasn't tempted to laugh. Much.

Stuart Grimes wasn't as taciturn as Ed Church, nor could he claim the other man's lazy stillness. Stuart waved his arms a lot. And his voice was loud most of the time.

Jonah took in those details automatically, saving what amusement or annoyance he found in them for later.

"Where are they, Jonah?" Stuart Grimes demanded. "Where are the kids? Why was Simon's car towed back to town, and why is it in the police garage now?"

Jonah was accustomed to the fact that many people in town called him casually by his first name, just as many used his title. It didn't really matter to him.

"If you'll just sit down, Stuart, you and Sue, I'll tell you as much as I know." Which was a lie but a necessary one. The only saving grace he personally found in the situation was that these two couples were friends all the way back to high school, and it was unlikely that either set of parents would blame the other set's kid for . . . whatever.

Small comfort.

He decided to start with blunt information, not because he was a cruel man, but because he knew the bottom line would have to be reached, and he preferred to reach it sooner than later.

"The kids are missing," he told their parents, keeping his voice matter-of-fact. "We have no evidence that anything happened to them, no signs of a struggle, nothing else to indicate they were taken away by force."

Monica let out a sob into her handkerchief.

"And Simon's Jeep?" his father asked. "It was in perfect working order."

Jonah nodded. "As far as we can tell, that's entirely true. There was gas in the tank, the tires were fine, it cranked easily when we tried it. Still, I have my best people going over it inch by inch to see if there's something not so obvious that might have stopped it."

With ominous timing, a loud boom of thunder rattled the windows, and it really let go outside, raining heavily.

Jonah hoped Sarah had been able to get all the pictures she could, because there sure as hell wouldn't be anything remotely resembling evidence at the scene when the storm passed.

"Were they eloping?" Sue Grimes demanded, showing less emotion except for the fierceness in her eyes and voice.

Jonah answered honestly. "Looks like it. The back of the Jeep was packed full of everything from clothes and a golf bag to a big screen and a goldfish bowl." He felt compelled to add, "I had one of my people get the fishbowl out and bring it up to this floor, to the lounge."

He didn't add that the solitary fish had seemed much more relaxed with more water in his bowl—and a bowl that was not in motion. He made a note to ask his people to look for fish food in the car.

In his usual lazy voice, Ed Church said, "We got the car was pulled off the main road, doors open, engine off. Robbery?"

Jonah wondered if Mildred Bates had a zoom-lens camera. Maybe they should have asked her for photos.

Maybe they would, before this was over with.

Shaking his head, Jonah said, "I don't see how. Too many valuables left in the car." He looked at Sue Grimes. "Amy's purse was in the front seat, undisturbed. There's several thousand dollars in her billfold. I had it and everything in the purse printed just to be sure; lotta smudges on the money, but otherwise no prints except Amy's."

Every student entering high school in Serenity got an ID with photo and fingerprints as a matter of both school and town policy.

He added, "Jean's holding it for you at the front desk; you can pick it up when you leave. I doubt it has any value as evidence."

Stuart Grimes said, "Where are the kids? It's not like there's a romantic trail off the side of the road to tempt them to stop. *Where did they go?*"

Jonah kept his voice even. "I don't know, Stuart. At this point, all I can tell you is what I have told you. The car was pulled off the road, doors left standing open, personal items and other valuables left in the car. Key in the ignition but engine off. And the kids gone."

"You didn't find a fucking *clue*? Not a footprint or anything to tell you what happened to the kids?" Stuart all but shouted.

"I didn't find anything that told me what happened," Jonah replied, honestly. "Maybe friends came by and picked them up, for whatever reason. Maybe they set out walking—for whatever reason—and stuck to the pavement so they didn't leave prints." He finished with that lie without a blink. "Look, when it comes to missing people, it's still early yet. We have to start calling their friends—we'll need your info and probably your help for that—and see if any of them have information worth sharing."

Or are willing to talk.

"And then?" Stuart demanded.

"Let's cross that bridge when we get there. The most likely explanation is that one of their friends knows where they are, and that they're somewhere waiting out the rain. So we start calling their friends."

"And then?" Stuart demanded again.

Jonah had never responded well to bullies, but his job had taught him to at least be calm. "Stuart, as I said, we'll take this a step at a time, following the procedures for missing persons. While this storm is pounding us and most of the other kids are either at home or with friends, we have an excellent opportunity to make phone calls. I assume you're all willing to help?"

"Of course." It was snapped almost in unison by everyone but Monica, who merely sobbed again.

"Okay, you all know the conference room is next door. There are several phones as well as legal pads and pens. Coffee too. I called before I got here and had two of the high school yearbooks left in there. Stuart is a senior and Amy a junior, so you can divide up the list like that if you want; even if you don't know names, look for faces you've seen with your kids more than others. However you choose is fine with me. Just please write down who you call and what they said. Jean's getting a list from the school with phone numbers, home and cell."

And it was a good thing Jean and Jack Rollins, the school principal, were . . . very good friends. He'd been willing to leave his coffee and his snug, dry house and slosh out to the high school for numbers he'd fax back to the police station.

There were, Jonah had thought many times, benefits to living in such a small town that virtually everyone knew everyone else. The downside, of course, was that nearly everyone knew everyone else's business. So if they didn't already, the whole town would soon know of an elopement that apparently didn't go as planned.

Jonah personally got the parents settled in the conference room and then returned to his office. All his instincts told him he wouldn't get much use from whatever the parents found—except to spread the news faster—but they needed to be busy, procedure needed to be followed, and he needed them out of his hair while he tried to think.

Sarah tapped on his door and came in. She didn't look the least bit wet, so either they had beaten the storm back, or water just slicked off her like a duck. It was something he had thought before.

She held a thumb drive in her hand. "You need to look at this."

"Ah, shit," he groaned. "Don't tell me this whole thing is even stranger than I think it is."

Without another word, she went around his desk to the credenza behind it, plugged the thumb drive into his computer, and called up the pictures on the drive.

"Take a look for yourself. I got every shot before the rain started."

Jonah swiveled his chair around and stared at the large screen of his computer. He stared for a long time, his gaze moving from photograph to photograph, each one clear, correctly lit, expertly focused. Very professional, obviously taken by an expert.

Except . . .

"Did you close the car doors?"

"Not until after I took those pictures," Sarah said calmly.

In each shot of the car, the doors were closed.

"And the footprints?"

"They were just as you saw them, same as I did, when I took the shots. The camera is working fine; I checked it as soon as I saw these. What the hell, Jonah?"

He really didn't know. Because there were no footprints in any of the shots. None. And he could tell from the wide shots Sarah had included that she had taken the pictures where they had both seen muddy footprints of two people.

Footprints totally gone. Gone as though they had never been there.

TWO

Judge Phillip Carson had called Serenity home for most of his life, minus the years away at college and law school and a five-year stint at a big legal firm in Atlanta.

He'd hated Atlanta. Hadn't thought much of the firm either.

Coming home to Serenity had suited him perfectly. Even a small mountain town of hardly more than five thousand people could always use another lawyer—and had definitely needed a judge. Since the county in which Serenity resided could claim only two other towns, both also small and with small populations, it had been more or less tacked in a judicial sense onto the larger circuit that was literally on the other side of the mountain. And that one contained several large towns, which made for a busy judge.

So it hadn't been very difficult for Judge Carson to convince the powers that be that it would just be a good idea all around for this smaller county to become a single district, and for the judicial circuit to have its own judge residing in Serenity. Unless something really unusual came up, he only had to leave Serenity to hold court in one of the other small towns maybe once or twice a month.

Holding court *in* Serenity—in the single courtroom on the second floor of the small police department—tended to consist of mundane traffic violations, the occasional half-assed assault between two drunks, and rare property damage from the handful of troubled high school kids they had to contend with seemingly every year.

But all in all, it was a peaceful town. That was what he liked about it. He had lots of leisure for his favorite sport, fishing. And though it looked hardly more than a wide creek, there were plenty of fish, so the stream that was less than a mile from downtown Serenity suited him perfectly. He'd staked out his special spot— which everyone in town knew and respected—and the walk out there and back two or three times each week was what he considered to be sufficient exercise.

Today, rod and tackle box in hand, he stopped in at the police station. "Is he in?" he asked Jean at the reception desk.

"He's in, Judge, but I've seen him in better moods."

"I'm not surprised." The information didn't deter the judge, and he passed through the nearly deserted bullpen to the chief's office. He didn't let the closed blinds deter him either.

He walked in without knocking, saying briskly, "Nothing new, I take it?"

Jonah looked up from the usual clutter on his blotter with a frown, but it was a general expression of mood rather than anything directed at the judge. He looked very tired and a bit haggard. "Nothing. I've reached out to every law enforcement agency in three states, issued a

BOLO, and took Sully's dogs out for miles around on three different days even though there wasn't much hope after that damned rain.

"There's been no ransom note. We've personally interviewed every single high school student in Serenity, *plus* all the teachers and the guidance counselor, and contacted distant relatives of both kids. We've searched both their rooms and their lockers at school. Everything points to a deliberate and well-planned elopement, nothing else. An elopement that just . . . stopped . . . near the edge of town."

"Nothing in the car?" The judge sat down in one of the visitor's chairs, setting the tackle box at his feet and propping his rod against the other chair.

"Nothing unusual. Once we went over everything and got it all out of the car, I had the parents back here sorting what belonged to who. Some stuff was obvious, but not everything. And nothing stuck out as not belonging to a couple of reckless kids taking off without much in the way of planning for the future." He didn't add that Monica Church had sobbed the entire time the parents had sorted their kids' belongings.

Jonah drew a deep breath and leaned back in his well-worn chair until it creaked. "Those two kids might as well have vanished into thin air for all the evidence I've found."

"Maybe they were just smart enough to lay down a false trail," the judge suggested.

Thinking of the vanished footprints that, so far, only he, Sarah, and Tim knew about, Jonah said, "From all I've been told, Amy was the brains of that pair—and she wasn't that smart. All she wanted was to get out of Serenity and out from under her parents' thumb, and it was the same for Simon. I'm betting they hadn't thought much beyond just getting out of here. No elaborate plan. They had relatively little money, relatively few skills, and like most teenagers, they thought they could build a life on that foundation. Somewhere other than Serenity."

"Stranger things have happened," the judge said mildly.

"Yeah, yeah, I know. And if either one of them had been in touch with *somebody*, I wouldn't be so worried. But they haven't. It's been a week, and nobody's heard from them. And since Amy left her purse behind, they only had whatever cash Simon had in his jeans. About two weeks' pay at most, his father thinks. That won't get them very far, especially if they have to rent a room somewhere."

He paused, then added, "Something else. Their cell phone usage— high as hell like every teenager's—stopped abruptly. Nothing after Saturday night, about the time they left. Which figures; probably Stuart letting Amy know he was waiting with the car. Nothing since. I mean nothing. The phones are either off or destroyed. And I have to lean toward the latter, because both had GPS locators in them; the parents had made sure of that *and* that the GPS was locked on at all times, so the kids couldn't disable without destroying the phones. A condition of them having their own phones, I gather."

"And no joy." It wasn't a question.

Jonah nodded. "How many teenagers do you know who can be more than a foot or two away from their cells? If they aren't in a pocket, they carry them in their hands. A lot of the girls don't even bother with purses anymore, just a little billfold-like thing on a long strap that holds their cell, driver's license, and car keys if they have a car, and maybe a few bucks or an ATM card."

He held up a hand before the judge could ask. "I know that because they volunteered the info and showed me the billfold things.

Most of the girls seem to have them. The twenty-first-century version of the fanny pack, I guess. Handy. But not helpful to me."

"Maybe they tossed their cells and bought burners," the judge suggested.

"It's a possibility, especially given the locked GPS signals, but who would they call except friends or family? I don't really know Amy, but according to her BFF, she would have called once they were out of town and on their big adventure, proud of herself for having pulled it off. The friend seemed sure. And worried."

"Because there was no call."

Jonah tapped his fingers on the stack of papers on his desk. "You signed the warrants so I could get the phone records of all the kids—*plus* everybody with a kid in town. And it's a sign of everybody's worry that they don't seem to mind. Anyway, I've pored over these records every day *and* had Sarah go over them in case I missed something. No strange numbers on any of these accounts. No unknown numbers. No untraceable numbers.

"We've also gone over their laptops or desktop home computers, and no joy there either." He sighed again. "Two very ordinary teenagers started to elope, and something stopped them near the edge of town. Not only stopped them—but took them."

"With no ransom demand."

"No. But . . . there are possibilities I'm not about to mention to the parents or anyone outside the investigation unless I have to. For one thing, there's a hell of a lot of money to be made these days in human trafficking, and kids in their age range are typical for the targets. I'm not talking about pretty girls sold to be sex slaves for some sicko, though there is that. I'm talking about something even worse.

Something I didn't know anything about until I took those FBI courses last year."

"I'm afraid to ask," the judge said.

"I wish I didn't know about it," Jonah responded frankly. "Even the FBI isn't sure if it's a huge organization or a bunch of smaller ones. Sort of like a bunch of secret clubs whose members are pedophiles, monsters into torture and snuff films, whatever horror you can imagine. The FBI has a unit set up just for the human trafficking, and they have young undercover operatives all over the country trying to infiltrate the groups."

"Jesus."

"Yeah. Dangerous as hell for the young agents. The FBI can't go in as buyers and commit crimes, so they have to send in undercovers to be potential victims."

"Jesus, who'd volunteer for that?"

"Some dedicated young agents, I'd say. As for the buyers . . . Pay a small fortune, and you can have your pick of attractive young people or kids, and do with them whatever you want, in a nicely discreet location and among other monsters with the same . . . tastes. The FBI hasn't yet figured out how these perverts communicate, how they're notified that one of the traveling groups will be in their area, but somehow they find out where to meet, at some very isolated location. Twenty-four to forty-eight hours later, the club is gone, the perverts are gone, and someone in the organization takes care of the cleanup and disposes of the bodies, most of which are never found."

"Nobody gets out alive?"

"Not according to the FBI. They believe some of the kids last for more than one . . . encounter . . . but eventually the client pays enough to kill to get off, and does just that."

"I wish I didn't know that," the judge said, adding immediately, "You think our two missing teenagers might fit?"

"Maybe some good news there. I was on the phone an hour yesterday with an agent in that FBI unit. The more I told her about the situation here, the less she thought they could have been targets of these traffickers. They tend to go for street kids, college kids, or clubbers in major cities. They apparently keep them under observation for a while, learn their habits and schedules, learn which kids are vulnerable, on the point of dropping out or burning out, or just don't have anyone to worry about them. Then they take them. Sad as it is to say, more often than not nobody even reports these kids as missing for weeks—if at all."

The judge frowned. "A stranger watching our kids would stand out here, especially if he or she watched for that long."

"Yeah, that's what the agent said. No way would one of the traffickers have taken a couple of high school kids a mile from their homes in a little mountain town. Just not where they hunt. Too high-risk for them."

"So you're back at square one."

"Yeah. All I know for sure is that they're gone—and there was no sign of struggle near the car. That's pretty much it."

"Then you're doing all you can."

"Tell my conscience that, will you? Then maybe I can sleep tonight."

The judge eyed him. "I'm a little older than you, so let me give you a piece of advice. Understand that you aren't going to win them all, find every bad guy, rescue every damsel—or couple—in distress. Even in a little town like this, there'll be murders you can't solve, other crimes you can't solve. And lost people who never get found."

"I don't like it," Jonah said. "It's not why I became a cop."

"Course not. Also why it makes you such a good one. But you won't win every time, Jonah, no matter how good you are. No one wins all the time. Do everything in your power, do your job. But don't let it eat you up inside." He rose to his feet, gathering his tackle box and rod. "You're a good cop, and that's good for the town. But nobody expects you to be perfect."

Jonah glanced at the clock on his desk and raised his eyebrows at the judge. "Thanks. Aren't you going out a little late? It'll be dark in another hour."

"Full moon. I get some of my best fishing then. And it's so peaceful. I very much enjoy being alone with the fish and my thoughts."

"Well, I hope you get lucky," Jonah told him.

Words that would haunt him for a long time.

AS HE HAD every night since the young couple had disappeared, Jonah worked late, going over and over information already burned into his brain, hoping to see something he'd missed, overlooked, or misunderstood every other time he'd studied it.

Nothing. Not a clue where those kids had gone.

Or where they had been taken.

Or any answer to the fairly spooky question of why both his watch and Sarah's watch *and* Tim's had stopped when each of them had reached the abandoned car, and why all their cell phones, still functioning, had all been missing the time spent out there.

As if they had stepped into a fucking time warp, or something else right out of science fiction.

"It's my night to work, not yours," Sarah said as she came into his office. "Go home, Jonah."

"You know, I *am* your boss," he reminded her.

"Yeah, yeah. Look, you can go home under your own steam, or I can call Tim and the tow truck." When he didn't even frown at that, she lowered her voice and kept it matter-of-fact. "A week in, we aren't likely to find anything new, and you know it. If nothing else, you need a good night's sleep so you can come back at it with fresh eyes in the morning."

"It doesn't seem right for me to just . . . go home," he said finally.

"You won't be any good to anybody if you spend another sleepless night in this office," she said.

"I slept. Sort of."

Sarah glanced at the old leather couch across the room from his desk. "That wasn't sleep, that was time on a medieval torture device. Unless you confessed you're a heretic, it was useless time."

Not even that earned a smile from him.

"Jonah. You've done every single solitary thing a cop could do on a missing-persons case."

"I haven't figured out the weird stuff," he said. "I'm not even sure keeping quiet about all that is the thing to do."

"I'm sure," she said. "Right now, we've got two teenagers missing, with clear evidence their intent was to elope. Both sets of parents *and* the rest of the town can understand that. They can find reasonable explanations in their own minds for the abandoned car, the inactive cell phones, the lack of any trail to follow."

"But add in the weird stuff . . ."

Sarah nodded. "Add that in, and your slightly uneasy town is going to wobble toward panic. Really fast. And what good's that going to do anybody?"

"If I could just figure it out——"

"From where I'm standing, I'm not sure anybody could figure it out. But one thing I do know is that you need rest, real, honest-to-God sleep, about twelve hours of it. Because no matter what you believe, nobody expects you to work on this or anything else twenty-four-seven."

"I think Monica Church does," he said seriously.

"Jonah. Go home. You stopped making sense a couple of hours ago."

He thought she was probably right. And he was too tired and discouraged to keep arguing with her. He did need to sleep. He needed a decent shower rather than the make-do shave and wash in the little bathroom off his office——though Sarah had been kind enough not to actually *say* that he looked like hell. He also needed to eat something that hadn't come out of a vending machine or a take-out box.

The Diner was still open even this late on a Saturday night, though nearly deserted, and Clyde was more than willing to get started on a burger and fries for Jonah. Then he came out to the front counter, reached underneath, and produced a bottle of Scotch and a small glass.

Mildly, Jonah said, "You don't have a liquor license, Clyde."

"I'm not charging you for this, Jonah. Drink it. Then eat and go home. Get some sleep. I've seen men in coffins look better than you."

"Nice."

"Truth." Clyde returned to the kitchen. He didn't have Waylon or Johnny playing tonight, so the Diner was quiet. There was a couple over in a corner booth finishing their own late supper and talking in low voices, and an expressionless teenage boy sitting at the far end of the counter with an open laptop before him.

Since Jonah had personally spoken at least briefly with every teen-ager in town, he recognized this one. Alec Lowry. Not a bad kid, but a not-so-good home life, and Jonah wasn't surprised to see him here because Clyde was generous with his Wi-Fi and liked to provide a safe place where kids could spend a few hours if needed.

Alec needed more than most, if Jonah was any judge. The favor-ite sport of his parents seemed to be arguing. Loudly. So he wasn't likely to find any quiet time at home. And there were certainly worse things he could be doing late on a Saturday night when he wasn't eager to go listen to or ignore the latest fight.

He probably wouldn't be missed there, sad to say.

Jonah brooded about that as he sipped his Scotch. It burned all the way down to his empty stomach, but he thought it probably would help him sleep once he ate.

He thought about two sets of parents who had, in their individual ways, been going crazy for a week now, and compared them to Alec Lowry's parents, who should never have had kids because they were too damned self-involved. If their son grew up to be a good man, as he showed every sign of doing, it would be because he'd virtually raised himself, not because they had.

"Here." Clyde slid a plate across the counter to probably his last customer of the day. "Eat." He raised his voice. "Alec, you want to earn a few bucks?"

The teenager looked up from his laptop, thin face finally wearing an expression as he smiled faintly. "Dishes?"

"There's a sink full," Clyde said. "Or you can stick around for sweeping and mopping. I could use the help."

Jonah dug into his burger and fries as the Diner owner went over to talk more to Alec, perfectly aware that Clyde was one of several adults in the town who looked out for the kids who got either bad parenting or no parenting at all.

A safe place to spend an evening, a good hot meal, and a little cash in their pockets from odd jobs could make all the difference in the world, as did a little time and attention from a good adult role model.

There were advantages to small-town life.

Usually.

IT WASN'T THE crack of dawn on Sunday morning when the phone rang, but Jonah was still conscious of a tickle of déjà vu as he fought his way out of the tangled covers to answer. And a cold, hard pit of something he didn't want to acknowledge settled in the base of his belly.

"Yeah?"

Without prevaricating, Sarah said, "Looks like another one, Jonah."

"Shit. More kids?"

"No. It's the judge. He didn't show up for his usual Sunday break-fast at Clyde's, and we all know he's a creature of habit. Clyde called me early, as soon as he started to feel uneasy. I went out and checked the judge's fishing spot." She paused, audibly drew a breath, and finished, "Everything looked absolutely normal and undisturbed. His chair, his tackle box, a string with half a dozen fish he'd caught just at the water's edge. His fishing rod leaning up against the chair with what looked like fresh bait on the hook."

"But no judge."

"No. It's a grassy path most of the way down from the road to the water, you know that, and we haven't had any rain since that gully washer the day the kids disappeared. No sign of footprints, his or anybody else's, except for one clear print just where he put the string with his catch in the water."

"String tied to the stake?"

"Yeah. As always. Nobody ever bothers that, not even the kids. Nobody else was out there, or had been, far as I could tell. Haven't seen another soul since I got back here. I took a chance and made the hike back to the judge's place, and everything looked normal. Key was in the normal place, so I went inside and took a quick look. Normal. Absolutely normal."

Jonah knew she was repeating the word deliberately. And they both knew why. The pit in his stomach was making him feel queasy, and not only because he considered Phillip Carson a good friend.

"One thing," Sarah added. "His cell was on his kitchen counter. Whether he forgot it or—"

"Probably just left it there. Whenever he doesn't expect to be called, or doesn't want to be, he just leaves the cell at home."

"Thought so. But we still need to take a look at his records and see when the phone was last used. I suppose the warrant he signed is good for his phone records too?"

Jonah honestly had no idea, but he knew the judge in the neighboring district, and made a mental note to call him and find out what they needed to observe the legalities.

"Okay, I'll take care of that a bit later. You talk to Clyde?"

"Asked him to keep his questions to himself, that you'd come talk to him later. We both know nobody else is likely to miss the judge unless we start shouting about it, at least for a day or two. Might not be such a bad idea for us to have that day or two without . . ."

"Without panicking the town?"

"Something like that. Missing kids with a clear intention of elop- ing is one thing; the judge is a fixture here. He goes missing, nobody is going to believe he just ran off."

"Probably right." Jonah fumbled for his alarm clock and squinted at the time. "It's after ten."

"Well, there really wasn't much for you to do here anyway. I figured you needed the rest, and I could take care of the preliminary look-see. Even went ahead and got pictures, for all the good it'll do us."

"I appreciate it." He swung his legs off the bed, absently noting that they were still wrapped, mummylike, in the covers. "What time did Clyde call?"

"Right at seven. Called me on my cell, not the station. Said the judge was always there when he opened up at six."

"Figure thirty minutes to walk from the stream to the Diner. He never uses lures in that stream; how fresh was that bait?"

"It's a worm, Jonah. All I can tell you is that it wasn't moving and hadn't dried out. He had a little can of live worms beside the tackle box." She paused, then added, "He had one of those little fisherman's battery lanterns beside his chair. The kind that's fairly powerful even though it's small enough to fit inside a tackle box. It was still on."

"So it was still dark when he . . . left."

"That would be my guess." She drew a breath. "The only thing the disappearances really have in common. Every victim was taken in the dark."

THREE

Jonah ran his fingers through his hair, trying to think. "Shit," he said again. "Did you say you were still there?"

"Judge's fishing spot, yeah. I knew you wouldn't want crime scene tape around the area, but I also figured you'd want to see it the same way I did. Only a few cars have gone by this morning on the way to church. Nobody's appeared to notice anything strange about me being here, and I'm leaning against the car all nice and natural. Just looking at the view. I'll stick around here. You can get to the Diner before church lets out. Have breakfast and talk to Clyde."

"Anything else?" he asked politely.

"Yeah. Bring me a coffee, will you?"

"See you in a few." He didn't wait for a response but cradled the receiver and fought free of the remaining covers so he could get out of bed. He had been told he was an extremely restless sleeper but had no idea why, since he could never remember his dreams.

In less than half an hour, he was showered, shaved, dressed, and out the door. Like the judge and even though both were bachelors, Jonah owned a house not far from the downtown area, with a small front yard, a garage, and a fenced backyard where the latest thing in barbecue grills lived on a spacious patio.

Though Jonah had never asked, he figured the judge owned a house rather than a condo for the same reason he did: a dislike of neighbors being *too* close.

They each knew more than they really wanted to about their neighbors through their respective jobs. There was no sense finding out more details they didn't need to know.

The Diner held only a scattering of customers, since church hadn't yet let out, so Jonah was able to claim his usual stool at the counter. *Am I becoming predictable? And is that a bad thing?*

"The usual, Chief?" a fresh-faced waitress named LaRae Owens asked cheerfully as she poured coffee for him.

Definitely predictable.

"Yeah, thanks, LaRae."

She nodded, smiled, and went off to serve somebody else, calling out Jonah's order as she passed the serving window to the kitchen, a bit quieter than usual because it was Sunday. And because Waylon and Johnny weren't singing back in the kitchen.

Jonah sipped his coffee and looked at nothing, his mind racing. Phillip Carson wasn't the sort for a joke, not like this, not when he knew how worried Jonah was about the kids disappearing. How worried the town was. So he hadn't vanished just to have fun. He didn't have family to speak of, at least not in Serenity, and if he'd been called away for a family emergency or because of his duties as a judge, Sarah would have known about it because the station was always notified of any change to his schedule.

If he *had* vanished as the kids had vanished, then victimology was not going to help find either the judge or the kids. Two teenagers attempting an elopement, and then a highly respected judge in his late forties who liked to fish at night? What did they have in common? Why would both be targets to be . . . taken?

They all lived in Serenity. They were all white, which was the majority demographic for the town, so possibly not something important to victimology. They had all been taken, apparently, sometime before the sun rose.

Jonah didn't know that the latter mattered; if he'd wanted to abduct someone, he probably would have chosen the darkness as a cover himself. And so late, between midnight and dawn, there was certainly less chance of being seen or heard, especially in a little town not exactly famous for its nightlife.

But . . . the unsettlingly weird aspects were true of all three disappearances. It was as if those three people had simply vanished in an instant. No signs of struggle. In the case of the kids, there had been footprints that had seemed decidedly strange when Jonah had seen them with his own eyes; the fact that the camera had not shown them at all just added to the eeriness of his memory of them.

The fact that both his watch and his cell had apparently been affected at the site where the kids had vanished, just as Sarah's and Tim's had been affected, was decidedly weird.

Jonah mentally kicked himself for not having asked Sarah if the same . . . situation . . . existed at the judge's fishing site. Though he'd find out soon enough, he supposed.

He hadn't realized he'd been lost in thought so long until a steaming plate of eggs, hash browns, and bacon slid in front of him, along with a smaller plate of toast.

"What the hell's going on, Jonah?"

It was Clyde, and he kept his voice low.

Jonah glanced back over his shoulder toward the kitchen.

"Alec's minding the griddle. Kid's a fair cook—and nobody can screw up breakfast anyhow. Where's the judge?"

"I have no idea," Jonah replied honestly, keeping his own voice low, his tone determinedly casual.

"So he's just gone? Gone like those kids last weekend?"

"That's how it looks. I'm going to meet Sarah at the stream as soon as I finish up here so we can put our heads together and try to figure it out. Wanted to ask you if he'd said anything to you recently. If he'd noticed anything odd, strange phone calls, a car he didn't recognize parked near his house or office, anybody following him."

Clyde leaned an elbow on the counter, looking very casual until Jonah met his very level, steely gaze—and reminded himself that even though he was only a few years older than himself, Clyde had served in Iraq back in the beginning.

"Not a word. Nothing out of the ordinary. And you do know, I hope, that he didn't talk to me about those kids going missing, not the way he must have talked to you, about details I imagine you've mostly kept to yourself."

"Yeah, I figured."

"I know how to keep my trap shut too, Jonah. Do me a favor and keep me in the loop about the judge as much as you can, okay? We've known each other a long time."

Jonah nodded.

"Appreciate it. Now eat your breakfast. You don't look much better than you did last night."

Without bothering to comment, Jonah merely dug into his meal, knowing he needed to eat even though he had absolutely no appetite. He was aware of Clyde returning to the back and his griddle, joking normally with the two waitresses working this morning and talking to Alec. And then he cranked up Waylon and Johnny—though a few notches lower than normal in deference to its being Sunday.

At least, Jonah figured that was it.

He finished his meal, also aware that more people were coming in for breakfast or brunch or lunch as the area churches were letting out. He ordered two coffees to go, paid his bill and left a generous tip, then managed to leave the Diner without anyone saying anything to him except good morning.

He had learned long ago that a preoccupied expression on a cop's face was enough to keep all but the most determined busybody from asking questions he didn't want to answer. He had perfected that preoccupied expression, though it certainly wasn't faked now.

He drove his Jeep roughly half a mile to the narrow side road that ran along the stream for a stretch, parking behind Sarah's cruiser. She was leaning against the front fender, hands in the pockets of her jacket, looking down toward the stream with a frown.

"Anything new?" he asked as he joined her and handed over her coffee.

"No," she said, gloomy. She took a sip of the hot coffee. "I just keep asking myself why the judge. Why those kids. What the hell's going on, Jonah?"

"I wish I knew. They're all white, they all live in Serenity, and they all disappeared sometime between midnight and six, as far as we can tell. All disappeared during the night. Those are the only common-alities I can think of."

"Shit."

He hesitated, then said, "Your watch—"

"Not wearing one." She didn't look at him. "But as near as I can figure, my cell lost the time I was here earlier, and the time I was down there using the camera. Seems to be working fine, it's just . . . about forty-five minutes off what it should be."

Jonah hesitated, then looked at his watch. He'd bought a new one rather than having the other one repaired. He was inordinately relieved when it was clearly working just fine. And then Sarah had to offer an explanation.

"I've been thinking, and I think there's some kind of perimeter. Because standing here, my cell hasn't lost any time. But it *did* lose the time I spent down there around his chair. Not sure exactly where the demarcation line is, assuming I'm right. Maybe your watch can tell us when you head down there."

Jonah wasn't exactly in a hurry to test her theory.

"You really didn't notice anything at all odd down at the stream? Other than whatever happened to your cell?" He could see from their position the judge's low beach chair and other things a few yards from the stream.

"Nothing. Looks like he just got up and left, peacefully. Leaned his pole against his chair, left his catch in the water, his tackle box and bait can closed. And just . . . left. How long do you think we can keep this quiet?"

"If we have to start asking questions, which we do? The whole town'll know by suppertime."

"And then?" Sarah sounded like she dreaded the answer.

"And then," Jonah said, "this place is going to go from uneasy to downright scared. It won't be pretty." He straightened away from her cruiser. "Before that starts, I want to get a look for myself. And then I want to get Sully's dogs out here, checking both sides of the stream at least half a mile in each direction."

He didn't want to even mention the idea that had occurred to him on the way here. That maybe the judge wasn't missing. That maybe they'd find him quickly enough. In the water.

Then Sarah said, "He wouldn't have waded out into the stream to fish, and I can't think of another reason he'd have willingly gone into the water. I looked as closely as I could and didn't see any sign of blood on any of the rocks, like if he'd lost his balance and fell."

"Still," Jonah said.

"Yeah. Still. With all the big boulders downstream, and the trees felled by last winter's storms, if he did fall in, his—he'd likely be caught somewhere along the way."

Jonah could hear in Sarah's voice that part of her would prefer to find the judge—in whatever condition—than have another inexplicably missing person.

He didn't blame her. He felt the same.

"Okay," he said finally. "We can be sure of a few things. The judge didn't leave a car parked by the side of the road. He wouldn't have left all his equipment and his catch behind, and he wouldn't have done that *and* accepted a ride from anyone."

"Maybe he got hurt," Sarah suggested. "He got a hook through one finger last summer, remember."

"Yeah. But if something like that had happened, he would have made sure to let you or me know about it. That's something I'm absolutely sure of. The only way he left here hurt and without letting us know would be if he was hurt . . . bad. Unconscious."

"And a Good Samaritan helped him but didn't report it?" Her voice was steady. "Doesn't sound likely."

"No," Jonah said grimly. "It doesn't sound at all likely."

As he took a step toward the stream, Sarah said, "You gonna test my theory?"

Jonah didn't want to, but he didn't admit that out loud. He just held his wrist up and pushed the cuff of his sweatshirt back so he could see the new watch, efficiently ticking away, then walked slowly down the path toward the judge's abandoned things.

When he was approximately six yards away from the little fishing site, his watch just . . . stopped.

May 30

Lucas Jordan scrolled through the last page of the report on his tablet and looked across the big desk at his boss with lifted brows. "And the police chief is only now calling us in?"

"It's happened in pretty short order," Bishop, Unit Chief of the Special Crimes Unit, said, calm as always. "A little more than three weeks, and the first disappearance had all the earmarks of an elope-ment, possibly set up in such a way as to throw off pursuit. No solid evidence there had been an abduction. The second, almost exactly a week later, the district judge—who likes to fish at night and knew all the details of the earlier disappearances. But an adult, and there was absolutely no sign of a forced abduction. Wherever he went, it could have been willingly."

Samantha Jordan, who hadn't even opened the tablet in her lap, looked at Bishop from her curiously dark eyes, unblinking. "The chief doesn't think he did that, obviously."

"No. But he could find no evidence to the contrary, just like with the teenagers. Then, three days later, on a Tuesday night just after ten P.M., a young woman named Luna Lang vanished. She left her husband at home with their sleeping infant daughter, to walk to the opposite side of their apartment complex, through an enclosed court-yard, to borrow a couple of jars of baby food from a friend and neighbor. She never got there. And, again, there was absolutely no sign of an abduction."

"Any of these places have security cameras?" Luke asked.

Bishop half nodded. "At the apartment complex. Grainy images the FBI lab is trying to enhance, but it looks like Mrs. Lang was visible, walking briskly, then passed into what's apparently a security blind spot. She never reappeared on the security cameras."

"How big was the blind spot?" Samantha asked.

"According to the chief, no more than fifteen feet."

Samantha blinked. "Damn."

"Whatever happened, happened fast," Bishop agreed. "And also according to the chief, in that blind spot were no windows or doors, or even shrubbery. No place for an assailant to hide."

"An enclosed courtyard."

Bishop nodded. "Pretty sturdy, tall iron fencing at the walkway out of the courtyard, with a gate requiring a keycard and a code. All entrances and exits are recorded on the main security computer. Now." He paused, then added, "This complex advertised itself as safe for young families just because of the general layout; it was designed with a few tricks to deter burglars or anyone else thinking about breaking in. From very thorny and well-lit shrubbery preventing any access to first-floor windows to first-rate door and window locks with individual security for each unit, plus excellent lighting all around the perimeter and inside the courtyard. Each apartment door is well lit all night, as are the open walkways on each of the four floors within the courtyard. No shadowy spots. And there's a two-man security team at night, one to watch the monitors and the other to patrol."

Luke lifted his brows again. "They worry much about security in a little place like Serenity?"

"They do now," Samantha murmured.

"Sam."

"Well, it's true, isn't it?" She looked at Bishop.

"It would probably be more accurate to say they've become obsessive about security. This apartment complex, for instance, had the fencing reinforced and the keypad code added, and began the process of updating the security system two days after Judge Carson vanished." He paused. "They were scheduled to update or replace security cameras and add several more to eliminate all blind spots in the courtyard and all around the exterior of the complex later in the week. Mrs. Lang disappeared before that could be done."

Samantha shook her head slightly, but said only, "And the next person to vanish?"

"Sean Messina, a car salesman, on the following Monday night." There was both a closed tablet and a stack of folders on Bishop's neat blotter. He never glanced down at them. "Messina and his girlfriend went to see a movie; there's an old-fashioned but renovated theater downtown and a multiplex out near the highway."

"They chose downtown?" Luke guessed.

Bishop nodded. "Messina's girlfriend told the chief it was because they could walk, on well-lit sidewalks, from their condo to the theater. They walked there without incident. The theater was about a third full, which Chief Riggs says is entirely normal on a Monday night when there's a new movie playing. The adults tend to leave the theater to the kids and teenagers during the weekends. Anyway, about halfway through the movie, Sean Messina left his seat and headed to the lobby, to use the restroom and get snacks at the concession stand."

Luke said, "Please tell me they have surveillance cameras in the lobby."

"They have. But Sean Messina never shows up on any of them. The entire lobby is covered, including the entrances to the theater and the doors of the restrooms. There is footage of him and his date arriving, getting sodas, and going into the theater. Sean Messina is never visible again."

Samantha said, "I suppose the emergency exits have alarms?"

"They do. And as far as Chief Riggs's technical people *and* the theater owner could determine, they were not tampered with at any time."

"When did his date realize he was gone?" Samantha asked.

"Approximately ten minutes after he left her. The movie was still running, but she left her seat and went in search of him. She went straight to the theater owner, who apparently also acts as projectionist and usher when needed, and together they searched the lobby and restrooms. Then he wisely locked the front doors, interrupted the movie to raise the house lights, and when there was still no sign of Messina, he called the police."

Slowly, Lucas said, "The first fully contained crime scene."

"Yes. Except that there was no sign a crime had been committed. No sign of a struggle, no exterior door opened—and no sign of Sean Messina. He hasn't been seen or heard from since. The chief even brought dogs in to clear the theater before he allowed other moviegoers to leave. They were very cooperative. And very shaken by what happened."

"And the dogs found nothing," Luke said.

"According to their handler, who was as baffled and uneasy as everyone else, as far as the dogs were concerned, their behavior clearly signaled that Sean Messina had never been in the theater."

Samantha frowned, the expression making her look even more sulky than the normal expression nature had given her. "He disappeared after he was never there?"

"Just telling you what's in the chief's report, Sam," Bishop said, still completely calm.

"Well," Lucas said after a pause, "it definitely sounds like our kind of case."

Samantha was still frowning, her unusually dark gaze on Bishop. "Give," she said.

He answered her readily enough. "There's a page missing from your reports. Not because I withheld it, but because I don't have it yet. All I have is the verbal report from Chief Riggs when he called me a couple of hours ago. Sometime after midnight last night, ten-year-old Vanessa Tyler apparently got out of bed to get herself a glass of ice water from the kitchen, which was not at all unusual for her. When her parents got up a few hours ago, they found a half-full glass of water on the kitchen counter, along with Vanessa's favorite stuffed bear. Her grandmother made it for her, and she always slept with it."

Bishop's gaze remained steady, but his voice had taken on a very soft, even, steely tone both the agents in front of him recognized. Like the scar twisting whitely down his left cheek standing out more than usual now, his tone was an indication of an intensity of emotion he very, very rarely showed in any other way.

"All the doors and windows in the house were locked from the inside. The security system, a good one, was active and showed no signs of having been tampered with. No screens were cut, no glass broken. But Vanessa Tyler is gone. She's the sixth victim to go missing this month. The first child. And so far, there is absolutely no evidence to indicate what happened to her. Or to any of the others. They're simply gone."

After a long moment, Samantha said with something of Bishop's almost preternatural calm, "Definitely a case for us."

ROBBIE HODGE LOOKED up from the tablet she'd been studying and frowned a bit at Miranda Bishop. Who, as was her usual habit, was sitting on her desk rather than behind it in the chair.

"You said two teams would be going?"

"Yeah. You two, plus Luke and Samantha Jordan."

Dante Swann, sitting in the other visitor's chair, looked up at Miranda and frowned as well. "Is Bishop briefing them?"

Miranda nodded, wearing a faint smile.

"Why?" Robbie demanded.

A little chuckle escaped Miranda. "Generally speaking, the newer agents find me . . . less intimidating. At least in the beginning. And a briefing isn't much more than relaying information. The four of you can go over everything on the jet. You should just about have time to do that before you land in Tennessee."

Dante glanced at his partner; they hadn't worked together for long, and it showed. As did something else, at least to Miranda's experienced gaze.

"Your abilities," she said calmly, "will only improve with practice. Field practice. We can only go so far in the lab, and experience has taught us that agents adapt quicker and with far more control when working in the field. Maybe because then it counts."

"That's what I'm afraid of," Dante muttered.

"Seen any spirits yet?" she asked him.

It was Robbie who said, "He has his shields up. Full strength. Can't you feel it?"

Miranda smiled faintly again. "I can. Don't push, Robbie."

"I'm not sure I even know how," Robbie confessed.

"You need to be aware," Miranda told her. "Your instincts are to reach out, even through your own shields. Born psychics tend to do that without thought or intent. It's a sense that's natural to you; your mind, at least at the unconscious level, doesn't operate with the same constraints most of us consciously impose on ourselves."

"Hey, were you trying to read me?" Dante was frowning at his partner.

"No. Not trying. I just knew your shields were up, that's all."

Matter-of-factly, Miranda said, "Dante has the stronger shield between the two of you. He also has a tendency to keep it up as much as possible."

It was Robbie's turn to frown at her relatively new partner. "You can't keep that up all the time. It takes too much energy, for one thing. And for another, with shields in the way, how will you communicate with spirits?"

"I'm really hoping there won't be any," he said with some feeling. "Spirits would mean our victims are dead."

Robbie looked back at Miranda. "Are you going to tell him or shall I?"

"Tell me what?"

Miranda said, "Serenity is an old town, Dante. Generations have lived—and died—there."

"So," Robbie finished, "the place is probably teeming with spirits, no matter what happened or didn't happen to our missings. Are you having fun yet?"

"With six missing people including a kid, no," he retorted. Then, to Miranda, he added, "I don't have spirit guides. A whisper here, a glimpse there; that's about it for me. I've never even had a helpful spirit point me in the right direction. Why send me?"

"You and Robbie need time to work together as a team," she answered readily. "And it's our practice to put a new team with a more experienced team when we can. We don't have many teams as experienced as Luke and Samantha."

"They could do this without us," he objected. "Samantha is scary powerful as a clairvoyant, and Luke's whole thing is finding people who are lost."

"We like to cover all our bases," Miranda said. "Luke's ability usually hinges on whether those who are missing are frightened or in pain; if they aren't, that sense is fairly useless to him. Sam is powerful, but there have been cases where her clairvoyance wasn't helpful. That happens, to all of us. As for you two . . . You may encounter a helpful spirit or spirits this time. And Robbie's an exceptionally strong telepath; that's not only one of the most reliable of psychic abilities, it's virtually always a good ace to have whenever gathering information by talking to people."

"It's cheating," Robbie muttered.

Miranda was unsurprised by the comment. Being one of those psychics born with her abilities, she had learned at a very young age to keep them hidden. Even though other telepaths here at the Special Crimes Unit at Quantico had worked with her for months now, she still struggled with the discomfort of "invading someone else's mind," as she called it.

"It's cheating," she repeated. "If they don't know. If I don't ask permission. It's an intrusion."

Deliberately, Miranda said, "Six missing people. Two of them teenagers. A judge. A young wife and mother. A young man with a frightened girlfriend. And a ten-year-old child."

After a moment, Robbie finally looked up and met her gaze. "The end justifies the means?"

"That's not what this is about. Your abilities are just tools, like the investigative and profiling techniques you've been taught. Like marksmanship, and interview techniques, and how to pick a lock if you have to."

Robbie smiled wryly at that.

Miranda nodded, more to herself than to the younger woman. "We never really know what tools will come in handy during an investigation. Or which psychic abilities decide to go AWOL just when they're needed. You may not need to even try to pick up someone else's thoughts, with or without permission. Because it isn't necessary—or because you tap into your abilities without even trying. That happens too. To the best of us."

Dante said, "Does this Chief Riggs know anything about our abilities?"

"Well, he was up here about a year ago, taking some of the courses we offer law enforcement officers around the country. He seems the type to make friends easily, and he talked to quite a few agents here. None of ours, I think, but that doesn't mean he didn't find out about the SCU. In fact, we're reasonably sure he did."

"Why?" Dante asked.

"Because he asked for us. Not a first-response team, not the BAU, not even the child abduction unit. Us. The SCU. And he was adamant about it. He called Noah directly." She paused, then added, "Noah and I both believe there's more to this than what's in Chief Riggs's reports. He struck us both as being shaken, and he's just not the type to easily shake. People disappear, it happens. Especially in the mountains. These disappearances seem odd, certainly, but what we've been told so far could easily indicate that these people, at least except for the little girl, just decided to leave and managed to do so without being seen."

"All within the same month?" Robbie said skeptically. "All in a little town that probably hasn't seen an unexplained disappearance in most if not all of its history? And all leaving when they were apparently in the middle of very ordinary, routine activities?"

"That does stick out," Dante agreed.

Miranda nodded. "We agree. Something very strange has happened—and may be still happening—in Serenity. Something the typical law enforcement officer isn't trained to understand or cope with. It's clear Chief Riggs knows that. How much he knows about the SCU . . . Well, you'll all find out soon enough. Grab your go bags. The jet's standing by."

FOUR

Jonah got word that the feds had landed on a semiprivate airstrip about thirty miles from town, and not half an hour later, a black SUV pulled into a parking slot in front of the police station, which was just off Main Street.

He stepped out onto the sidewalk to meet them, and to say he was curious would have grossly understated the matter. Four people were getting out of the vehicle, two men and two women, all casually dressed but all also wearing guns on their hips.

The driver was a tall, well-built blond man with unusually intense—and just plain unusual—green eyes. He moved quickly, with the springy step of a man in excellent shape and with energy to spare. And he was the first to reach Jonah.

"Chief Riggs? I'm Lucas Jordan. Luke."

"Jonah."

They shook hands, and then a very fair-skinned woman of medium height with a slight build, short black hair, eyes the closest to black Jonah had ever seen, and a sulky mouth that turned her almost beautiful when she smiled joined them on the sidewalk.

"My partner and wife," Luke said. "Samantha."

"You always introduce me as your partner first," Samantha said, observation rather than complaint.

"We were partners first," he said simply.

"Ah." She nodded, then extended her hand to Jonah. "Sam," she said.

Jonah shook hands and was just thinking how these two were unlike any federal agents he'd met before when the other two joined them on the sidewalk, equally . . . unusual.

The man Luke introduced as Dante Swann was slightly above medium height, with dark brown hair and very pale brown eyes that were almost gold—and seemed almost to glow, which was more than a little disconcerting.

"Dante?" Jonah managed.

"My mother was a classical scholar and loved his poetry. Go figure." He shrugged. "I tried to just be Dan for a while, but—"

"You aren't a Dan," Sam said absently as she stood looking around what she could see of the town. There hadn't been very many pedestrians on Main Street and there were none at all on this side street.

"Apparently not," Dante agreed, taking a step to the side to introduce his partner.

Robbie Hodge was tall, very blond, and very beautiful. She could have made a fortune as a model. Her merely polite smile made Jonah wonder if his toes were actually curling inside his boots.

Surely not.

Putting various thoughts aside to chew on later, he told the team,

"A town this size doesn't need a very large police department, and since I've called in all the auxiliary personnel I have, it's more than a little crowded in there. If it's okay with all of you, I've commandeered the space next door, right over there, for the duration. Used to be a real estate office, but it's been vacant for a couple months. I've got a big round table, evidence boards, Wi-Fi, and landlines already set up, along with two new computers. There's a kitchenette in the back as well as a restroom and a lounge. And I've got workmen coming in a bit to hang blinds over that big window in front. I figure we don't need passersby looking in. Because they would."

"Panic setting in?" Sam said, more a statement than question.

"That started more than two weeks ago, when the judge disappeared. It's been growing worse and worse. The only happy people in town—though they do try hard to hide it—are the owners of our one electronics store."

"A run on security systems?"

"Yeah. On complete systems and on various components to enhance and strengthen existing security systems. And locksmiths are installing new door locks at a pace I've never seen before. I don't think there's a house or condo in town that doesn't have an extra dead bolt on every exterior door." Jonah knew he looked tired and grim; he just hoped he didn't look as grateful as he felt at the arrival of these agents. He was not too proud to yell for help, especially when he didn't have a clue what was going on in his town, but no man wanted to look like he felt totally helpless, after all.

Luke, clearly the lead agent, exchanged looks with the others, then said, "It'll be dark in a few hours. All the sites of the disappearances were within a mile radius of downtown, right?"

"Yeah."

"Okay. Well, we brought some equipment with us, but we can unload that and get set up later. I assume you've stepped up patrols in Serenity?"

"Doubled during the day; after dark they're doubled again, and I have officers on foot, in teams, covering as much as possible of the downtown area. The town council told me to forget the budget and get whatever and whoever I need, but there just aren't many trained auxiliary deputies, and I don't like using jumpy volunteers. So I've done what I could. Stretching resources as far as they'll stretch."

"It's all you can do until we find some kind of pattern in all this," Luke said.

Jonah nodded and said, "Your hotel is just a couple of blocks away. And they'll hold the rooms till whenever you're ready to check in."

It was Luke's turn to nod. "Good enough. Normally, we'd split up and take different sites, but in this case, I think we should all probably see the site of each disappearance at the same time. And in order."

"That could be important?"

"At this stage, there's no telling what may or may not be important," Luke said, matter-of-fact. "Sometimes we start with the most recent case and work backward, mostly because the freshest crime scene is the most likely to hold some important information or detail. But in this case . . . we can't really call them crime scenes. According to your reports, nothing was disturbed at any of the scenes, no blood, nothing suspicious. Just missing people. Might as well start with the first scene and work up to Vanessa Tyler's disappearance last night."

"Her parents are basket cases," Jonah said. "My second's been with them all day, as well as their pastor, with various relatives and friends coming and going. I had to follow the missing-child protocols and put out the Amber Alert for surrounding areas, and I have people manning the tip line."

Robbie tilted her head slightly as she looked at him. "But you don't believe either will help find Vanessa."

"Nessa," he said in a rather automatic tone. "They call her Nessa. And, no, I don't expect either to help. If this was a child abduction, just simply that . . . But it isn't. It's the sixth disappearance in less than a month, and even though they were all different, they all have . . . things . . . in common. Whatever happened to Nessa, it's happened to five other people. I don't want us to focus on just the disappearance of a child, as difficult as that may be. They're all gone. They all need to be found."

Luke nodded. "Understood. And agreed. When did you put out the Amber Alert on Nessa?"

"I waited as long as I could," Jonah said frankly. "It's a second marriage for Caroline; Matt is Nessa's stepfather—though he adopted her legally. Her biological father, Curtis Hutchins, hasn't been part of her life since she was a toddler. He was abusive; Caroline left him with the baby and came here, where she had family. Filed for divorce, uncontested, and got full custody. She and Matt were married a bit over a year later."

"Hutchins was a suspect?"

"To Caroline he was. Probably still is. She's convinced even after nearly nine years that he got in somehow and abducted Nessa."

Luke said, "You're sure he didn't. Because her disappearance matches these others in certain . . . details?"

"That. And the fact that shortly after noon today we tracked down Curtis Hutchins. He's doing life in a Nebraska prison. Aggravated murder, nothing to do with a child."

"I'd call that an alibi," Dante murmured.

"Yeah. Once I more or less persuaded Caroline he couldn't possibly have taken Nessa, of course she and Matt both wanted the Amber Alert. But I kept it low-key."

"To delay the media descending on us," Sam said.

Jonah nodded. "It gives us a little breathing room. But if I'm wrong, if Nessa's disappearance isn't connected to the others and somebody did simply abduct that little girl . . . I know the odds on stranger abductions of children. Delaying the Amber Alert could have signed her death warrant."

SINCE IT WAS quicker to drive than walk to the spot where Amy Grimes and Simon Church had vanished, Jonah led the way in his Jeep, with three of the feds following in their SUV.

Lucas Jordan rode with the chief.

Almost as soon as they pulled out onto Main Street, Luke said, "You seem very sure Nessa's abduction wasn't someone local."

It wasn't exactly a question, but Jonah answered anyway.

"No registered sex offenders in Serenity. I know those monsters can hide in plain sight and often do, but I also know my town. I grew up here. Look, we went through the paces. We questioned neighbors, friends of the family, and Nessa's friends, asked all the right questions of all the right people. I believe a stranger who watched Nessa long enough to be able to get into that house, take Nessa, and get out without leaving so much as a fucking *hair* behind, even assuming that was possible, would have been noticed.

"That leaves a stranger abduction—and I have the same reservations for that, for the same reasons plus one more. Because her disappearance was too similar to five other disappearances this month for me to be able to ignore that."

"How do the parents feel now that the biological father has been eliminated from suspicion?" Luke asked, looking around as they drove.

"The whole town knows about the disappearances; even though I tried to keep details quiet, once others were nearby—girlfriends, husbands, parents—most of those details got out quickly. The Tylers believe Nessa's abduction is connected. They want answers, naturally. And the sooner the better. They've also scared themselves more than necessary by going onto the Internet and reading stats on abductions, especially child abductions. Why do people *do* that?"

"They think they want to be informed, to understand." Luke shrugged. "Though it usually just scares them more, as you said."

"I get it. I just don't like it. People still believe every word they read on the Internet is true, the way they used to be able to trust newspapers. It's hard as hell to convince them to read critically and check sources. It also wastes my time," he added.

Calmly, Luke asked, "Have you managed to keep the real oddities of the disappearances under wraps?"

"The oddities of people disappearing into thin air, no," Jonah said after a moment. "Conspiracy theories are popping up like weeds."

"And the rest?" Luke smiled faintly when Jonah shot him a quick look. "You asked for the SCU. For us, specifically. We're all assuming there are details you didn't put in your reports or tell Bishop. Details you've been keeping to yourself. Details that make you certain these disappearances are connected."

"My second knows," Jonah said finally. "Sarah Waters, lead detective. She discovered the kids' car abandoned at the first site, where we're going now, and was the first to reach the stream where the judge disappeared. She knows all the . . . oddities."

"And you don't want to tell us what those are."

Jonah sent him another quick look. "It isn't a test or any of that bullshit. It's just . . . I don't want any of you influenced by our knowledge or perceptions. People disappearing into thin air is bad enough; I don't want my imagination running wild. At least not any worse than it already has."

"I don't disagree," Luke said. "About not telling us, I mean. History is filled with disappearances, with people walking away—and apparently vanishing without a trace. But six people in one small town in less than a month is definitely outside the norm."

"It's certainly outside the norm for Serenity. We don't have a disappearance on record until this month. Not a single one, not even runaways." Jonah hesitated for a moment, and then said, "The spot where we found Simon Church's car is just up ahead. Before we get started, I should probably confess that I have a pretty good idea of what's so special about the Special Crimes Unit."

Mildly, Luke said, "We more or less assumed."

"Because I called Agent Bishop directly?"

"That—and your visit to Quantico last year. The SCU started out as being something of a guilty secret the Bureau wanted kept at all costs, but the years and the successful cases have made us more respectable, even a solid plus for the FBI. We still tend to keep our abilities quiet in public, but at Quantico and even among most law enforcement organizations we've worked with in recent years, we've been more or less open about them. Not to the extent of putting too many details in official reports, you understand, or giving interviews to the media."

Jonah nodded. "I asked around, and that's what I heard. Your unit has investigated all over the southeast, but especially in the Blue Ridge mountains. You've earned a lot of respect. Cops I know are too hard-nosed to believe in the supernatural talk about your abilities like they're just useful skills."

"They are," Luke said. "And that is the point. We have abilities that are completely natural to us. And when we can, we use them as investigative tools. Sometimes they help; sometimes they just make a situation more difficult."

"I have questions," Jonah admitted. "But I expect I'll have plenty of chances to ask them."

"Probably. We aren't shy, so don't hesitate. But it might be easier to absorb if you get the information in smaller-to-digest pieces rather than all at once."

"Noted."

Jonah pulled his Jeep onto the wide shoulder of the road and stopped it. He and Luke got out, and Jonah waited until the black SUV pulled in behind him and the other three feds got out before he said, "Simon Church's car was parked on the shoulder about twenty yards straight ahead. I've still got the car in the police garage, so you can see that later. I should warn you that just after we found the car and moved it into the garage, we had a hell of a storm with inches of rain. Whatever footprints or other signs there might have been were certainly washed away."

Sam shoved her hands into the pockets of her jacket and frowned at him. "There were photos in the file, when the car was still here. Presumably taken before the rain. No sign of any footprints, and no mention of them."

"True," Jonah said. And that was all he said. He didn't exactly look stubborn, but it was clear he had nothing else to say for the moment.

To his people, Luke said, "Let's just walk the area, okay? Keep an open mind, see if we notice anything helpful."

Jonah waited at the Jeep, leaning back against the front, not showing much expression except weariness.

As soon as they were a few feet away, Sam said, "We being tested?" She was still more than a bit touchy about that sort of thing, especially given her background as a carnival "seer."[1]

"No," her husband and partner replied. "He's not asking us to jump through hoops, Sam. He hasn't offered details, but it's clear Bishop was right about there being things Jonah didn't put in his reports. There's something odd about every one of these scenes, something connecting them. Whatever it is, he couldn't explain it, and he wants to know if we find the same thing."

"Without prejudice."

Luke nodded. "Without prejudice. Are you sensing anything yet?" Samantha was a touch clairvoyant, which meant that she generally only had to shield when she was touching something connected to a crime or other violent event. She had, however, been working with

---

1 *Hunting Fear*

other SCU clairvoyants as well as Luke in teaching herself to sense more intangible things—such as the mood of a small town.

"I feel that the whole damned town's on edge, but it's a general sort of uneasiness and bafflement. Plus a lot of fear. But faint. What about you? Sensing anything from the missing?"

"You know my shields are up."

She did. "Yeah, but you've gotten better at picking up on fear or pain even with them up."

"I didn't want to try until we got to the scenes."

"Well," Sam said, "here we—" She stopped so abruptly that Lucas stopped as well, half turning to look at her.

"Sam?"

After a long moment, she said in a distant-sounding voice, "What?"

Luke glanced at the other two agents, who had stopped just behind them. Both looked curious—and guarded. Typical for new agents. He looked back at his wife.

"What are you sensing, Sam?"

She looked up at him, blinked, and then her eyes closed and she went completely limp, only Luke's quick catch keeping her from hitting the ground.

"WELL, I KNEW you all had some kind of abilities, psychic abilities, but I didn't expect them to knock any of you out."

"They don't, as a rule—though we do have a couple of agents who suffer from blackouts. But Sam can be exceptionally powerful, and unlike most clairvoyants or seers, if what she senses is unusually strong, sometimes she . . . goes somewhere else."

"Somewhere else? Like where?"

"A galaxy far, far away," Samantha murmured as she opened her eyes, blinking several times with a frown. She was in an unfamiliar vehicle—she assumed Jonah's Jeep, since it had been closer—mostly sitting up in the backseat.

The door was open and Luke was standing there beside her. She looked at his hand holding both of hers in her lap, then turned her head enough so she could see his face. He didn't look quite as grim as he might have, which told Sam she must not have been out long, and he wasn't showing any external sign of strain.

"A galaxy far, far away?" he said to her, dryly.

"When I was coming out of it, I could hear you and Jonah talking," she said. "And I couldn't resist."

"So where were you?" Jonah asked in the tone of a man who wanted answers. "The future, or now?"

"It wasn't a vision. Nothing from the future."

"Then the here and now. What was it?"

"I have a question first." Samantha looked at her fellow agents one by one. "Anybody else feel anything unusual up there?"

Rather surprising everyone, including herself, Robbie immediately said, "Some kind of energy. I could feel the hair on the back of my neck stirring. And really faint, there was sort of an uncomfortable crawly sensation in my skin."

"Any idea what kind of energy?" Luke asked her.

Robbie shook her head. "I haven't really learned to differentiate. "But . . ." She drew a quick breath. "For just a few seconds, I could hear whispers."

"Saying what?" Sam asked.

"I don't know. I was caught off guard. It happened too fast, and they were too faint."

"Sam?" Luke was watching her steadily. "What did you sense?"

"Something dark," she replied slowly. "Something really, really dark. And really, really hungry."

FIVE

Jonah didn't quite understand when Luke told him that they would need to wait until the following day to again approach the site where Simon Church's abandoned car had been found.

"Sam might get something from the car, though," he added. "After she's rested a bit."

"I don't need to rest," she protested, getting herself out of the Jeep under her own steam and rather relieved when her legs remained steady. "And even if trying again here is useless for the time being, we still have four other sites where people disappeared. One of us could pick up something at any of them. The judge was next, right?"

"Right," Jonah said.

Telling herself she was only reading the frustration on his face, Robbie said, "It's like static electricity."

"What?"

"When psychics pick up on an energy signature. If it's a place, then tapping into that energy once is like—walking across carpet in your socks and touching something metal. You get shocked the first time. But then the static has to build back up for the same thing to shock you again."

"Okay," he said slowly. "I get that. I think."

"We're happy to answer questions as we go," Luke told him. "But when we get to the areas where people are likely to be all around the site of a disappearance, we might want to be discreet."

"We *definitely* want to be discreet," Jonah said. "Sarah is the only one of my people who knows about your unit; nobody else at the station could even access the law enforcement FBI database, because it's password-protected. And I've told nobody in town. As far as they're concerned, you're FBI agents, period."

"Probably for the best," Robbie said. "Prevents those what-kind-of-freak-show-have-I-wandered-into glassy-eyed stares."

Jonah looked at her but didn't comment.

Before the silence could become obvious, Luke said, "Sam, why don't you ride with us to the second site." It wasn't really a question. Or a suggestion.

"I told you I'm fine."

"Still."

"I didn't get a nosebleed. And I'm not tired. Stop fussing."

"Since when was that an option? Come on, let's go. We'll be losing daylight soon."

Samantha sighed but climbed back into the Jeep's backseat while Luke went around to the front passenger seat and Dante and Robbie returned to the black SUV. In just a couple of minutes, they were turned around and headed back toward town.

"Who's the lady in the cast?" Samantha asked.

Without looking as they passed the house, Jonah said, "Mildred Bates. If it weren't for that cast, she'd have joined us back there."

"Town busybody?" Sam guessed.

"Yeah, pretty much. She's not malicious, but she does like to know what's going on. Sounds awful to say, and no pun intended, but it's a break for us she's laid up with that cast." He paused, then changed the subject. "What was that about nosebleeds?"

"I get them sometimes," Sam answered readily. "If I push too hard. Reach too far."

Luke said, "Most of us pay some kind of price for our abilities, Jonah. They always come with strings. Pounding headaches and nosebleeds are fairly common. Especially—"

Jonah glanced over at him as the fed broke off. "Especially?"

Sam leaned forward, an elbow resting just below the headrest of Luke's seat, and said, "Especially for those of us not born with our abilities," she said.

"Sam, you don't have to," Luke said without turning his head.

"Oh, I'm not going to offer details. No offense, Jonah, but I don't know you that well."

"Okay," he said, obviously puzzled. "No offense taken."

"It's just that those of us not born with psychic abilities, even latent ones, usually have them triggered at some point in our lives. Almost always because of trauma. Emotional, psychological, physical. Sometimes all three. The more traumatic the trigger, the stronger the abilities tend to be." She paused, adding, "As Luke told you, I have strong abilities."

Jonah heeded the warning and didn't question her about that. All he said was, "Are any of the four of you born psychics?"

"I am," Luke said. "Though I didn't know about it in the earliest years of my life."

"Sometimes," Samantha murmured, "we're latent as children, born with . . . possibilities. The abilities are there, often full-blown, but we don't know about them unless and until we experience some kind of trigger."

Jonah glanced at Lucas but didn't ask. "Okay. Anybody else?"

"Robbie is. And she was aware of being different pretty much as soon as she could understand the concept."

"That must have been . . . difficult," Jonah ventured.

"Most of us don't exactly look back on rosy childhoods," Samantha said matter-of-factly. "One way or another, these abilities can and usually do put us through hell."

Lucas exchanged a look with his wife, then said to Jonah, "Both Robbie and I are able to tap into very specific energy signatures. Unlike Sam and Dante, who have more diverse abilities, we tend to focus very narrowly in order to use our abilities effectively.

"Robbie's a telepath, able to read about half the people she encounters, at least when she does her version of dropping her shields. That's a high average; most telepaths are lucky if they can read a quarter or less of those around them."

"And you?" Jonah asked after a moment.

Luke said, "What I am doesn't really have a name. It's partly telepathic and partly empathic. What I *do* is home in on the specific electromagnetic energy signature of fear."

"And his specialty," Sam said, "is finding lost people."

"People who are afraid," her partner and husband said. "People who are in pain. Even before I joined the FBI and the SCU, I was using my abilities to find lost people, though in those days I barely had any control at all. I'm better now, thanks to Sam and the SCU." He paused, but instead of elaborating on that, he added steadily, "But I can't find people who don't want to be found. And I can't find the dead, at least not by using my psychic abilities."

Jonah asked slowly, "Do you feel the difference? I mean, would you know if the missing person just didn't want to be found—or was dead?"

"Sometimes."

"Then—"

But Luke was shaking his head. "No, I haven't picked up anything here, not so far."

"What does that mean?"

"Maybe nothing. We haven't been to all the sites yet. I haven't been here long enough to get a sense of the place, and I usually need to do that. And . . . I've never been able to read anything, feel anything, from people who are drugged or otherwise unconscious."

"Unless they're having nightmares," Sam reminded him quietly.

"Yeah. I do pick up on nightmares sometimes. But like any other psychic, I have abilities that are limited. People often mask or suppress their fear, especially men. I'm less likely to tap into those people. Like all the other psychics in the unit, my abilities also limit themselves, and no matter how much I practice, how hard I try, how hard I push, I can't get past those boundaries. There are some people I just can't read, no matter how much pain they're in or how afraid they are."

"That must be tough," Jonah said finally.

"Yeah," Luke said. "It is."

WHEN THEY REACHED the site where the judge disappeared, Sam hesitated, then said, "I think I'll wait here by the Jeep. I want to see if any of you sense something. I think I distracted everybody at the first site."

Jonah was reasonably sure she had—and before any of them had reached what he and Sarah believed was the perimeter of . . . whatever it was. He had also noticed that only Robbie was wearing a watch—nondigital, like his own—and he really wanted to know if her watch would stop.

"I'll hang back too," he told the others. "We bagged the judge's chair, rod, and tackle box, but you can see where he always sits. Couple yards from the water just to the left of that wooden stake there at the edge. It's where he always ties his catch, and nobody ever moves it. Not even kids trying to be funny."

"Well, he's a judge," Sam murmured. She watched the others move toward the stream, in a line parallel to the stream rather than in a group, and said to Jonah, "What is it you expect them to find?"

"Whatever's there," he replied promptly.

Sam sent him a look. "That was a very Bishop-like answer. You two don't know each other, do you?"

"I've only talked to him on the phone," Jonah replied honestly. He kept his gaze on the agents moving toward the stream. "You said before that you sensed something dark and hungry. You ever sense anything like that before?"

"Not exactly like that."

"What do you mean?"

"I mean . . . evil is always dark in some way. Always . . . hungry, grasping. Once you sense it, touch it . . . it's familiar. Even if it's not quite the same as before."

"So what you sensed back there is evil?"

"Yeah."

Jonah started to ask her to elaborate, but then the three agents approaching the stream stopped suddenly. Robbie, in the middle, lifted both her hands and slowly moved them as if she felt some kind of barrier. Luke and Dante were both looking at her, and both were wearing frowns.

They were almost exactly six yards away from where the judge always parked his chair.

"Shit," Jonah breathed.

"Energy bubble?" Sam's voice was remarkably calm.

"You tell me."

Still calm, Sam said, "You knew whatever that is had a defined perimeter, didn't you? How?"

"That," Jonah said, "depends on whether the watch Robbie is wearing has stopped."

"Energy affects electronics," Sam said, more considering than surprised. "Some places hold on to energy. So do some people. We have an agent who blows out every lightbulb in a room if she gets upset and drops her shield."

Steady himself, Jonah said, "All I know is that watches stop—and cell phones lose time."

Samantha didn't even appear startled. "How much time?"

"Far as I can tell, all the time you spend inside that perimeter."

"There's one at the site of every disappearance?"

Suddenly struck, he said, "All except the Tyler house. There are several clocks in that kitchen. Oven, microwave, even a plain old wall clock. They looked fine. My watch didn't stop. And I don't remember my cell losing time. Why didn't I notice that?" He pulled his cell phone from the pocket of his Windbreaker and looked at it, compared it to his watch.

Sam waited until he put the phone away again, swearing under his breath, then said, "You didn't notice because last night a little girl was taken. Kids always hit us the hardest."

He nodded. "Even those of us who aren't parents. Yeah, it's something I've noticed before. Though, thankfully, I haven't had to go through it many times."

Sam turned her head and looked at him, brows lifting in a silent question.

"No, it wasn't here. I trained to be a cop in Nashville, and worked there a few years before I came back here. Plus, I've taken advantage of things the FBI has offered, from seminars to being temporarily attached to federal task forces around the country."

"Including child abductions?"

"Yeah. After three different cases, I decided I didn't want to be a part of those particular task forces again. Though I have taken part in others over the years." He shrugged. "It's a small town, and I love it here, but it isn't—usually—the best place to keep a cop's instincts sharp."

Sam nodded. "I get it. And points to you for taking the time and trouble. A lot of small-town police chiefs wouldn't bother. Not their circus, not their monkeys."

Jonah smiled faintly but said only, "I want to be a good cop. Besides,

I enjoy a challenge. Usually." He returned his attention to the stream, where Robbie was slowly walking what appeared to be the perimeter of energy—or whatever it was. She didn't go into the stream, so she walked a half circle on the stream's wide bank.

The two men didn't follow but stood watching her intently.

"They can't sense it?" Jonah asked Samantha.

"Luke doesn't pick up energy from places or things, just people. As for Dante, he could probably sense it if he dropped his shields. Most mediums tend to be pretty good barometers for negative energy. But it can be dangerous for them."

"How?"

"Mediums open doors," Sam said matter-of-factly. "Depending on your belief system and experience, those doors lead to a spirit realm, another dimension, maybe even another time. Hell, maybe all three. But wherever or whenever it is, what's usually waiting on the other side of those doors and eager to come through them is energy of some kind. Sometimes human. Sometimes not. And very few mediums can control whatever comes through those doors. Negative energy is very destructive."

"Is that what took my missing people? Negative energy?"

"I doubt it," she replied. "What Robbie's sensing, what affected your watches and cell phone is probably residual energy from a very bad person or people. Or evil acts committed. That's what usually creates negative energy. Or makes energy negative."

"You've lost me," Jonah confessed.

"Well, I'm not the scientific type, but one thing I've learned is the law of physics most of us have to cope with in some way, and on a fairly regular basis. Energy can't be destroyed, only transformed. With the right conduit, otherwise harmless energy can be turned dark, negative. The right conduit tends to be an evil person, an evil act, or an evil force."

She frowned. "But the energy here has lingered, hasn't it? The judge vanished over two weeks ago. The teenagers more than three weeks. I would have thought the energy would have dissipated by now. Especially since it's outside."

Jonah didn't even know what questions to ask next, so he was more than a little relieved when the other three agents rejoined them at the Jeep. Samantha immediately told them about watches and cell phones, about what had been different at the Tyler house, and then asked Robbie what she had sensed.

"Definitely energy. My watch stopped. And—" She pulled a cell phone in an unusual rubberized case from her pocket and looked at it, then reached over for Jonah's arm and calmly compared her cell to his watch. "That look about right to you? We were down there about ten minutes?" she asked him.

"I think so."

"Time lost. That's a new one." She released Jonah's arm and returned her cell to her pocket.

Luke was frowning as he looked at her. "You didn't say if it was negative energy."

"I didn't know. I didn't drop my shields," she told him. "What I felt through them was too strong to risk doing that. I'm a receiver, remember?"

"Is that a . . . special kind of telepath?" Jonah asked.

"It's a matter of degree," she told him. "Most telepaths have to drop their shields and then focus, concentrate. I drop my shields and it all just comes rushing in."

"All what?"

"The thoughts of roughly half the people within about a hundred yards of me," she replied. "Like a loud party suddenly erupting in the next room. A lot of noise, but nothing makes sense." She shrugged. "So I never completely drop my shields if I can help it. I just . . . open a little window. When I have to."

"During a case."

"Yeah, usually. Or in the lab. We're constantly working to learn better control, or figure out if there's a different way to use our abilities. I just . . . don't like trying to pick up someone's thoughts if it isn't necessary. It's an invasion of privacy." Her chin firmed somewhat stubbornly.

Sam said, "Some of our telepaths feel the same, though not all of them. And some clairvoyants, like me, hesitate to touch objects we know were part of or near a scene of violence. Those headaches and nosebleeds, remember?"

Jonah had a strangely surreal moment when he realized he was discussing with four federal agents psychic abilities he had never believed in.

Until now.

IT DIDN'T TAKE them long at all to check out the courtyard of the complex where Luna Lang vanished—and to find a smaller energy "bubble" there as well. Just in the security cameras' blind spot.

A bubble where time was lost.

Jonah wasn't positive but believed the bubble was the same size it had been when Mrs. Lang had disappeared. There was some discussion about experimenting by having one or the other of them stand in the bubble, both to find out if they picked up anything unusual and to see if time continued to be lost.

But Lucas was reluctant to subject any of his team to a paranormal event they didn't understand—yet—so he elected to leave the area be. It wasn't roped off by crime scene tape, but there were several orange cones marking the area, all with signs stuck in them saying PLEASE WALK AROUND.

"Does that work?" Luke asked the chief.

"Not sure. I had one of my uniforms stand watch for the first couple of days—with orders to stand back and within the existing security camera's view at all times. He reported nothing unusual, and also that the residents of the complex were giving this whole area a wide berth. No teenagers live here, just small kids being watched *very* closely by parents or nannies, and when the complex manager told me they were continuing to install more security cameras, including that one"—he pointed to one up high, which very obviously covered this entire area—"I decided the cones would be enough to keep people away. So far, so good."

Sam said, "One thing about nervous fear, it does a lot to minimize curiosity. Or at least keep it internalized."

So that was settled.

Jonah had called ahead so that the downtown theater owner, Kent Ferguson, was there to unlock the front door and let them in at this odd afternoon hour.

"Is the downtown area always this deserted on a Wednesday afternoon?" Luke asked.

"Not quite this deserted, even though several of the stores follow an old tradition and close up around noon on Wednesdays. But since these disappearances, there isn't a lot of loitering to pass the time. People get out, go to work or do whatever else they have to do, and then go home, in broad daylight if possible, and with company. We've suggested everybody buddy up, not just the kids, and most are taking the advice to heart."

"Curfew?"

"Midnight. Another strong suggestion, even though most had already set their own curfews—considerably earlier. I'm sure Kent will mention that."

And the theater owner did, the instant he swung the door open for them. "Jonah, when are things going to get back to normal around here? I can't sell enough tickets to even bother with popcorn."

Jonah was tempted to say something about the little girl who had vanished the night before, but he'd been at this job too long to lose his temper that easily.

"We're working on it, Kent," he said, calm. "Do you mind turning up the house lights in the theater and waiting for us here in the lobby?"

"Sure, sure. Anything if it'll help . . ." He didn't repeat his earlier complaint, perhaps realizing just how it sounded. Just bustled off and left Jonah to lead the way into the theater.

"Sorry I didn't introduce you," he told the agents. "But trust me when I say you're better off when Kent *doesn't* know your name."

"We have thick skins," Lucas said absently as they stood in the aisle and looked around the theater. "Two doors back here, two emergency exits down front."

"Yeah," Jonah said. "And everyone who noticed him said that Sean Messina left for the lobby through the door on this side. The one we just came through." Realizing, he added, "And no bubble of energy here. Or did I miss it?"

"No," Lucas said. "You didn't miss it. There isn't one, as far as I can tell. Interesting. And you said the Tyler house was the same. So, the open areas hold the energy while the enclosed ones don't."

Half under his breath, Jonah muttered, "Why do I think that's a very bad sign." It wasn't a question.

Robbie took a step back and turned to eye that entrance/exit. "The door has that dark little vestibule thing so people coming in or going out don't spill light into the dark theater. So if he *did* go out this door, that's really the only blind spot before the lobby cameras would have picked him up. What's that, about twelve square feet?"

"Less," Jonah said. "There was a couple in the back row here— another young couple—and they both knew Sean and his girlfriend. They swear whatever scene happened to be playing on the screen just then was bright enough so they saw him, recognized him, even waved to him. They said he used that door. But he never went *through* the door into the lobby, at least not according to the cameras."

"Just vanished into thin air," Luke said. "But no change in energy for the area. We all walked through that space just now, and I don't think any of us picked up anything out of the ordinary. Did we?"

The other three agents shook their heads.

"I'm going to go out on a limb," Luke said, "and guess we won't have a reaction at the Tyler house either, especially since Jonah noted the clocks weren't affected. Whatever happened to these people, an energy signature was left behind only outside."

"Which," Samantha said, "is very, very strange."

SIX

When they left the theater, they split up, with Dante and Robbie getting the key from Jonah and going to start unloading the SUV and setting up their temporary command center, and Luke and Sam going with Jonah to the Tyler house.

They met Jonah's second, Sarah Waters, who was undoubtedly exhausted but didn't look it. She was a tall, slim woman with very dark hair worn up so it was impossible to guess its length, sharp blue eyes, and a lovely face that was curiously doll-like in its delicacy and would have looked more natural within the pages of a fashion magazine. Her excellent figure looked more model than cop as well, even with the still-crisp police uniform she wore. She greeted them with the information that relatives were with the parents in the upstairs den, making missing-child flyers.

"At least it's keeping them occupied," Sarah told Jonah and the agents. "They've been just about going out of their minds all day. And I didn't see the harm, with the Amber Alert out now."

"You've kept in touch with the station?"

"Of course. Nothing coming in on the tip line except the usual crank calls and a few insisting they saw Nessa hundreds of miles away in some unlikely spot." She shrugged wearily. "If it was within the realm of possible, I had one of our people reach out to law enforcement in those areas so they could check. Every single one of them came up empty."

"What about media?"

"Well, assuming Nessa's abduction was tied in with the others, which we are, we've been lucky with the media. Local is staying quiet as per your request, and regional is caught up with numerous cases, including that serial in Virginia, the one law enforcement believes they're finally close to catching after nearly a year and too many bodies."

"And national?"

"Election year coming up, so there's that. Plus a train derailment last night that's still burning crude, a couple of idiot drug dealers barricaded in a Chicago house threatening a shootout with police— and tornado season has started early and with a vengeance in the Midwest. We're barely a blip on the radar."

"Let's hope it stays that way. Go home, Sarah."

"Look, I want to—"

"You want to keep working the case. And you will. Tonight. But you worked the late shift last night and you've been up all day. Go home, get a few hours' sleep and some food into you. Head back to the station around midnight or later. We'll either be there or next door."

Sarah finally nodded. "I told Caroline and Matt they needed to stay here. Just in case. And whatever relatives aren't out putting up those flyers before dark will stay here and make sure they aren't left alone. I'll stop at the station and send one of our people to stand guard at the front door; it's probably useless security-wise, but at least the family will know we're nearby."

"Okay. Thanks. Go home and get some rest."

She nodded, then left Jonah and the agents standing in the side of the open-concept space that was the living area.

"She's a good cop," Jonah said, keeping his voice low. "Sarah was the one to notice there was a defined perimeter around all the outdoor sites where someone went missing." He paused, then added, "Neither one of you has said—not that you had the chance, really—but I gather there's no unusual energy here."

Samantha shook her head. "The opposite of what it should be, just like at the theater. The inside spaces are clear—and the outside spaces are holding on to energy that should have dissipated long before now." She was studying the area even as she spoke, frowning slightly.

"Energy from *what*?" Jonah asked. "Tell me how someone or some*thing* could have taken these people? It's like something swooped down out of the sky and carried them away—except that two of them vanished even with roofs over their heads."

"I don't have a clue," Samantha said frankly.

Jonah eyed her. "I was looking for something a little more helpful."

"Sorry. Though there is still a chance I can pick up some kind of useful information yet."

"How?"

Luke didn't appear very happy about it, but said, "Sam is a very powerful touch clairvoyant and seer, remember? Even though she's sensed energy in some of these places, her true ability is that she picks up knowledge from touching objects involved in crimes, or the belongings of victims."

Jonah eyed her again, curiously now. "Always?"

Sam shook her head. "Had this thing most of my life, and still can't really control it. But like most of us, I've found that the more traumatic or violent the event, the more likely I am to pick up something."

A rather unreadable expression in her very dark eyes nevertheless gave Jonah the impression that whatever she "picked up" from those violent or traumatic events was usually not pleasant, but he didn't question. He figured that time and observation would answer at least some of his questions. So he merely nodded.

"Okay. Well, anything we could even remotely classify as evidence is bagged up back at the station. I'll have it sent next door to our makeshift command center. I assume we'd all rather you not . . . try to pick up information in a police station."

"That wouldn't be my first choice, no."

Luke looked at her, frowning. "Are you sure you shouldn't rest first, Sam?"

She smiled faintly. "We made a deal, remember? Even if I collapse at your feet—which admittedly I've already done once today—I still get to decide if I'm okay to try to use my abilities. As long as I'm conscious, my decision."

"I have veto power."

"Yeah, but only if I'm showing signs of too much strain. Nosebleed, sensitivity to light, pounding headache. I don't have any of those. So I get to decide."

Because he couldn't help himself, Jonah looked at the very intense fed and said, "How on earth did she get you to agree to that?" Then he remembered these two were married and added hastily, "Never mind, nosy question."

Luke took his wife's hand, neither of them seeming anything but amused, and said to Jonah, "Some things really are better left as mysteries. Let's go try to figure out the ones that need to be solved."

DANTE STEPPED AWAY from the evidence board, where he had constructed a neat timeline for the disappearances, and rubbed the back of his neck as he studied it.

In a conversational tone, Robbie said, "I hope you realize that the longer you keep your shields at full strength, the more likely they are to desert you when you really don't want them to. Like when you're sleeping."

"Pot, meet kettle," he murmured.

She ignored that. "I'm just saying, there's no negative energy here, so maybe it would be a good idea for you to rest your shields, that's all. I checked; this building was constructed less than twenty years ago, and nobody ever died here. No deaths in previous buildings at this location, and it's not some kind of Indian burial ground or anything."

"So there are no spirits here?" He turned his head to look at her; while he had worked, she had set up, on a small table against one wall rather than the larger round table, one of the laptops they'd brought from Quantico. "Have you ever worked with a medium before?"

"Not as a partner, but in a group, sure. You know as well as I do that Bishop sort of mixes and matches until he gets a good fit." She frowned. "I wonder why he thought we'd be a good fit?"

"Maybe he's still mixing," Dante suggested. "Members of the team generally *have* to work together before anyone—including Bishop—knows whether they'll work *well* together."

"Are you saying we don't?" She was curious rather than offended.

"I don't think either of us knows yet. We haven't really had to do anything so far that required a collaborative effort. But, for future reference, most mediums will tell you that whether someone died in a place has absolutely nothing to do with whether spirits are present. As a matter of fact, according to Bishop, and based on both lab and field studies, one thing we're reasonably sure of is that mediums tend to attract spiritual energy. Whether we're trying to or not." He rubbed his neck again. "This place could be filled with spirits, gathered from all over town and God knows where else, waiting for me to open a door for them."

She couldn't help looking around rather warily, even though she knew she'd see nothing out of the ordinary. "Do you intend to keep your shields up regardless?"

"Regardless of what?"

"Regardless of whether this case suggests or even demands that we investigate spiritual energy."

"I don't know," he said finally, adding, "If there's no negative energy here, why don't you drop your shields?"

"I meant what I said about seldom if ever dropping them completely," she replied. "But I do have a window open. That's how I knew your shields were still up."

"Maybe you just can't read me."

"Actually, I can." When he frowned slightly, she shrugged. "You, Luke, Sam—and Chief Riggs. I can read all of you. Riggs is clearest, since he only has the bare shield nonpsychics develop—especially if they're cops."

"You can read Luke and Sam?"

"Yeah—probably because both have abilities they generally have to concentrate to use, so neither needs much in the way of shields. I mean, they're sort of guarded people by nature, both of them, but they have an emotional and psychic link that's just a bit like neon, to me anyway."

"Like Bishop and Miranda?"

"No, not like that. Bishop and Miranda's link is a link between two telepaths, and exceptionally deep. Luke and Sam haven't been together as long, and neither one is a telepath, so the link is different. But they're still connected. Not quite two halves of a whole, but stronger together than they are separately."

Dante was still frowning. "What about my shields?"

With a slightly apologetic gesture, Robbie said, "That's why I wanted to warn you to give them a rest now and then. They're slipping, Dante. Not much and not often, but if you're not completely focused on keeping them up, like you were at the stream, then . . . they slip."

"And when they do, you read my thoughts?"

"It's more like catching your thoughts. Or, rather, not catching them. I don't focus on them or anything; they're more like whispers kind of slipping past me. And only when I have a window open."

He sighed. "Does that help you, to open a window?"

"Yeah, usually. I don't like doing it with lots of people around, so I tend to wait for quieter moments. If I don't open a window now and then, my shields tend to slip too, and usually when I'm least prepared for that to happen."

"Like when you're asleep."

"When I'm asleep. Or when something unexpected happens."

"What do you mean?"

"Well, look at us now. We're doing ordinary things we tend to do on cases, the usually boring gathering of information and getting it organized so it becomes useful to us. You've combed through various files to assemble information, developing a timeline; I've set up this laptop to receive more info from Quantico—which is actually scheduled to come through in the next hour, according to a brief e-mail from Bishop."

After a moment's thought, Dante said, "The security footage?"

"Hopefully examined and enhanced by the techs at Quantico so it's useful to us, yeah. And Bishop said he was sending along some aerial views of Serenity as well."

"He did? Why?"

"I didn't ask."

"Bishop never does anything without a reason," Dante said slowly.

"That's what everybody says."

"So . . . what? He retasked a satellite to get aerial images of this town?"

"Well, I doubt he went online and used one of those find-your-house-on-a-map sites."

"Robbie, retasking a satellite is a big deal. As in a national-security-sense big deal. Those birds tend to be busy doing things like watching enemies or potential enemies, tracking storms, facilitating communications, and God knows what else."

With a shrug, she said, "I guess he believes it'll help us, or that we really need it for some reason he suspects or knows and just hasn't had the chance to tell us yet. I mean, he has to justify doing something like that, right? To the Director, at least?"

"I would think so. But I don't actually know. Remind me to ask Luke about it. He was part of the earliest group of psychics Bishop found and recruited, so I assume he'd know."

Robbie tapped neat pink fingernails on the table beside the laptop. "You know, when I first joined the unit, one of the other agents warned me that I would always be able to trust what Bishop tells me—but that he almost always leaves stuff out. Sometimes fairly important stuff."

"I was told the same thing," Dante admitted.

"So . . . what do you think he left out about this case?"

Dante hesitated, then said, "From all I've heard, we probably won't know whatever it is. Until we fall over it."

"Or into it," Robbie said.

"Yeah," Dante agreed somewhat hollowly. "Or into it."

HE NEVER MOVED until it got dark. Never came out.

The darkness was what fueled him, fed him. What gave him his power. The darkness allowed him to work.

He was aware of the hunters, those who belonged here and those who had come to join the hunt. They didn't disturb him.

He had the darkness.

The weapons they wielded were puny by comparison.

They just didn't know that. Not yet.

He passed by his Collection on the way out, all of them still and silent behind the bars.

In the darkness.

His Collection that was not . . . quite . . . complete. He needed to hunt again. Tonight, in the dark, he needed to hunt. To choose his prey.

And then decide when and how to take her.

SAMANTHA CLOSED THE take-out box that had held a rather good dinner and pushed it away, saying absently, "That Diner guy is a really good cook."

Jonah, sitting on the other side of the round table from Sam, had closed his own box some time before and was staring at the evidence board with the timeline. In an equally absent tone, he said, "Yeah, he really is. Listen, does anybody else think there's something weird about having a timeline when something at most of the abduction sites messes with time?"

"We don't know that's what's happening," Robbie objected, still working on her supper. "It's what *seems* to be happening." She waved her fork for emphasis.

The chief turned his gaze to her. "Do you have another explanation?"

"I don't have an explanation at all. I've never seen anything like it." She looked at Lucas. "You've been at this the longest, right? Can you explain it?"

"No, lost time is a new one on me, except for time lost during a blackout. None of us have blacked out, so that explanation won't fly. But most of us in the SCU have dealt with things we couldn't explain— at the time. If you can't explain a thing, leave it and look at the case another way. Very often, the pieces don't seem to fit together until you have them all. Then they fit. Then the puzzle makes sense."

"Victimology?" Sam suggested. She had been talked out of touching any items belonging to the victims for the time being, as requested by her husband, who wanted to "use our brains before the extra senses."

He hadn't fooled anyone, including his wife. He'd wanted to give her more time to recover from the strange collapse earlier in the day, to get some food into her system. And to give them all time to become more familiar with the facts—such as they were—of the disappearances.

Luke nodded an agreement with her suggestion. "We have an energy signature we can't explain, but not at all the abduction sites. We have missing people, but we don't know if they're still alive, or dead. We don't have a suspect or a motive. The victims are the only thing we have to profile. We have to look for something they all have in common."

Recalling the FBI courses he'd attended, Jonah said, "Isn't most profiling done on the basis of crime sites?"

"No, it's a pretty individual thing. You work with what you've got. In most cases, the crime scene is apt to provide a lot of information. Other times, especially if you don't have a crime scene but a dump site, or someone just missing, then you have to concentrate on victims."

Samantha said, "To study a hunter, you study his prey."

Luke nodded again. "At first glance, the only things connecting these victims is that they were all white, and they all lived in Seren-ity." He frowned suddenly. "Two of them were *leaving* Serenity."

Jonah wanted to correct the past tense usage but couldn't bring himself to interrupt.

Dante asked, "Think that could have been his trigger? Two teen-agers leaving town?"

"It's worth considering. If he has abandonment issues, and espe-cially if he was close to either of those teens, their leaving could have been the stressor. Something had to set him off. You don't just wake up one day and decide to start disappearing people, leaving no clues behind. This is something you work up to."

Dante said, "Think he's had practice runs? If not here, then some-where else?"

"Maybe."

"Not here," Jonah protested. "I would have known."

Robbie said, "I imagine you would have. And assuming he lives here, he probably wouldn't have wanted to take anyone local until he was sure he could do it. So we should check missing persons for—what?—couple hundred miles all around?"

Sam was making notes on a legal pad. "At least."

Jonah frowned, but before he could speak, Luke was continuing. "He's moved awfully fast, taking six people in less than a month. Not much of a cooling-off period. Except . . . He took Luna Lang just three days after he took the judge. The other abductions were more widely spaced. He also took her earlier than the others, before midnight."

"Not sure about the judge," Jonah pointed out. "He walked to his fishing spot just before dark, and he was there long enough to catch a few. We don't know *for sure* that he wasn't taken before midnight, since he wasn't missed until morning."

"True," Luke conceded.

"And Sean Messina disappeared before midnight too. The movie started at nine." He frowned. "Why on earth did I decide a midnight curfew was early enough?"

Sam said, "The downtown area is practically deserted *now*, and it's barely nine. You don't have to be psychic to feel the tension and fear; once it gets dark, most people are very obviously going to stay home."

"Yeah, you're right. But all this time I've been thinking the dangerous hours were after midnight. Now, all we really know is that it's either likely or certain that these six people disappeared sometime after it got dark, and before dawn."

Robbie said, "In the dark. The dark can be a friend, if you're bent on stealthy. Easier to hide. Easier to watch. And easier to make off, without attracting notice, with someone you've grabbed."

"After first knocking them out?" Sam asked with obvious interest.

"Sure. I mean, lots of options. Just because we haven't found a weapon doesn't mean he didn't have one. The traditional blunt instrument, something heavy he could easily carry. A Taser. Some drug in a hypodermic he could inject before they realized what he was doing. Even a choke hold, assuming he's strong enough and quick enough and has the knowledge. We can't check any possibility off our list as far as I can see."

Dante said rather plaintively, "Aren't we getting further and further away from finding things these people actually have in common?"

"We seem to be," Sam agreed.

"What does that mean?" Robbie asked, adding, "I haven't taken any of the profiler courses yet, remember?"

"As profilers, we need to ask the basic questions first," Luke said.

Samantha said, "Why these particular people in these particular places at these particular times. Even if we haven't figured it out yet, they *have* to share a common characteristic. Something that made each one of them a target."

Brooding, Jonah said, "Two teenagers eloping, a judge doing some night fishing, a young wife and mother going to borrow baby food from a neighbor, a car salesman out on a movie date with his girl-friend, and a ten-year-old girl who got up sometime during the night to get herself a drink of water."

"Are we sure about that?" Dante asked suddenly.

Jonah looked at him. "That she got up to get herself a drink?"

"Yeah."

"Well . . . it was apparently a habit with her. The fridge in the kitchen dispenses cold water and ice, and that's what she likes. The stuffed bear she always slept with was on the kitchen island, beside a glass half full of water, with her fingerprints on them."

"She's been printed?" Luke asked.

"No, the kids aren't usually printed until they hit high school. Process of elimination. We dusted her room, eliminated prints belonging to her parents, and concentrated on objects they said she handled a lot. Pulled a clear set of kid-sized prints from a lacquered music box she apparently loved. The prints on the glass in the kitchen were a match."

"Sounds like you have a solid crime scene unit," Dante ventured.

"It's a two-person team. And they are, unfortunately, getting better with practice."

SEVEN

Nobody commented on Jonah's grim statement. There was a moment of silence, and then Lucas spoke again.

"You've already checked into missings for a couple hundred miles all around Serenity, haven't you?"

Jonah nodded. "Yeah. When Sean Messina was taken. I looked for missings that were in any way like those here. Came up dry. Within a *five*-hundred-mile radius, there were about a dozen reported missing. A few turned up as bodies, killed accidentally or otherwise; a few are still missing but didn't just vanish into thin air, and the rest turned up more pissed than grateful that someone had reported them missing and gone looking for them."

With a sigh, Sam crossed through some of her notes.

"Sorry," Jonah told her.

"Don't be. You've saved us needless work. And based on that, plus other indicators, we have to assume the guy is here in Serenity, probably grew up here or at least has lived here quite a while, long enough to not stand out as being a newcomer, and that he has a personal reason for taking these people. If you're abducting people in or close to home, you aren't taking strangers. It's too high risk to take people who have or might have a connection to you, especially not just for the sake of taking someone."

Dante said, "You also aren't an experienced predator, right? Experienced predators never hunt where they live."

Sam was nodding. "Almost always the case, yeah. If they're stranger abductions, we're dealing with a whole different kind of bad guy."

"I just . . . I just can't believe anyone local could be doing this," Jonah said, still resisting. "How could somebody be *this* disturbed and go unnoticed? By family, friends, neighbors. By me. How could I not see it?"

"Evil hides," Sam reminded him. "More often than not, behind something familiar, something nonthreatening. That's its ace, being able to hide. And . . . most people don't believe in monsters. So they aren't looking for one, especially close to home."

There was a brief silence, with Jonah obviously pondering the existence of human monsters while the feds looked at him with varying degrees of sympathy.

It wasn't an easy thing to accept, that a monster could walk around in your town looking and acting just like everybody else.

Not an easy thing at all.

Finally, Lucas said, "Your people did very thorough interviews of anyone connected in any way with the missing people, right up to the latest abduction. I assume they've been working just as hard on Nessa Tyler's abduction?"

"Yeah. Everybody I could spare canvassed the neighborhood all day *and* talked to as many people as we could find who even knew the family. Her teachers and other students at school, every parent who ever had her in their home for a play date. We even checked alibis on the out-of-town relatives who joined the family for support. No flags, no suspicions. Once it got dark, I didn't want my people out knocking on doors, so they've been doing phone interviews all evening. So far, still no red flags. At all."

Dante asked, "Besides those family members, are there any strangers in town?"

"The four of you. That's pretty much it."

Luke asked, "What about Mrs. Lang's husband? Did family come to Serenity to support him?"

"His family lives in Serenity. His parents, brother, and sister-in-law have been trading off time so he's never alone and has help with the baby. Neighbors have helped out too. Dave and Luna have always been a very well-liked couple."

Samantha leaned her chair back, laced her fingers together over her middle, and turned her head to gaze steadily at her husband and partner. "Strike three."

"What?" Jonah asked, baffled.

Luke said, "Everything we're hearing, learning, just increases the probability that someone in this town is behind the abductions."

"How is that possible?" Jonah asked after a moment, still struggling against a reality too painful to readily accept. "One of my neighbors just suddenly decides to abduct people? Someone smart enough or with some kind of weird ability to circumvent security systems, including cameras? And—the weird energy, the missing time, people vanishing into thin air. Plus the strangeness of those photographs Sarah took at the scene where Amy and Simon disappeared."

He had shared those very odd photographs, and their bafflement over the open car doors not showing, the footprints not showing: seen by their eyes, but not by the lens of a camera.

Samantha said, "No way to explain any of that yet." But her tone was just a bit elusive.

Jonah looked at her. "All of you looked at those pictures, and all of you seemed as baffled as Sarah and me. Have you come up with a theory or something since?"

With a shrug, Sam said, "Just something I'm mulling in my mind. It may turn out to be worse than useless, so I'd rather make sense of it myself before offering it even as a theory."

"Sam, you know profiling, investigating, is a collaborative effort," her husband said matter-of-factly.

"Yeah, I know. I just . . . want to sit with this awhile longer myself. At this point, it's just a cockeyed theory with absolutely no evidence to back it up."

"Don't wait too long," Luke advised her.

"No, I won't."

Robbie said, "In any case, it's pretty clear a stranger would stand out in Serenity, in the day *or* the night, especially given the likelihood that he watched the victims for quite some time before he put his plan into action."

Lucas nodded. "Jonah, you and your people have talked to just about everyone in town, and you said it yourself: Aside from us and Tyler family members with alibis, there just aren't any strangers here."

Making a last-ditch protest, Jonah said, "You're telling me someone I *know* is doing this?"

"*Know* in the broadest sense, probably," Luke said. "Even in a town
this small, there are bound to be people on the periphery of your life.
Not friends or neighbors or coworkers. Maybe you'd recognize a face,
or even know a name, but not really give them much thought because
your life and theirs haven't really intersected. There's been nothing
to make them memorable. Maybe they live a bit farther out, don't
come into town too often. Don't get into trouble or otherwise draw
your attention.

"We all have people like that in our lives. Vague recognition, but
no interest. No real knowledge. What may be vitally important to
them, an experience, an event, could easily be something that barely
scratched the surface of your life. And whoever this is, he probably
learned early how to go unnoticed. Maybe he grew up in an abusive
home, and drawing attention meant a beating. He learned to be quiet,
still. To blend in. At a guess, he's in his thirties or forties; he's too
patient and too careful to be younger."

Samantha took up the not-quite-musing, her voice as thoughtful
as Luke's had been. "The judge wasn't a small man, and both Sean
Messing and Simon Church were in good shape, athletic. So this guy
has to be able to handle size and muscle, either with his own muscles
or by some other means."

"A gun?" Jonah suggested.

It was Robbie who said, "Six people . . . a child, a teenager, a young
wife and mother; I'm betting at least one of them would have cried
out, made some kind of commotion, if they'd seen a gun. The men

probably would have struggled, one of them at least. Hunting is common in this area, right?"

Jonah nodded.

"Then so are guns. Especially these days. We don't fear what's familiar, as a rule, at least not quickly enough to react. Besides . . . the judge was out in the open. The two teenagers in a stopped car with no sign of damage to indicate someone forced them to stop. Luna Lang crossed through about fifteen feet of a security blind spot and vanished. Sean Messing in a theater. I just . . . I just can't believe that every single one of them could have been taken by force, without any kind of a fuss and without leaving some kind of evidence of that behind."

"It doesn't seem likely," Luke agreed.

"So," Samantha said, "we're back to trying to figure out what all these missing people had in common."

With a sigh, Jonah said, "I thought we were doing that."

"We were. But I'm reasonably sure all of us kept in our heads the notion that these people were taken by a stranger, because even though stranger unsubs are more difficult to find, let alone capture, it's the monsters hiding in plain sight that frighten us the most, because we don't know who to trust—even when the faces are familiar.

"Now we have to consider what a member of your community might have in common with these missing people when viewed by one of their own neighbors. Somebody they all know. Somebody who may have been watching them for years."

Jonah was startled. "Years?"

"Without knowing what he's doing to these people, it's almost impossible to theorize. But given that we believe he's a local, and somehow connected to these missing people, the chances are good that whatever's driving him has been in him for a long time. Could be a mental disorder, but I would have expected that to manifest before now, and obviously; you or someone else would have noticed. So it could be simple resentment or hate."

"Those kids didn't do anything to make somebody hate them," Jonah objected. "Not the teenagers, and certainly not Nessa Tyler."

"It only has to make sense to him," Dante spoke up to say. "A madman has his own mad logic."

Slowly, Luke said, "The one answer we need as soon as possible is, for now, at least, the hardest one to figure out. We don't know *why* he wanted these people. I've never heard of a serial abductor except for the few who abduct kids or teenage girls and keep them literally in bondage, for years."

"Saw the most recent one like that on the news," Jonah said, looking a bit queasy.

"There have been worse cases. When abduction or even slavery isn't the goal, but murder is. Torture is. What really doesn't fit here is the range of victims. We've got three men if we count Simon Church, two women if we count Amy Grimes, and a ten-year-old girl. I've never heard of any serial killer with tastes that broad in his victims."

"Which," Dante said, "is yet another argument that this is personal. These people were targeted."

"Yeah," Samantha said, "but for what? What did they do to get on this guy's radar?"

Lucas said, "We don't know if they're dead or alive. If they're dead, where are the bodies? If they're alive, where is he keeping them? How is he controlling them? It's been weeks for the teenagers; is he feeding them? Torturing them? In a town so tense the slightest sound draws instant attention, why has no one heard anything, or seen anything the least bit suspicious?"

Samantha said, "He has to have a fair amount of room, and it has to be a remote location . . ."

IT WAS THE strangest thing, Robbie decided. The room around her, brightly lit, just faded out, darkening around the edges. The darkness slowly crept toward her, and she couldn't move, couldn't ask the others if they couldn't *see* what was happening.

Couldn't help her *stop* it.

The darkness was going to swallow her up, she knew that, felt it, and watched helplessly as it swallowed up the others one by one, creeping up to them, over them, like some hideous black sludge, moving in terrifying slow motion, until they vanished and only the black was left. Only the darkness. She could hear her heart beating, but nothing else.

Nothing except the eerie sounds of that thick, smothering darkness flowing toward her, rustling softly as though it were whispering to her.

It was . . . almost seductive.

Wait for me.

Can you hear me? I know you can. You aren't like the others.

We can . . . together . . . and we . . .

. . . belong together . . . you know . . .

. . . we do . . .

Listen to me . . .

She didn't know where it came from, but Robbie was aware of the certain knowledge that if she listened to the whispers, if she let them in, she would die.

The blackness was creeping toward her, rustling, whispering, and all Robbie could think to do was slam her shields up as hard as she could, making them as strong as she could make them, because she couldn't let it in . . .

"DANTE IS A medium," Luke was saying. "Able to communicate with the dead. When they want to communicate, that is. And even then, they often have nothing helpful to say. Something else we've learned."

What? We've already talked about this. Haven't we?

Half nodding, Dante said, "The universe doesn't like to make things too easy for us, apparently. Even with these extra senses of ours, we still have to work to get what we want and need."

Wait a minute. I know we've talked about this. Because Jonah was curious and didn't seem freaked out. Though right now . . .

Jonah nodded, more uncertain than anything else.

Maybe he's more freaked out than he shows. Maybe he always was.

"Robbie is a telepath, able to read minds," Luke said. "Not all minds, of course; even our strongest telepaths can only read sixty to seventy percent of those around them. Sort of like trying to tune in on a particular radio frequency; not all people are on a frequency a particular telepath can receive."

What the hell . . .

Without any ability at all to stop it, Robbie heard herself saying, "Like all of us here, and most agents in the SCU, I have mental shields, so I can generally block out thoughts even on my frequency when I want to. And I usually want to, in case you were wondering. I believe it's an invasion of privacy to read someone else's thoughts without their knowledge or permission." She sounded more than a little defiant.

Wait. I got over that. Got past it. Mostly. Didn't I? Because it's the work, just like Bishop said. It's a tool I use in the work, to help put the bad guys away.

Luke said, "Robbie is our problem child; she's still trying to decide if her abilities are a gift or a curse."

No, I'm not!

Robbie felt weirdly detached from what was happening, and yet she knew she felt irritation when she said, that *other* Robbie said, "They aren't a gift *or* a curse, they're just abilities natural to me. And I just have to practice more to use them effectively. Miranda said so. And Bishop. Besides, Dante is the problem child. He really doesn't *want* to talk to dead people."

Not really arguing, Dante said, "Well, it's unsettling."

"I can imagine," Jonah said, his expression saying he really, really couldn't.

All right, this has to stop. Because it didn't happen, not like this. I'm positive it didn't happen like this. He's trying to trick me, that's what it is. Trying to . . . what is he trying to do? Pull me into a different time? A different . . . reality?

Is that even possible?

Does it have anything to do with losing time in the bubbles of energy?

If I concentrate really hard, I can stop this. Him. I can push back the darkness. I can. I know I can.

Robbie concentrated as hard as she could, putting everything she had into shoring up her shields. And even so, even with everything she had, there was an instant when the darkness around her swirled suddenly in iridescent flashes, shifted—

And she was standing on the sidewalk of downtown Serenity, in the shadows of a dark building. Now, or on a different, equally dark night. She wanted immediately to move, to get to the pool of light up ahead, the light from one of the old-fashioned streetlamps.

But she couldn't move a muscle.

She could hear her heart beating again, hear her own gasping breaths—and then she realized that wasn't her, she wasn't hearing herself, she—

The woman staggered into the pool of light, both her hands at her throat. A strange gurgling sound came from behind her hands, and for a moment it seemed she would turn and stare at Robbie, something Robbie hoped desperately would not happen. Because she couldn't look away, she could only stare at the woman as she sort of tilted, like her balance was affected by something.

And then she just dropped, the light hitting her in such a way that she was unrecognizable as anything but a heap of darkness in the vague shape of something human.

"WHAT?" ROBBIE BLINKED, looked around the room. The bright, becoming-familiar room of their makeshift command center.

She looked down to see a hand on her arm, and followed it up to focus on Dante's concerned face.

"Hey," he said. "Where did you go?"

She didn't find the question strange—which *was* strange, or should have been.

"How long was I . . . away?" she asked.

Dante looked across the table, and she followed his gaze to see familiar faces and a puzzled Jonah-face that was becoming familiar.

Sam answered her question, saying simply, "About five minutes."

"It seemed longer," Robbie said, dimly astonished at her own calm voice. "It really seemed a lot longer than that."

"You don't have visions," Dante said.

Robbie thought about it, nodded slowly. "Yeah. But that's not what it was."

"Then what was it?" Luke asked.

Robbie spared a moment to recognize that as hard as she'd tried for most of her life to *not* use the psychic abilities she'd been born with, it was immeasurably comforting to be among people who were utterly matter-of-fact about such abilities.

"I think . . . I think he's psychic."

"The unsub?" Sam asked.

"Yeah."

"What?" If anything, Jonah looked horrified.

"He got into my head. Not all the way, just . . . far enough. He tried to trick me. Tried to convince me that things . . . didn't happen the way I remember them happening. Us talking. About our abilities. And I knew that if I let him do that, let him convince me what he showed me was real, then he'd win."

"What would he win?" Dante asked.

"Me." Robbie nodded slowly. "Me. He was . . . it was a test. To see if he could control me. Like he controlled them."

AMY GRIMES FELT as if she had been . . . sleepwalking. All her senses were deadened, dull, and her memories were awfully fuzzy. She remembered leaving town with Simon.

Starting to leave town.

And then . . . nothing.

Or at least nothing she could hold on to. Thoughts and scenes and sensations flitted through her mind, some bright, some dark, and she didn't know which of them were real.

It took all her effort, everything she had, to force her eyes open, and when she did, the scared little girl who lived always in the back of her mind flinched, then whimpered.

It was dark.

Darker than dark. Darker than dark could ever be. The darkness had substance, weight. It smothered sound. It had power.

Power to hold her. Because she couldn't move, no matter how hard she tried. She thought she was moving her eyes, darting them around, seeking even a sliver of light, but she wasn't sure that was what she was doing because the darkness never changed.

There was no light.

There was no escape.

She didn't even know if she was alone here. Wherever here was. She had no sense of anyone near, heard no sound—

Simon. Was he here? Was he close?

She wanted to call for him, to make some kind of sound, but she was still unable to move. Unable even to open her mouth. The whimper of that little girl in her mind was trapped in her head. And even that was growing fainter. Fainter.

Amy had the dim sense, suddenly, of someone else. Someone who, like that terrified little girl, was in her mind. Someone who had abruptly taken notice of her, as if he had been distracted for a time and only just realized she was aware.

Impossibly, the darkness got even darker, heavier, until Amy didn't think she was even able to breathe. It was in her mind, and it covered over thoughts and questions and panic and fear. It covered over the whimpering little girl.

It covered over everything, black and powerful.

Until Amy wasn't even aware of herself anymore.

Until she was . . . until she was . . .

Gone.

EIGHT

Jonah leaned forward at that, his expression shifting from horrified to questioning, intent. "Them? You mean my missing people?"

"I think so. I was trying to block him, trying to shore up my shields. And he was testing them, my shields. He tried to scare me. He tried to make me feel helpless. Then it was almost like . . . seduction. Promises. Like he thought he could tempt me."

"To go to him?" Luke asked.

"To give way to him. To let him control me." Robbie drew a breath and let it out slowly, really beginning to understand. "Another SCU agent told me that during a few cases over the years, there had been some . . . He said Bishop called them minor skirmishes. Of mind control. But that they'd only seen it between two psychics who were either deeply bonded or related by blood. And even then it was always an uncertain thing, impossibly difficult to control."

Luke was nodding. "Bishop's never been completely convinced

it's even true mind control. He thinks it's like hypnosis. We can't be hypnotized, but another psychic, with the right abilities, could . . . manipulate our reality. In theory."

Robbie jabbed her index finger in his general direction. "Yes. It was like that. I saw and heard myself, and you guys, having a conversation I *know* we never had, at least not like that. But it was so real. And I was fighting so hard to push him out, using all my strength, that when I finally did—it was like a rubber band snapping. I wasn't in that reality he created, and I wasn't here . . ."

She turned her head and looked toward the big window whose new blinds protected them from the curious gazes of passersby. "I was . . . out there. Like I overshot, somehow. I was on Main Street, just around the corner, in the shadows of a dark building. But I could see ahead of me the light from a streetlamp."

"Robbie?" Dante's voice held concern. "You've gone pale."

She tried to get a hold on herself. "Yeah. Um . . . I saw something, and I'm honestly not sure if it was real or—or something he threw at me in that last minute."

"What did you see?" Jonah asked, still intent.

I like him better here in my reality, where he's not freaked out by what I can do.

She tried to ignore that realization. "I saw a woman. She sort of staggered out of the darkness between two buildings and into the circle of light on the sidewalk."

"Who was she?"

"I wasn't close enough to see. Or maybe it was the dark, and the light falling the wrong way. I don't know. She had her hands up to her throat, and I heard a sound coming from her. An awful sound.

She seemed to lose her balance. And then she just dropped like a stone."

"Robbie—"

"I don't know who she was, but I know she was dead. I know he killed her. I just don't know if it was real." She hesitated, then said, "I think . . . I think she's dead because she was in the way. He had to be close to try to manipulate my mind. He had to be close, and she almost caught him. Maybe she did catch him. Maybe that's why he killed her. She caught him, and he didn't have time to do anything else. Didn't have time to control her. So he had to kill her."

Jonah was beginning to look uneasy. Very uneasy. "I think maybe we'd better walk out to Main Street."

"I think you're right," Luke said, getting to his feet.

Rather desperately, Robbie said, "It might not have been real. It might have just been another trick. And even if it wasn't, I can't swear that it was even here, in Serenity."

Sam said, "You're a telepath; have you ever found yourself, even in spirit, somewhere else?"

"No," Robbie said slowly. "No, this is the first time anything like that ever happened."

"Then," Luke said, "odds are, it was our unsub. And if it was, we need to understand as much as we can about his abilities pronto. But first, we need to find out if what you saw is real."

Samantha and Dante were also getting to their feet, all of them adjusting or just touching the guns they wore in a kind of automatic reassurance.

"We need to be sure, Robbie," Sam said.

Robbie pushed her chair back and stood, vaguely surprised that her own hand reached to touch her gun; she hadn't thought about her training, about the familiarity created by hours and hours of practice at the gun range. She hadn't wanted to carry a gun, but now she was very glad she did.

And that she knew how to use it.

JONAH GOT TO her first, while the others, guns drawn, scanned the area all around the streetlight. The downtown area was still quiet and still, and for now at least all the light came from the streetlights and the flashlights all of them carried.

Robbie stepped closer to Jonah, who was kneeling beside the woman. Her body was positioned so that it had required the light from his flashlight to show them she was indeed dead, her throat slashed from ear to ear and a pool of blood all around her upper body.

"Who is it, Jonah?" Robbie couldn't see her face, mostly because she hadn't been able to look too closely.

"Annie Duncan." Jonah sat back on his heels, the streetlight's glow making his face look gaunt. Or maybe it wasn't the streetlight. And it was as if all the feeling had been squeezed out of his voice. "She was one of my officers."

Lucas seemed to flow out of the shadows to join them. "Sam and Dante are checking the other side of the alley, but so far the only thing visible is some blood." He paused, holstering his weapon, then added unemotionally, "Arterial spray on the wall, looks like. The unsub must have cut her throat in the alley, then let her go. She couldn't have walked more than a few steps. In fact, I'm surprised she made it this far."

"Why was she here at all?" Robbie asked. "She isn't in uniform, but I don't remember her being one of your plainclothes cops."

He didn't really have those, Jonah reflected, glad for something to occupy his mind. Unless he or Sarah decided to work out of uniform, which was the norm for him and an occasional thing for her. Otherwise, other than Jean at reception, and a couple of other non-cop administration people who only worked part-time, all Jonah's people wore uniforms.

"She shouldn't be here," he said finally, without looking up at Robbie or Lucas. "She was one of a handful who'd been working the phones since dark and on duty since the first shift. I'd told her and a couple of others to go home and get some sleep."

"When was that?" Luke asked.

"When I checked in at the station on my way to get our takeout. I double-checked on the way back, and they'd all gone home. Or, at least, weren't at the station."

"That was a bit after seven," Luke said. "It's nearly ten o'clock now. She should have gotten home."

"I sent them in pairs," Jonah said automatically. "If one of them lived alone, the other officer was to go in with them and check out the place, just to be sure. Annie lived alone."

"Who took her home?"

"Adam Sheffey. He's married with a couple of toddlers—and had one hell of a security system installed barely a week ago. Also has a very protective family dog." Jonah shook his head slightly. "He's a good cop. He would have checked out Annie's place thoroughly before leaving her alone there."

"She's out of uniform," Robbie repeated. "She must have gotten home safely, Jonah. Had time to change. Maybe she came back out to get something to eat."

He was shaking his head. "She enjoyed cooking. When the rest of her shift would send out for a pizza or some other takeout, she'd always have something homemade in the break room fridge. Usually somebody tried to wheedle her into swapping takeout for her food, because she was such a good cook."

"What other reason would she have to come back here?" Robbie asked. "Far as I can see, she isn't even carrying her sidearm."

"I can't think of a reason. She's been a cop ten years; she'd know better than to come out, alone and unarmed, at a time like this."

Dante and Samantha rejoined them then, both holstering their weapons.

"Nothing," Dante reported to Lucas. "It's all pavement or gravel, and other than what was in the alley, there's no sign of blood. No footprints either, bloody or otherwise."

"I can get Sully out with his dogs," Jonah said, more or less automatically.

"There might be a faster way," Samantha said.

HE WATCHED THEM from his vantage point, unsurprised that they moved as easily as any well-practiced team. They didn't stop to gather any of Chief Riggs's people, which gave him pause. He would have expected the telepath among them to be weakened by his attack.

Uncertain, at the very least. Bothered. Unwilling to trust her own instincts and thoughts and urges.

But she seemed very focused and very certain, leading them cautiously but steadily along Main Street until they reached the circle of light from a streetlamp.

And the crumpled body of a woman on the cold concrete sidewalk.

He wanted to linger, to watch them work the scene. He wanted to know if they used standard police work or their extra senses. He really wanted to get a better idea of what those other senses consisted of. Besides the telepath. But her steadiness made him feel just a bit uneasy about remaining so close to her.

She was strong. Stronger than he had expected.

And he wasn't quite certain what that would mean.

But for now, for this night, he knew that if he wanted his work to continue, he needed to fade back into the night. And possibly reconsider his options.

Because he had connected with the telepath's mind. He wasn't sure if she knew what that meant.

But he knew.

"NO WAY IN hell," Lucas said with some force.

Samantha's tone was calm and reasonable. "It's the quickest way, and you know it. Maybe I'll get a sense of the unsub and maybe not, but at least we can find out why Annie was out here when she should have been safely locked in at home."

"It's too dangerous, Sam. She's *dead*. Last time you tried something like this, it nearly killed you."

"That was different."

"Was it?"

"Luke, we don't have time to argue. With every moment that

passes, the energy in her brain dissipates more. If I wait too long her memories will be out of reach forever."

Robbie was looking at Dante. "You don't get a sense of the recently dead, do you?"

He shook his head. "Not so far." He didn't look too eager to try this time.

"It's safer if I try." Samantha was still looking at her partner and husband. "I've been at this a lot longer. I have more control."

Not entirely sure what was going on, Jonah said, "You aren't a medium too, are you?"

"No. But a clairvoyant can often pick up energy from a crime scene. Or a death scene. Even a dying brain has energy. Maybe especially a dying brain. Our brains have energy, electrical impulses, and they don't just stop the way a heart stops. It takes a few minutes for that energy to dissipate. Luke, I have to try and you know it."

Robbie said to Lucas, "You know the signs if she gets in too deep. If that happens, pull her out. But we need to know, Luke. Even a rookie agent can be sure of that."

Their team leader hesitated, then swore under his breath. "I'll be close," he told Samantha. "I see *anything* that looks like you might be in trouble, I'll yank you out. Got it?"

"Got it." She knelt down on the other side of the body from Jonah, and looked at him steadily. "You up for this?"

"I have no idea," he said frankly. *A dying brain? Christ.* "Just tell me what *not* to do so I don't screw up whatever it is you're trying to do."

"Lean back, and don't touch her."

"That's it?"

"That's it." Samantha barely waited for the chief to lean back and for Lucas to kneel at her side. She drew a breath and let it out slowly, then leaned forward and, without any sign of squeamishness, placed one hand across Annie Duncan's forehead and the other over the bloodstained sweatshirt just above her heart. Then Sam closed her eyes and bowed her head, almost as if praying.

Jonah hadn't been told not to talk during this . . . procedure . . . but the silent attention of the others was a good indication to him that he should keep his mouth shut. And all he could think about for several minutes was how on earth he was going to tell Annie Duncan's parents she'd been brutally murdered.

How could a parent ever recover from that?

And what about Nessa Tyler's parents? The Grimes and Church families? Judge Carson's many friends and the far-flung family he seldom mentioned? Sean Messina's family and girlfriend? Luna Lang's husband and infant child?

He told himself that his missing people weren't dead, couldn't be, that this group of very matter-of-fact FBI agents with their odd abilities was going to help him find his people alive.

All of them.

Because he was pretty sure he couldn't live with any other outcome.

Even as that realization surfaced, Samantha sucked in a hard breath, and even in the poor light of the streetlamp, he was certain he saw her normal pallor increase.

A glance at Luke's face told him only that the other man was grimly watchful, but not yet ready to pull his partner and wife from . . . wherever or whenever she was.

In Annie Duncan's dying moments? What kind of hell must that be? How could anyone still breathing get that close to a violent death . . . and return to tell the tale?

SAMANTHA NEVER HAD any preconceived notions whenever she focused on an object used in violence—or a person whose life had been brutally destroyed. Not anymore. She had discovered the use-lessness of that peering into a crystal ball as a carnival seer. No matter what she expected back then, using abilities still raw and mostly untried, reality was always something else.

Lesson learned.

She didn't think about what she might see or hear because it was always different. Always unique.

And sometimes horribly painful.

Annie Duncan died in agony and darkness. Not just pain, and not just night. In her final moments of consciousness, she could feel him behind her, flesh and bone like her. Except not like her. Dark. Something once human coated in darkness, like a sludge of . . . evil. And strong. So strong. And cold. And inescapable.

You shouldn't have been watching, little girl.

Wait. Who?

For a strange and dizzying instant, Samantha knew that their psychic unsub had abruptly become aware of her. It didn't make sense, because she was in Annie's mind, in Annie's memories of what *had* happened, so how—

Annie tried to force words past the forearm pressed against her throat, but couldn't. Wanted to tell him she hadn't seen anything, anything at all. Too tired to cook but hungry, she had taken a short-cut from her condo to the favored local pizza place, walking instead of driving because she'd thought the walk would do her good, clear her head, so preoccupied with her thoughts it hadn't even occurred to her to bring her gun. Something had been nagging at her, and she just couldn't make it come clear in her mind. Something she had read in a report or a statement, something someone had said to her or something she'd said to herself—

She didn't really feel the knife, not immediately. Just his forearm removed, and before she could say anything at all, there was some-thing else preventing her from speaking. She put her hands up and felt the horrendous opening of her throat, felt the hot blood flowing over her hands, and her legs went weak.

And then the agony came, and the terror, and she hardly felt him give her a shove so that she stumbled the last few feet through the alley and toward the light she could see ahead. Light that was dim-ming with every staggering step she took. Her life flowing redly between her fingers.

It was too soon. She hadn't done everything she wanted to do. There was nobody here to say good-bye to. She wondered if anybody would mind her leaving. If anybody would mourn. Her parents. Oh, God, her parents . . .

Darkness was closing over her, and she barely felt the cold hard-ness of the pavement as she fell. In those final seconds, she wasn't thinking of sins or regrets or even things left unsaid. Except one, because that one thing might bring the little girl home, might bring them all home, and she was the only one . . . the only . . . the . . . only . . . one . . . who . . . knew . . . It was getting so dark. Why was it getting so dark . . .

"No!" Sam knew her voice was shaking, but only because she was shivering so violently. Luke had already put his jacket around her and was holding her back against him, his hands firmly gripping her wrists, and she didn't have to look at her fingers and palms to know they were marked by frostnip.

Which only happened when she got too close to evil.

Or too close to death.

"Dammit," she whispered.

"I had to pull you out, Sam." His voice was rough.

She nodded and let herself relax against him. "I know. And it was . . . it was the last seconds anyway. She was almost gone. But . . . *dammit*. Something had been bugging her. Something she'd seen in the reports, or read in a statement, something someone had said to her. And in the very last seconds of her life, she realized that whatever it was could help bring that little girl and the others home. But she was slipping away even then. If I'd followed—"

"You'd be dead," Luke said. He pulled her even closer, crossing her arms over her chest while being careful not to further hurt her cold, cold hands.

Samantha didn't argue.

Catching a glimpse even in the dim light, Robbie said, "Your hands are white where they were touching her. Why?"

Lucas answered. "It's frostnip. If she goes too deep, that's one of the things that happens. If she's holding an object, it marks her with its shape, as if it were colder than you can imagine. The marks can last for months."

"No nosebleed this time," Sam offered. "And my head's just a little sore, not really pounding."

"Maybe, but you're frozen clear through and exhausted. I can feel it. Jonah, she's done for at least ten or twelve hours. I've got to get her warm and she has to sleep."

It was Robbie who said, "You two go get checked into the hotel, then. Take the SUV. Dante and I will help Jonah and his people here, and then we'll find out what Officer Duncan's been working on. Maybe we can figure out what was bugging her."

Lucas got to his feet, bringing Samantha easily with him. "It'll probably be close to lunchtime tomorrow before we're back working," he warned.

"I don't need that much sleep," Sam said, ruining the claim with a yawn. "Jesus. Maybe so. Listen, you guys—rope off that alley till daylight, and don't let anyone go in there, even your crime scene team. One of us needs to check that out. Hell, maybe all of us. I know we didn't see anything with flashlights, but he was right behind her, and if he didn't leave footprints in her blood, then he was definitely pressed back against the wall when he was holding her in front of him. I'm not sure what it is, but something about that alley is definitely bugging me."

After glancing down at the dead woman, Lucas said, "In that case, I'm not letting you out of my sight for the duration."

"There's something else," Sam told them, her voice growing fainter. "The unsub . . . he knew I was in Annie's head, her memories."

"How could he know that?" Dante asked.

"Dunno. But he did. Not sure if he knew which of us it was, except I think he'd recognize Robbie. I don't understand how it could work like that . . . but I felt him become aware of me. Just before he cut Annie's throat."

NINE

Either because he didn't realize the significance of what Sam had told them or merely because he had more pressing issues on his mind, Jonah didn't question what Samantha had reported. Sounding unutterably weary himself, he said, "I'll send a couple of uniforms and the CSU. And alert our coroner. He's a semi-retired surgeon who spent a few years as a medical examiner down in Florida; he knows his stuff."

"Good," Lucas said.

"I have to go notify her family. After I tell my people at the station. They're going to take it hard. Annie was well liked."

Robbie opened her mouth to offer to come along but then stopped herself when Lucas caught her eye and shook his head slightly.

Lucas said, "Robbie and Dante will stay here and make sure no one disturbs the scene." He paused, then added, "Along with the usual equipment and supplies, we brought along one of those small, collapsible tents they use over in England to protect—and shield—victims while the medical and other technicians work on them. Respect for the dead as well as preserving as much of the scene as possible and shielding the victim from curious eyes. Probably a good idea to use it here, since this area is so public. So visible. We'll be drawing a crowd here soon. It could take hours before she's ready to be moved, maybe not even until daylight or close to it." He didn't add that shielding Annie Duncan's body from anyone other than police might at least lessen the shock of her murder.

Maybe.

"Thanks," Jonah said, briefly but with real gratitude. He gave a last look toward his fallen officer, then turned and headed back toward the station.

Speaking low to Lucas, Robbie said, "I might have been able to help. I doubt he's had to make many notifications like this one."

Sounding very sleepy now, Sam said, "Don't sell him short. For a small-town police chief he's gotten himself some big-city experience." She pronounced those last three words very carefully, adding just as carefully, "Pretty sure he's done this before. Just . . . not here in his hometown."

Knowing she was about to go out, Lucas said to the other two, "Help Jonah and his people any way you can without stepping on anybody's toes. *But stay together.* And I mean within sight of each other. Especially out here."

"You know something we don't?" Dante said.

"Ask Robbie. As soon as I get Sam settled, I'll check in with you two, but I'll stay with her. Unless we get a break soon, this could drag on awhile. It'll be best to split the duty whenever we can, especially since this unsub does his hunting at night. When Sam and I come back, you two can get settled into the hotel and get some rest."

"Copy that," Dante said.

"I'll come by and drop off the tent on our way to the hotel."

This time, Dante merely nodded, and barely waited until Lucas and Samantha were out of sight before looking at Robbie with lifted brows. "Ask you?"

"You know, I think that telepathic part of how he does what he does is a lot stronger than he'll admit," she said.

"Robbie."

She sighed, glanced down at the murdered cop, then returned her gaze to her partner. "The bastard got into my head, Dante. He didn't make me do anything—except have to sort my way through a few false memories and then see this poor woman stagger out of that alley and die on the sidewalk."

Dante waited, frowning.

"With everybody in the room then, I had my shields up—and the window closed. And yet he got in."

"You're a strong telepath," Dante said slowly. "Maybe he homed in on that."

"Yeah, well, that's probably what has Luke worried. Has me worried too. Of all of us—at least in theory—I should be most conscious of any attempt to manipulate my mind. The one most likely to sense another presence before that presence can have any effect on me."

"But you didn't."

"Not at first. Not for too damned long. I was too busy feeling shaken and uncertain because my memories were . . . stirred up and spread out in a different way. No lies. What was said was said, more or less.

Only not like *that*. And what it means is that monster is a scary-powerful psychic able to manipulate memories, manipulate reality. Individual reality, at least. And if he can do that to a psychic with pretty strong shields . . ."

"He could really do a number on a nonpsychic with little or no shielding."

"Exactly. Like, maybe, our six missing people?"

"YOU'RE SURE?" BISHOP asked.

"I'm sure he got inside Robbie's head," Lucas replied, keeping his voice low even though he knew that Samantha was deeply asleep in the next room. "From what she said, the first thing he did was manipulate some of her memories. She said there were no lies, no deceptions, just information . . . rearranged."

"Not something we've seen before," Bishop said slowly.

"Yeah, I was kind of hoping you might have encountered it even if we haven't. This creep really is unique?"

"He didn't make Robbie do anything."

Long accustomed to his unit chief's habit of answering some questions obliquely and some not at all, Luke merely said, "Far as we could tell, no. Maybe just a test, to see if he could get in and mess with her mind. But he did give her a memory she shouldn't have had, or maybe a vision. She was standing on the sidewalk watching as Officer Annie Duncan staggered out of an alley and collapsed with her throat cut."

Since Lucas had already related information about the murder, Bishop was aware of what had happened.

"Do you think he was showing her that as it happened?"

"If not in the moment, then damned close. Sam said Officer Duncan's body was still warm."

"I know you don't like it," Bishop said, "but Samantha's ability to retrieve memories is also unique."

"She retrieved memories from a dead woman's dying brain, Bishop. Just the idea is something out of a horror movie and we both know it. At best, it pulls too much of her own life force from the psychic, and at worst she could be pulled into the energy escaping the brain and end up God knows where. Now, you and the doctors and whoever may find that fascinating, and *maybe* something new can be learned about the brain, even about the death process, but Sam's the one taking the risks. Both her hands were frostnipped, and she was out before I could get her up here to our room. She came close, really close this time."

"You said she went out earlier in the day. Do you have any idea what caused that?"

"As far as I can tell, there's a choice between at least two possibilities, and I don't like either of them. First, Sam reacted to that energy bubble—though why it knocked her out when Robbie was able to sense the energy without it harming her is anybody's guess."

"And the second possibility?"

"Same as with Robbie. He got into her head somehow. But Sam isn't a telepath, and she had a lot of experience in her carnival years in warding off negative energy, plus what she's learned in the SCU since then. Maybe she pushed back without even thinking about it, but the effort took enough of her own energy and strength that she went out before even she could realize what happened. It is pretty much her default response to using too much energy."

"True."

"Also true that it would have taken a tremendous amount of energy to knock her out like that, so quickly."

"I would say so."

"And she's certain he was aware of her later, Bishop. While she was tapping into the last of Annie's memories, experiencing her murder. How is that even possible?"

"I don't know," Bishop said.

"You want to venture a guess?" Lucas tended to be intense often enough for it to be fairly usual, but to speak to his unit chief and a man he respected deeply with that snap in his voice was ample evidence of just how worried about Samantha he was.

Bishop paused, but not out of temper as his thoughtful voice indicated. "We know that when minds touch they leave . . . bread crumbs. Even if Samantha wasn't aware of the contact earlier, he apparently *did* try to get through her shields. Maybe he did. Not far, obviously, but maybe just far enough to leave a bread crumb or two. And when Sam was using her abilities later to get what information she could from Annie Duncan, the unsub somehow became aware of that and . . . followed the bread crumbs."

"That's a lot of qualifiers."

"It's that sort of situation."

Lucas sighed. "So . . . he wasn't sensing her when she was reliving Annie's memories just before Annie died because those memories were in the past; the unsub just managed to become a part of Sam's process."

"That makes more sense, doesn't it?"

"I'm not sure anything in all this makes sense." Lucas sighed again. "Sam has a better shield than I do, but I know damned well she'll insist on using her abilities again. And soon. We have evidence bagged from the scenes of four of the six sites of the disappearances; I talked her out of touching any of that today, but with a murder added to the abductions, the clock is moving faster, and we both know what she'll do."

"If we don't, we should after all this time." Bishop paused, then said, "When she first went out, when he presumably touched her mind or some part of it, it was during the day, right? You were walking the scenes where the missing people disappeared, during the day."

"Yeah." Lucas frowned, repeating, "Yeah. So he strikes after dark, but could be keeping an eye on us during the day as well. Shit."

"Could have been just the one day," Bishop suggested. "Because you all got to town today and he either knew or heard you'd be arriving. It would have been news and spread around town very quickly. Maybe he just wanted to watch you work."

"And test our defenses. So he knows we're psychics."

"He knows Samantha and Robbie are. No way to be absolutely sure he tested you and Dante. In fact, he probably didn't. Too many men believe women are the weaker, more vulnerable targets, especially predators like this one; he may have simply tried them first for that reason."

With a certain grim satisfaction, Lucas said, "Well, he's got a lot to learn, doesn't he?"

"Even so, you're right to worry about Samantha. We both know she has a tendency to go deeper than she needs to."

"We also both know that she'll do what she feels is right, no matter how dangerous it might be."

"True."

"You want to tell me how I can protect her from herself?"

"Luke, we're both married to strong women. And we both know they can take care of themselves." He paused, adding wryly, "We both also know that knowledge doesn't put a dent in the worry. Look, you're there with her, and you know the danger signs. Don't hesitate to pull her out if you have any doubts at all."

"I never have."

"We both know that too."

Lucas sighed. "This unsub has been active for nearly a month, with six disappearances—and no bodies found. No way to know if his victims are alive or dead. We checked all the records we could find, and so far there's nothing remotely similar to this unsub either at an earlier time here or anytime anywhere else in the southeast."

"I took it nationwide," Bishop said. "No hits. Unless he made some drastic changes, he started in Serenity less than a month ago. And that's likely where he'll finish."

"I told Robbie and Dante to stay within sight of each other at all times. Also told them we'd split shifts, at least unless and until there's a break in the case. This unsub being psychic ups the stakes. A lot. I don't want any one of us vulnerable because we're tired." Lucas knew more than most the dangers of being tired—and psychic.

"Good. Now take your own advice and get some rest. You know you don't have to stay awake to watch over Samantha."

They had that in common too.

"Yeah, I will." Luke paused, then added, "This town's been keeping it together mostly, but this murder is going to change everything."

"Yes. Get some rest, Luke. Check in tomorrow."

"Right."

"THIS STRONG WOMAN is worried," Miranda said as her husband pushed the speaker button on the phone to end the connection and then came to join her on the sofa in front of a low fire. Nearly June or not, there was still patchy snow all around their comfortable mountain aerie.

"So am I, love," Bishop confessed. "But Luke has more than proven he's one of our top team leaders. Together, he and Sam are a formidable pair."

"I know that. I just wish . . ."

"That we could tell them? Warn them?"

It could help.

It could also make things immeasurably worse. We agreed, remember?

Aloud, she said, "We could have warned them he's psychic."

"They figured that out quickly enough."

"What about the price, Noah? The price of our silence. If he touched Sam's mind and Robbie's . . . he'll try to use that to his advantage. And if he was powerful enough to drop Sam in an instant, then he's too powerful."

"I know that. And so does Luke."

"If they'd known in advance, they would have been more guarded. He might not have gotten in at all."

Bishop pulled his wife even closer. "We both learned long ago the difference between prediction and prophesy. Do you really believe anything we could have told them would have changed a future we both saw?"

"I don't know. No . . . I suppose not. It's just . . . so many of our people have to go through some sort of baptism of fire, either before they join the team or after. They work their asses off to make the world better. To save lives. To destroy monsters. The universe made them psychic, and God knows that's enough of a burden. Why these . . . tests?"

"I can't speak for the universe."

Miranda gave him a look.

"But if I could, it would probably be in clichés. What doesn't destroy us makes us stronger, for instance. You're stronger for what you've been through, as brutally painful as some of it has been. So am I. So is every member of the team."

Steadily, she said, "Yeah, but sometimes, if things get really bad, people do get destroyed."

"We didn't see that."

"We saw the possibility."

He was silent.

"We saw darkness, Noah. A darkness neither of us has ever seen before. What if they aren't strong enough to fight that?"

"They have to be," he said simply.

She half shook her head. "We've been incredibly lucky as a unit; if our agents weren't psychics, half of them would be dead."

"Not half," he objected.

Miranda couldn't manage a smile. "I just . . . I have a bad feeling about this one. Over and above what we saw. That maybe our luck has finally run out."

"You know I don't believe in luck."

"I know. Still."

"You want to go down there, don't you?"

"I think . . . we need to be closer than we are. Not in town, not visible, but nearby."

"And if he senses us?"

That did conjure a smile. "If he senses us, love, he pretty much has to be that 'perfect psychic' you've been waiting for. And if he's that, if darkness instead of light got your perfect psychic, then we have to fight him with everything we've got. And much better to meet him on our terms than on his."

"You've got a point." He paused. "Then again, he could just be your garden-variety psycho with one of our tools in his toolbox. Or something like one of our tools. Something more than telepathy."

"Either way, I think we need to be closer. Not because Luke and the others can't handle themselves, but because of what we saw. I don't know how they're going to handle *that*. Do you?"

"No," Bishop admitted. "I don't. Especially Luke. He's good at finding people. Not good at losing them."

ROBBIE AND DANTE did their best to help Jonah and his officers as they went about the grim task of looking for evidence on and around the body of their fallen comrade, but they quickly discovered that their best was simply to keep their distance and keep a respectful silence.

"Sorry," Jonah said as he paused briefly near them. "They don't really blame you, it's just . . ."

"It's okay," Robbie said, keeping her voice low and matter-of-fact.

"We get it. Nobody died until we came to town, at least that they know of. They've needed somebody to blame for weeks. We can take it."

Jonah frowned. "It's irrational, and in their right minds they know it. Once her—once Annie is taken to the morgue at the clinic and Dr. Calder gets started on the post, I'm calling a meeting at the station. Probably best if you two don't come."

Dante was nodding, but Robbie said, "Don't be too hard on them, okay? They need time to process what's happened. So do you."

"Yeah. My head gets that." He continued on.

Robbie sighed. "Why do I get the feeling he's blaming himself for Annie's murder?"

"You're not reading him?"

"Are you kidding? After this maniac got into my head before, I closed up tight as a drum. I don't want to read *anybody*."

"Listen, it was you who told me that's not healthy."

"Over the long term, it isn't," she replied. "But it's night, his favorite time to hunt, and I'm betting he's close enough to watch this. This is the show he's been denied so far. A spellbound audience for his work. And I really hope he isn't realizing it."

"I don't like the sound of that."

"No, me either. If he decides he likes this show more than his abracadabra abductions, we're really in trouble. Does he want to stay mysterious and watch the town slowly tear itself apart? Or would he rather do this again and watch it happen faster?"

"You think that'll happen? Destroy the town?"

Robbie waited while two cops with set expressions walked past them without a glance, then said, "It's already happening. When people disappear, those left behind can hope. But with every day that passes and he isn't caught, there isn't even a decent lead, and more people disappear, hope turns in on itself. Maybe the cops aren't working hard enough? Let's blame them. The FBI should be able to find people, right? Let's blame them. Or maybe . . . maybe it's somebody they know. Neighbor suspects neighbor. Friend suspects friend. Spouses suspect each other." Robbie paused, then finished, "Murdered bodies start turning up, and muttered questions and deflected blame won't be enough for these people. Things will start to get loud and ugly."

"That does not sound fun."

"No. It won't be. Not for anyone." Robbie sighed. "Small towns depend on community more than cities do. Neighbor helping neighbor. Everybody coming together in a crisis. But this . . . it's been weeks and they feel helpless. After this murder, helpless is going to turn to angry."

"Great."

They were standing near the opening of the taped-off alley, which gave them a clear view into the tent where Annie Duncan lay as well as a good look at how much more active the downtown area had become, and not just with cops.

They were certainly frightened of the predator hunting among them, but this, this brutally murdered officer, was the first tangible evidence the people of Serenity could actually see. Even if all they *saw* was a small white tent with grim-faced CSU and other officers moving about, as well as the coroner, who had gone into the tent for a while but now waited patiently, expressionless, leaning back against the tailgate of an old black hearse with a magnetic CORONER sign clapped to each of the front doors.

Dante said, "They really weren't prepared for all this, were they?" He looked around at the yellow POLICE LINE DO NOT CROSS tape, behind which were gathered a goodly number of Serenity's citizens— excepting children, presumably left home with at least one frightened adult behind a locked door.

It was after midnight, but the downtown area was brightly lit, by streetlamps turned up to full wattage and storefront lights on as well. The downtown Diner had even reopened, offering coffee and sandwiches to the working cops.

"Nobody's prepared for this," Robbie said. "They read about evil in a book or see it on TV or a movie screen. And if they're very unlucky, something bad done by evil will happen to someone they know—which is more than close enough. Nobody wants to see evil up close and personal. Except us."

"I don't really want to *see* evil," Dante confessed.

"You know what I mean. We hunt evil. Professionally. We go out looking for the monsters other people wish didn't exist."

Dante eyed her. "You're a glass-half-empty sort of person, aren't you?"

"Only at murder scenes." She shifted restlessly, frowning. "Dammit, I feel so helpless doing nothing."

"I don't think any of these cops want us helping," Dante reminded her.

"No, but—" She saw Jonah coming back from wherever he'd been and stepped out to meet him. "Hey. I don't think our being here is doing anyone any good," she told him, keeping her voice low. "If you'll post officers at each end of this alley and keep it taped off for later, Dante and I will go back to the command center and start working through whatever information we've gotten so far. I know there was a delay in getting Bishop's info from Quantico, including enhanced video from the security cameras, but we should have that by now, as well as more files from your people."

Jonah nodded, and before she could bring it up, he said, "I'll go myself to Annie's desk and gather up everything she'd been working on, and bring it over as well. If you're right that she had some kind of realization, surely one of us will see it."

"I hope so," Robbie replied, adding, "Jonah . . . he's probably watching all this."

The chief's expression didn't change. "That crossed my mind. But I'm reasonably sure he'd notice if I sent out my photographer to get shots of the crowd."

"I'm sure too. But just standing here, we've had a good chance to look around. Most of these businesses have some kind of camera or cameras covering their entrances and even the parking spaces in front; please tell me they aren't dummy cameras."

He swore under his breath. "I should have thought of that. No, there used to be a lot of dummy cameras along Main, but not since people began disappearing. Everything is wide-angle to cover as much territory as possible. Sarah and I have reviewed footage after every disappearance, just to be sure. I'll have her pull the tapes and put in new ones to keep running. She'll bring what we have so far to the command center."

"We'll be there."

TEN

Sarah Waters delivered the promised security tapes less than half an hour later and elected to stay at the command center and help the agents. She had, of course, put herself back on duty as soon as Annie Duncan's murder was discovered, which meant she'd gotten next to no sleep.

Still, Dante reflected, she seemed to wear the same bright-eyed, brisk, unrumpled look that Robbie always managed—and just as effortlessly.

Dante wanted a shave and a shower. And he wouldn't have minded a nap. He also suspected he looked decidedly rumpled but refused to ask and have that confirmed.

"I can review the security tapes, since I know most everybody in Serenity," Sarah said, "but until we can narrow things down so I have some idea of *who* to look for, it seems fairly useless."

"Yeah," Dante said. "There was no camera covering that alley, front or back, we checked. If he's on the recent security tapes, blending in with the crowd of townsfolk watching, we'd never know it. Not yet, at least."

Robbie looked at the piles of folders on their round table and sighed. "Who was it that said we'd be a paperless society shortly after computers came along?"

"I don't know," Sarah said, "but he was obviously an idiot. Even when we *do* store information on a computer, we always have hard-copy backups. Always. Boxes and boxes of files in the basement."

Robbie nodded. "For the zombie apocalypse. I'm the same way about my books. Buy the e-versions for my tablet, but always buy a hardcover or paperback copy as well, for the shelves."

"You're weird," Dante told her without looking up from his computer station.

"Yeah, yeah. Come the zombie apocalypse, you'll be at my house looking for something to read by candlelight. Bring wine."

"Come the zombie apocalypse, I'll probably be looking for guns and food," Dante said. And then he looked up to frown at her. "How did you pull me into that?"

"It's a gift. Sarah, did you have a chance to eat before coming back on duty?"

"Yeah. I even managed a nap, though I don't think Jonah believes that."

Robbie sat down at the table, pulling the top dozen files off a fairly tall stack. "He's looking pretty haggard. Normal for him?"

"It's become a familiar look these last weeks," Sarah said frankly as she sat and reached for files. "But before then . . . no. He's a good chief, a good cop, and he works hard to do right by the people in this town. But he also knows how to delegate, and knows he needs rest to function at his best. Least he did. Until the teenagers vanished, and all this started."

"He wanted to believe it was a stranger, didn't he?"

Sarah paused in studying her topmost file and frowned. "You know, I'm not sure. I think maybe he knew all along that it was somebody here in Serenity. He's the kind of cop who knows *why* people do the things they do, if you know what I mean."

"A natural profiler," Robbie said.

"I'd say so. It's been minor things until this started. Something got stolen, he knew whose door to knock on. Kids causing trouble at the high school, he seemed able to sit them down and talk to them— and whatever he said, it stuck."

"What other kinds of crime have you guys had to deal with?" Robbie asked.

"Usual. Vandalism, petty theft, a few domestic disturbances over the years. Nothing like this. Nothing even close to this."

In the same casual voice, Robbie said, "When the teenagers disappeared, that was weird about the car doors and footprints." Jonah had of course filled them in hours before on the other "oddities" of the various disappearances.

"Very weird," Sarah said with some feeling. "You don't know how much I'm hoping you guys can explain it—with or without psychic trimmings."

"How do you feel about psychics?" Robbie asked.

"Total believer," Sarah replied calmly and without hesitation. "Born and raised. My grandmother had the sight, and the whole family paid attention whenever she had something to say. And it was none of that vague you'll-meet-a-dark-man bullshit either. Very specific. I came home from college once—went to UC Berkeley in California, so I didn't get home often—and she told me flat-out to stop dating the guy I'd had only a couple of dates with. She'd never seen him, and I hadn't mentioned him, even though I liked him. But she was adamant. 'Stop. Do not see him again.'"

She had Dante's attention now as well, both feds listening intently.

"I asked why, of course."

"What did she say?" Robbie asked.

Sarah looked at Robbie. "She said, 'He's a killer. He will kill at least a dozen young women before the police find the evidence they need to put him away.'"

HE HATED THE blood. The way it smelled, the way it felt on his clothing, his skin.

He hadn't realized there would be so much blood.

But she'd surprised him in what he'd thought would be a safe place, what with the curfew and all. As close as he dared get to the feds' makeshift command center.

So he could touch the telepath's mind.

Play with it a bit.

He didn't need touch or even line of sight, but he did need to be close enough. He wasn't sure exactly what his limits were, since this wonderful ability was fairly new to him, but he had sensed her when he'd reached the alley, so that had been close enough.

Until Annie Duncan picked the alley as a shortcut.

He couldn't believe she'd done that. Couldn't believe she hadn't even worn her gun.

Stupid bitch deserved to die.

But he hadn't liked killing her. Too messy. And not part of his plan.

He stood in the shower for a long, long time as soon as he got home, soaping his body again and again, using the hottest water he could stand. It hurt some of the scars still not completely healed, but he didn't mind pain. If he'd minded pain, he'd probably be dead or addicted to painkillers by now.

He was neither.

The pain had only made him stronger.

And given him The Gift.

A Gift he intended to use to its fullest. After all, why else had he been singled out?

That was one of the things he'd wanted to discover in touching the mind of the telepath: how she had received her gift. But that information, that memory, had been buried deep, and he hadn't been able to find the event that must have changed her life.

Not yet, at least.

He'd have to try again.

But he'd have to be even more careful now. Even more cautious in what he did, how he moved. Cops went insane when one of their own was murdered, he knew that. They'd be out in force every night, and they wouldn't hesitate to start shooting if a shadow moved the wrong fucking way.

The darkness that had been his friend could become his enemy, if he wasn't careful.

But he wasn't done yet. He still needed to figure the telepath out. And that other one, the odd one who had somehow reached into Annie Duncan's dead mind and found too many details of her death.

That was . . . strange. Unnerving. That was a kind of Mind Trick he didn't understand. And didn't like.

There should be rules, after all. Even about Mind Tricks.

Especially about Mind Tricks.

He soaped up his body one last time, finally sure he had rid himself of the stink of blood and death.

There were plans to be made.

And he was running out of time.

"WOW," ROBBIE SAID. "I gather she was right."

"Was she ever. I was majoring in law enforcement, so remaining silent about something like that really went against the grain. I asked her if I could stop it, alert the police, do *something*, but she said some things had to happen just the way they happened. This was one of them. Nothing I could do to change the outcome."

Robbie and Dante exchanged glances.

"What?" Sarah asked. "Don't believe me?"

"Oh, we believe you," Robbie said immediately. "It was the other thing you said your grandmother said. That some things have to happen just the way they happen. It's sort of the mantra of the Special Crimes Unit."

"You mean you deal with that kind of shit all the time?"

"Yeah. Not fun."

"Frustrating, I call it. And not a little bit scary when it comes to killers. One of the girls on my campus who was killed about two months later was a friend. She was his third victim, first college student. I never knew she was dating him, so I never got the chance to warn her. And I would have, no matter what Gran said. But . . . The police got close once or twice, but it was still almost two years before they caught that bastard."

"Please tell me he was convicted," Robbie begged.

"Of ten counts of first-degree aggravated murder and aggravated assault. They couldn't prove he killed the first two victims, but the police were sure, and I think they convinced the families at least enough to give them some peace. In any case, he was arrested, charged, and with his guilt being a foregone conclusion, everybody agreed to a plea deal that locks him up forever and a day."

"Not long enough to bring any of his victims back, but better than a death penalty."

"I agree," Sarah said. "Even if the system was working smoothly, which it most definitely is not, with the death penalty you get months, even years, of appeals, and after all that a few brief minutes of a needle or a gas chamber or the chair or whatever—and it's done." She paused, adding, "I always thought killers should be locked away in tiny cells with nothing to do but think about their crimes until they die."

"I agree," Robbie said.

"I'm not arguing," Dante said, but absently, his attention back on his computer.

Robbie looked at him with a frown. "You sound preoccupied. What are you doing?"

"Reviewing the security videos from the courtyard where Luna

Lang vanished—and the ones inside the Tyler house. Tyler really did get a top-notch security system: great outside cameras, and inside cameras covering all the common spaces and every single bedroom doorway—but the inside cameras are programmed to be on only from eleven P.M. to six in the morning, unless someone changes the programming. Outside, twenty-four-seven. And the outside cameras cover all the windows as well as the doors. Outside lighting is excellent, and on a timer from dusk to dawn."

"That's certainly extensive," Robbie said. "If not a little paranoid. But given what happened . . . Did the FBI lab do a good job of enhancing the videos?"

"Tyler's system is digital, so much clearer than your usual security cameras to begin with. The ones in the apartment complex courtyard were your garden-variety middle-grade cameras, slightly out of focus and grainy. The lab improved them considerably."

He still sounded preoccupied. Robbie looked at Sarah, then said to him, "Dante? What is it?"

"Mmmm."

"Dante, use your words."

He looked at her rather blankly for a moment, then said, "You know the woo-woo stuff with car doors being open but photographed as closed, and footprints being visible but photographed as not being there at all?"

Robbie groaned. "Don't tell me we have more useless information from those recordings."

"No," Dante said. "Not useless. I think. But I'm damned if I can figure out what I'm looking at."

Robbie and Sarah immediately left their files and came to peer over his shoulders at the computer screen. He was using a split screen, and rewound both videos so he could start them at the right point. Then he started the tape on the left side of his screen, at normal speed.

They saw Luna Lang, the young, attractive wife and mother, dressed casually in jeans with her hair tied by a ribbon at the nape of her neck. She was walking briskly along the courtyard walkway to go to her neighbor's condo. Everything about her looked utterly and completely normal.

Then normal stopped.

She stopped. Very abruptly. There was no sign of anyone else. No movement. And for several moments, she just stood there, her back to the camera. Then she turned and suddenly looked directly up at the camera. Her face was expressionless.

Like the face of a doll.

"Anybody else just feel a chill?" Sarah murmured.

"Oh, yeah," Robbie responded, her gaze fixed on the screen.

Luna Lang moved quickly toward the camera, a visual that was disconcerting in and of itself. It was well above her head, and it was also obvious that she stood on something, though what was difficult to tell. But as they watched, she slowly changed the angle of the camera. Still wearing absolutely no expression, eyes blank.

She apparently got down from whatever she'd been standing on, disappearing from that camera's range for a few seconds. But then she reappeared on a second camera, which showed her holding a lightweight metallic outdoor chair.

Seconds later, she was adjusting that camera as well, moving it slightly, slowly. There was a quick glimpse of her as she got down and moved the chair.

And then nothing.

Sarah swore under her breath. "There wasn't a blind spot. Not until she moved those cameras. How could we have missed that? How could the security guards have missed it?"

Dante answered readily, even though he still sounded a bit preoccupied. "On the original video there was some static, just a few seconds of it, not uncommon enough to worry the guards at the time. And one section of that walkway looks pretty much like any other section. But once Mrs. Lang disappeared . . . that's why Jonah had it sent out for enhancement. This is what the enhancement uncovered."

The two women exchanged looks, and it was Robbie who said steadily, "He was controlling her. Somehow, he controlled her, made her change the angle of those cameras. Maybe even made her come to him."

Sarah straightened slowly. "She sure as hell wasn't herself. I knew—know—Luna Lang. She's very expressive, always has been. But this . . . I've never seen a human face so blank. Even the dead have more expression."

Robbie said, "If that's his psychic ability, mind control, then it's definitely unique. Human minds just aren't that easily controlled. I mean, magicians and mentalists make it look easy, and the reality of hypnosis has convinced more than one person that it must be easy to actually control another mind just by suggestion—but they're wrong. Almost no one can be hypnotized against their will, and even those that want to and can be can't be forced to do anything their conscious minds would reject. And psychics can't be hypnotized at all."

"Really?"

"There are more psychics in the world than you might expect, and the SCU has studied a good number of them. Enough to conclude with fair certainty that psychics can't be hypnotized."

"Even by another psychic?"

"Especially by another psychic."

"But you said he was in your head. Earlier, before you guys went out and found Annie."

"Yeah, that's what's bugging me. I still don't believe I was hypnotized, but he was definitely in my mind. Maybe trying to find out how much control he did have."

"And it was enough to scramble your memories?"

"Not scramble, exactly. Everything made sense, it was just . . . it played out a different way, and I knew that wasn't right." She scowled. "Damn, this is difficult to explain. Especially when I haven't figured it out myself."

Dante said steadily, "Want another puzzle piece to add to the rest?"

"Not really," Robbie said, but leaned down again to look at the other side of the paused split-screen. "Nessa?"

"Yeah. Watch." He set the video in motion.

The camera was placed up high so that it covered the entire large kitchen as well as the space beside it, what designers called "keeping rooms" but which were basically just open dens with fireplaces and TVs.

"That light over the island stays on all night. And there are night-lights along the hallways and stairs, mostly because it's a habit of Nessa's to get up. I asked," Dante said. "The cameras can go to infra-red if the rooms go totally dark, that's how the system's programmed, but—well, just watch."

There was no movement for a few seconds, and then a little girl in print pajamas, her long hair hanging down her back and her favorite stuffed animal under her arm, came barefoot into the kitchen. She put her toy on the center island, used a strategically placed kitchen stool to climb high enough to reach an upper cabinet, and got a glass for herself.

She filled the glass from the refrigerator's dispenser, then stood sipping for a moment or two.

Then she went completely still.

"Shit," Robbie breathed.

"Wait for it," Dante said, still steady.

The little girl's head tilted slightly, as if she were listening to someone. Then she put her glass on the island, walked around the island and to a distant corner—and appeared on a different camera, this one in what looked like a mudroom.

"The light isn't normally kept on in there at two in the morning," Dante said. "Which is when this recording was time-stamped."

They could all see the door that probably led to the garage, see the security keypad beside it—

And then everything went black.

"She didn't go near a light switch," Sarah said. "How long—"

"Ten seconds," Dante said. "The room stays totally dark for ten seconds, and then—"

And then the lights in the room came back on. Nothing looked disturbed. The door was still closed. The security keypad was still blinking the red light that indicated it was active.

Nessa was nowhere to be seen.

"I reviewed recordings from all the other cameras," Dante told them. "Inside and outside the house. The *only* cameras that record

Nessa when she gets up are in the great room and the mudroom. You don't even see her in the hallway outside her bedroom, or on the stairs. You see her come into the kitchen, and you see her in the mudroom heading for the door. And then she vanishes."

"You don't see her in the garage?"

"No. Infrared recordings for out there during the night: two cameras, one trained on the door to the mudroom, the other trained on the double garage doors. No motion at all recorded out there. No sign of Nessa once she leaves. However she leaves."

Robbie straightened and then moved restlessly away from the computer. "Well, it had to be the same, somehow. The same as Luna Lang. He got her to do whatever it took to make herself mysteriously vanish. Sarah, you guys printed the security keypad?"

"All of them." Sarah had also straightened. "Nessa knew the code, but Caroline and Matt said she almost never touched the keypad. Still, we checked. Smudges mostly, what you'd expect from keypads touched two or three times a day by at least two people. And the smudges were only on the numbers that are part of the code."

"I guess the cameras were out of her reach."

"Very much so. And the nearest ladder was in the garage, high on a rack. A ladder much too heavy and unwieldy for a ten-year-old girl to manage."

"Even if she'd had time." Her frown deepening, Robbie swung around to look at the other two. "Time. Jonah said none of the clocks were affected in the Tyler house."

"The videos are time-stamped," Dante said. "That was something else I checked to make sure. No missing time on the recordings. When the mudroom goes dark for ten seconds, the camera's clock keeps time. It doesn't stop or slow down. Neither do any of the other clocks."

"So," Sarah said, "whether Nessa got herself out of the house or he got her out, it was managed without somehow tampering with any of the cameras."

"Or maybe," Jonah said from the front doorway, "that's exactly how he got her out. By tampering with the cameras."

ELEVEN

Robbie stared at him, still frowning. Then her frown cleared, and she swore under her breath. "We've been missing the obvious, haven't we?"

"I think we were meant to," Jonah said, closing the door and coming the rest of the way into the big room. He still looked tired, but it was clear his mind was working just fine. "Want to spook an entire town, have people disappear seemingly into thin air. Which any decent magician can do."

"No mirrors or trap doors," Sarah offered, still frowning.

"Who needs mirrors or trap doors when he can hack into a security system?" Jonah said.

"Goddammit," Dante muttered. "You're right; at the Tyler house, that's the only thing that makes sense. And all he had to do at the condo complex was insert a line of code for a few seconds of static and then have Mrs. Lang move a couple of cameras a few inches."

"Just about any computer geek could have done that," Jonah said. "It's a basic system, and even though it's hardwired in, there aren't exactly dozens of firewalls. It's an apartment complex, not a bank. And not a theater; those cameras would have had to be hacked for Sean Messina to get out of the theater unseen. And they were installed a good ten years ago."

"So not too difficult to hack," Robbie noted.

"Not difficult at all. Now, the Tyler house, that would have been a lot harder. That would have taken some skill. Sounds almost impossible. Until you remember that security systems are designed to keep people *out*. Not in."

Dante was rubbing his jaw absently. "Yeah, okay, but it still would have taken some skill to orchestrate the garage and outside cameras so the images remained frozen long enough for Nessa to get out and away, and yet keep the time stamp going."

Jonah nodded toward the evidence board, where the shadow of a man's outline represented their unsub—with no information beneath it. "So now we know three things about him. Can't really prove he's psychic, not in a courtroom. But now we know he's good with computers and understands security systems. I can name off the top of my head a couple dozen men who barely know how to use their cell phones."

"It's a good start to the profile," Robbie said. "Now we're beginning to understand this guy."

"Wait a minute," Sarah said. "Luna looked hypnotized. And we didn't see anyone around her."

Robbie sighed. "He wasn't within sight of me when he was messing with my memories. But that didn't stop him from doing a pretty fair job, despite my shields. I seriously doubt Mrs. Lang had any shields at all. So . . ."

"She would have been easy," Jonah said. "Nessa certainly would have. The only one of the others I would have called strong-minded is the judge."

"Contrary to popular opinion," Robbie said, "the more intelligent someone is, the easier they are to hypnotize. I'm guessing our psychic unsub would have been able to handle the judge too. At least long enough to get him away from his fishing site and maybe trussed up in the trunk of a car."

"Which tells us something else about him," Dante said.

Sarah looked at him, brows raised in question.

"Control is an issue with this unsub. He's turned people into his puppets, mindlessly doing his bidding. I'm guessing he has little to no control over any of the people in his normal life. And that there's probably someone he'd love to control but hasn't yet gotten the nerve to try."

Clearly uneasy, Sarah said, "How far would he take that when it comes to our missing people? I mean, okay, let's say he used a little bit of psychic control and some decent computer skills to abduct these people. And then—what?"

None of them wanted to consider worst-case scenarios, but it was Robbie who finally said, "Since we don't yet know why *these* people were taken, what their connection to him—and to each other—is, why these particular people were his targets, we can't even speculate about what he did after he abducted them."

"No," Jonah agreed. "We can't. All we can really know is that none of their bodies have turned up. Yet."

HE HADN'T REALIZED how tired he was until he was showered and had to force himself to eat something. Had to eat. Had to keep his energy up.

But he realized just how tired he was when he heard faint sounds coming from his Collection, and had to concentrate hard for several moments until they were still and silent again.

He had been able to keep them still and silent even while he slept, but that was a different thing. He supposed, having done some reading on the subject, that what he used then was a kind of posthypnotic suggestion, planted deeply in their minds.

Maybe too deeply. The girl was, as far as he could tell, the only one who never stirred.

Maybe he had gone too deep with her.

He thought about it, but not really with any anxiety. After all, it was *his* Collection. It didn't matter what they wanted or needed. They belonged to *him*. He only fed them because it pleased him to keep them alive.

For now, at least.

SARAH WAS FROWNING again. "Wait a minute. The first abduction. The teenagers. Simon Church's old Jeep isn't exactly crammed with electronics, unless you count those god-awful loudspeakers he jerry-rigged in the back. Nobody could hack into that thing except with an axe."

"True," Jonah conceded. He half sat on the conference table after finding a small space free of file folders. "But there's still the mind-control thing. Or whatever it is. Hate to say it, but neither one of those kids could come close to winning an academic scholarship, and they were both very self-centered."

"Easy targets," Dante noted.

Sarah hadn't stopped frowning. "Say you're right about that. We are still left with two very large elephants in the room," she said. "The first is those photographs I took that didn't show the open car doors *or* the footprints both Jonah and I saw. And the second is those energy bubbles."

Robbie shook her head. "I still think those energy bubbles have something to do with him and his abilities. I don't know why it's only outside and not inside, *or* how it monkeys with time like that. But I'm certain he's the cause."

"And the photographs?" Sarah's voice was a bit tense.

Dante murmured, "The more intelligent the person . . ."

"You think he played one of his little mind games on me?" She didn't *quite* snap the question.

"Don't shoot the messenger," he said, holding up a placating hand. "But at least until he killed Officer Duncan, this unsub was apparently a two-trick pony. Computers. And some kind of psychic mind control. We really haven't seen anything else from him in the way of skills."

It's not difficult at all to cut someone's throat.

Nobody said that. Out loud, at any rate.

Jonah said, "Sarah, we know there was time for him to take those kids wherever he took them and still get back to the car before you found it."

"Okay. But you saw the open doors and footprints too, Jonah. And there was *not* a lot of time between you leaving and Tim getting there with the tow truck."

Nobody said anything, until finally she swore and said it herself. "Him too, huh?"

Jonah spoke carefully. "It was just before that cloudburst. You took the photos quickly, and Tim got the car hooked up to his tow truck quickly. If the unsub *did* have to . . . mess with your memories, both of you, it wouldn't have been for long."

"All he really had to do," Robbie said, "was stall you two long enough to close the car doors and rake away the footprints—but leave the memory of that in your mind and Tim's."

Sarah remained stubbornly silent.

Robbie tried again. "I doubt he can create images on film, not that specific, at least. The energy he leaves is too . . . uncontrolled." A thoughtful expression crossed her face briefly, but then she shook her head slightly and finished, "You took photos of the scene as it actually was; you only *remember* the way it looked when you found it, and showed it to Jonah."

Grim, Sarah said, "Any way you can prove that?"

"In court? No." Robbie sighed. "But I can probably prove it to you. Telepathically."

"So you can read more than surface thoughts," Jonah said.

"Memories sometimes. Especially if the person I'm reading has been . . . fretting about something. And I can usually project those memories back to whoever I'm reading. Look, Sarah, it's up to you. I can keep my focus very narrow, and look only for those memories."

Not exactly protesting, Sarah said, "Is it dangerous for you to try reading me with the unsub around somewhere?"

"I'm not so sure he's near enough to matter," Jonah said. "It's not dawn yet, barely twenty-four hours since he abducted Nessa Tyler. And it's been a very busy twenty-four hours for him. He has to be feeling the strain. Seeing Samantha go out the way she did is all the proof I need that psychic abilities take, sometimes, more energy than a psychic has to give."

Robbie was nodding slowly. "He abducted Nessa, touched Sam's mind at least once and probably twice, messed with my memories, murdered someone . . . And if he's keeping our missing people alive, he has to do whatever it takes to accomplish that. You're right. He can't keep up that kind of pace, not unless he's a hell of a lot more powerful than any psychic *I've* ever met. He has to eat, to sleep."

"So," Jonah said, "maybe this is our chance to try to get ahead of the bastard." He looked at his second. "Sarah, I hate to ask, but it would help if we could cross off one more supposedly spooky thing from our list of what he can do. We're never going to figure out who he is unless we know what he *isn't*."

"Okay, okay." Sarah drew a breath and let it out. "Just . . . don't expect me to like it."

Keeping her own voice brisk, Robbie said, "I'm not a touch-telepath, but probably best if we're both sitting down when I try this."

"When you *try* it?"

"Well, I know I can read you, but that doesn't necessarily mean I can read you right now. Control is one of the things we struggle with." She looked suddenly at Dante, brows raised. "Maybe part of the unsub's control issues?"

"Maybe. If those energy bubbles are what's left over when he uses his abilities, it could be he doesn't have as much control as he thinks he does, and is . . . spilling . . . the energy he can't fully control."

"That's all we need. If Sam says his energy is negative, I believe her. Especially since we know now that he's a killer. I hadn't thought . . . but killing Officer Duncan could have added to that negative energy. I wonder if he even realizes."

Sarah said, "Hate to interrupt, but can we please get this over with? Just because I've been comfortable with the idea of psychic abilities doesn't mean I'm all that anxious to have my mind read. No offense," she added to Robbie.

"None taken. I'm still not entirely comfortable with reading people, and I've been able to do it all my life." She sat down at the table, while Sarah sat down immediately to her left.

"What do I do to help?" Sarah asked.

"Sounds trite, but close your eyes and think about that morning. When you found the car, and the teenagers gone. Just think about that, okay?"

"Got it." Sarah drew another breath and let it out slowly, closed her eyes, and concentrated. It was a Saturday, early Saturday, and she was doing an easy patrol alone because she'd wanted to get out of the station for a while. Just an easy patrol on a peaceful morning—

WHAT THE HELL is the Church boy's old Jeep doing out here? Honestly, I would have thought him too lazy to be up and about so early. Unless it's late for him . . .

Huh. Why're the doors open?

She pulled her cruiser off the road and far enough back not to disturb any evidence—just in case there was some. She even unsnapped her weapon holster once out of her cruiser, though that was, she told herself, just a precaution.

She felt . . . odd. The hair on the back of her neck was stirring, and she didn't know why. She wanted to call out for the Church boy but knew she was close enough to wake Mildred Bates, and that was the last thing she wanted. Even though it was more likely than not the dratted woman would be up any time now.

She approached the Jeep warily.

Engine off, but key in the ignition. The back packed full of stuff, like somebody was moving. And in the front passenger seat, a girl's colorful, bespangled purse.

Amy Grimes. She was very proud of her gaudy purse, carried it everywhere even though most girls her age had ditched purses in favor of little pouches just big enough for cell phones, driver's licenses, and maybe a credit card or a few bucks.

Sarah pulled a pair of nonlatex gloves from the inner pocket of her lightweight jacket and put them on. Amy Grimes's purse contained an equally bejeweled cell phone, the usual girly stuff—plus what looked like several thousand dollars in cash.

An elopement. Of course.

So . . . where were the soon-to-be-wed teenagers?

Sarah walked around to the driver's side—and that was when she saw the tracks down the gentle slope of the embankment and to the flat below.

Footprints. A large pair and a smaller pair. Weirdly precise footprints that just . . . stopped.

Sarah stood looking around for a few moments, puzzled but also conscious of that uneasy sense of things being not right.

Amy wouldn't have left her purse like that, especially with so much cash. Simon Church wouldn't have left his Jeep just sitting on the side of the road, keys in the ignition as though inviting it to be jacked.

Not that carjacking was the sort of thing that went on in Serenity. Still.

She sat gingerly in the driver's seat and started up the engine. Seemed to be working fine. Tank was full of gas, according to the gauge. Nothing in the car said there was anything wrong. Except for the absence of the teenagers.

Sarah turned off the Jeep and got out, and after a slight hesitation she walked farther down the grassy verge so that when she went down the sloping embankment, it was not close to the footprints. She walked around the area carefully, noting that last night's rain had left everything soaked, the dirt now mud that clung to her shoes.

She was careful. She circled widely, looking for any sign that the kids had gone beyond the point where the eerily precise footprints had stopped.

No signs they had. No signs of anyone else, at least since the rain. Absolutely no sign to tell her what had happened here.

Except that two teenagers appeared to be missing.

It wasn't a conclusion Sarah jumped to. Simon Church was inordinately proud of his old Jeep and had a habit of twirling the keys around one index finger.

The keys were in the ignition.

Amy Grimes was inordinately proud of . . . well, herself. Her possessions. And she was a girl who liked to make plans.

Sarah doubted that any plan of Amy's would include leaving her prized purse and a wad of money behind.

It would have been easy, of course, to call the Church and Grimes families and ask if their kids were home, safe and sound and, if so, could they please tell Simon he'd left his car inexplicably here and Amy had left a purse full of cash . . .

Sarah returned to her cruiser, sighed, and made the call that would undoubtedly wake up Jonah. And then——

"Skip ahead, Sarah. Jonah arrives, you both check out the scene, and he asks you to take photographs and call for the police tow truck. Isn't that the way it happened?"

An odd voice, Sarah thought. Soothing and yet . . . an order. So she skipped ahead.

Yes, that was the way it happened. Jonah left in his Jeep, and Sarah was making adjustments to the camera before taking the pictures——

No. When Jonah left, she was already down the embankment and on the flat, placing a ruler beside the footprints before photographing them. Wasn't she? She thought she had been doing that. But here she was, near the hood of her cruiser, making adjustments to the camera, just fiddling, really.

And then Tim came with the tow truck, and they stood there talking for just a minute or two, she was sure it was no longer than that, because thunder was rumbling and they both knew they had to hurry to beat the storm.

So then Sarah took pictures of the car with the doors open, so Tim could go ahead and close them and get the Jeep hitched to his tow truck while she took photographs of the footprints on the bank and down on the flat.

And Tim helped her up the bank, both of them cursing the mud on their shoes, and——

"That's not the way it happened, Sarah. Concentrate. When Jonah left, you *were* down on the flat, placing a ruler beside the footprints. What happened then?"

Annoying voice now. Annoying command.

No, I was by my cruiser, fiddling with——

"Sarah. You're down on the flat. You're bending over to place a ruler beside the footprints. Jonah saw that. He's driving away now. What are you doing?"

For a moment, it seemed that all Sarah's memories flipped and rolled in her head, a confusion of what was real and what had been . . . given to her. Stuck in her head, in her mind, by an alien voice she . . . almost . . . recognized.

Almost.

I . . . pick up the ruler and stick it in my back pocket. And then . . . I look at the pictures I've taken, and I delete them.

"Why, Sarah?"

Because . . . he told me to.

"Who told you, Sarah?"

I . . . I'm not sure. I think I know his voice, but . . . it's strange in my ears. In my head.

"Listen more closely, Sarah. Do you know who he is?"

I . . . No. He doesn't want me to know. He's nearby, over in the bushes, but every time I try to see him . . . it gets dark. So dark I can't see anything at all. I don't like the dark.

So I do what he wants. I go back up the bank, and wait for Tim. And when Tim comes, we . . . I thought we talked, but I think . . . I think we just stood there. For the longest time, we just stood there.

And then, when he told us to, we could move again. I took pictures of the Jeep so Tim could close the doors and hook it up to the tow truck. But I took the pictures after Tim closed the doors. And then I took pictures of the bank and the flat.

"Did you see the footprints, Sarah?"

Yes. No. No, they were gone. But he told me to take the pictures. He told me the footprints would be there. I didn't want to believe him, but I had to.

"Why did you have to, Sarah? Why did you have to believe what he told you was the truth?"

I had to . . . because . . . he said if I didn't . . . if I didn't believe with my whole heart and mind that the footprints were there . . . he'd know. And he'd leave me to drown in the darkness.

"Sarah—"

He'd leave me to die. Alone. In the darkness. Where no one would ever be able to find me again.

TWELVE

Sarah was pacing the floor, fuming. Robbie eyed her with more than a little sympathy.

"I'm sorry. It's not much fun to realize you can't even trust your own memory. Believe me, I know."

"That son of a bitch. That sorry son of a bitch." Sarah swung around abruptly to face the others. "Okay, how do we go about finding this bastard?"

Robbie nodded toward the files piled all over the conference table in the center of the room. "For now, old-fashioned police work. We have to go over these files, one by one. In fact, we should double up, make sure at least two of us study each file. Jonah, you and Sarah know this town better than anyone, so one of you should look at every file. Dante and I are strangers to the town, which means we may spot something important that anyone belonging here would take for granted."

Jonah nodded toward a file box he'd set on a chair near the door. "What about Annie's files? And her notes. As a matter of fact, I got just about everything I could from her desk."

Robbie thought about it briefly, then said to the chief, "Whichever of you—you and Sarah—knew her best should go over those files separately. And whether or not you find anything, Sam should go over them when she gets here. She's the one who caught at least a glimpse of Annie's memories. She may see something all the rest of us miss."

"Sarah knew her best," Jonah said.

Sarah was nodding. "She was on my shift, usually. Jonah and I switched it up so we each got a couple nights off every week, and Annie was pretty much on the same schedule. I'm talking first and second shift; we kept a skeleton staff on the third shift because it was so quiet here. Until the disappearances started. Since then it's been all hands on board and you rest when you can. We even have a few cots scattered around the station, in the break room and a couple of unoccupied offices and storage rooms. At least half the cots tend to be occupied whenever you walk through. Lotta overtime."

Dante said, "I doubt the town council complains."

Jonah grunted. "They're nervous as hell and want me to hire on more officers. But not locally. I'm not putting inexperienced people on the payroll, not at a time like this. I've put a call out to a few police chiefs and sheriffs I trust, asking if they can spare an officer or two for what I hope is no more than a few weeks at most, at double pay."

Sarah frowned at him. "Am I getting double pay?"

"Yes. And we should have another dozen officers here by tomorrow—I mean Friday. The town will foot the bill to put them up at the hotel for the duration. At least then we'll have enough manpower to fill all three shifts with experienced personnel, and everybody will get some decent rest."

Jonah looked at his second's continued frown and sighed. "Yes, I know I need to rest. If you *swear* to me you got some sleep—"

"I swear. I slept at least three hours, and you know for me that's as good as eight."

"Okay. Then I'll leave you all to start going over all the files. I'll go home and get a few hours' sleep, and be back late morning."

"Make it noon," Sarah suggested. "I'll be fine until then. Plus, Lucas and Samantha will probably be back here by then." She looked at the two feds, adding, "And the three of us will probably be more than ready to crash for a few hours."

"Works for me," Robbie said. "Good night, Jonah."

He smiled faintly, but took the hint. "Do me a favor, and all of you stay here, together, at least until it gets light. Call me immediately if anything changes, or you find something we need to act on without delay. Got it?"

"Got it," Dante said. "Good night, Jonah."

Jonah managed another smile, then lifted a hand and left their makeshift command center.

"There goes one tired man," Dante said.

"Yeah," Sarah said. "But he's got better sense than to waste any off time not actually resting. He'll sleep. Now—how are we going to go through all these damned files in some kind of logical, reasonable way? We need a system."

In the end, they came up with an easy system. Each file folder had a sticky note attached, and whether it was one of the cops or one of the agents, once it was studied, that person made a note of having done so, along with time and date, on the note. They also each kept legal pads, jotting down any notes they felt might be important or need to be further investigated.

By the time they were done, Robbie had said, "Each file will have been studied by a cop and a fed."

And, hopefully, they'd have various notes to study, *and* be able to narrow down the amount of paperwork on the table. They were, after all, starting with files of anyone they could link in any way with any of the victims. The second step, assuming they found no solid connection, would be to separate out the files of all adult men roughly between the ages of thirty and fifty. It was an arbitrary age range, Robbie had confessed, adding that when Luke and Sam returned, they might be able to narrow it more because they were far more experienced profilers.

Dante said, "What happens if we find nothing that raises a red flag in any of our minds in any of the files?"

"Let's not borrow trouble," Sarah begged. "I just want to stay busy and focused so I'm not worrying about whether that bastard is trying to worm his way into my mind again."

"Awful as it feels," Robbie told her, "at least we can be pretty sure now that nobody disappeared into thin air, that footprints didn't magically vanish when photographed and car doors didn't shut on their own. Everything was stage-managed to look more eerie and . . . otherworldly . . . than it actually was. At best a distraction for us. At worst a calculated move to further spook an already shaken town."

Sarah let out a sigh. "It's too late now, but in the morning, either Jonah or I need to go see Mildred Bates. The neighbor with the cast. She was watching that morning, the whole time Jonah and I were there, and while Tim was there with me. As many times as I've cursed those binoculars of hers, she may actually have seen something helpful."

Robbie pursed her lips. "But it wouldn't be anything obvious, because otherwise she would have called one of you. Right?"

Sarah nodded. "Trust me, she doesn't hesitate to call the station if she thinks anything's going on. Which makes me feel pretty certain that if the bastard was actually out there, he stayed out of sight in the vegetation down below the bank. Still, she might have seen something she didn't think was important at the time, or since then."

"Any information could help us," Dante noted. "It's not like we've got a whole hell of a lot to go on so far."

Sarah went to get the file box Jonah had filled from Annie's desk and brought it back to the conference table, sitting down in a chair with a fair amount of clear table space in front of her. "So we really don't have *any* kind of a profile on this guy yet?"

Dante said, "If you mean the white male, age range, occupation sort of stuff that usually helps make up a profile—no, not really. Not reliably. That's why we're at least initially working with a really wide age range. We can guess he's white only because all the missings are and it's the majority demographic for Serenity. And it's a guess, if an educated one, that he's probably in his thirties or forties, maybe even older, because he's been too patient and too clever to be younger."

Robbie sat down at the conference table as well, continuing, "In a small town like this, we're bound to have way too many overlaps when it comes to victimology: same church, same doctor, same bank, shop at the same stores, kids go to the same schools—that sort of thing. So that doesn't really help. But he picked these people, he went out of his way and to considerable trouble to abduct these people, these *particular* people, for a reason, and that's what we have to look for. Somewhere, somehow, there's a specific connection between the missing people that will lead us to the man who abducted them."

NESSA WASN'T EXACTLY sure what had happened. She'd gotten up to get a drink, she knew that. But then . . . then there was a time she didn't remember. And now she was here.

In the dark.

Nessa had always feared the dark. Always. It was why her daddy had made sure she never had to walk through a dark house to get to the kitchen for the chilled water she usually wanted in the middle of the night. Her mama had said there was water in her bathroom, after all, and Daddy was spoiling her, but not in that voice that said she really meant it.

There were perks to being an only child.

But none of those were going to help her now, here. Wherever *here* was.

She was afraid of the dark, but Nessa was old enough to know there were worse things, so she made herself squash the fear, made herself not think about it. She could do that, she knew.

At least for a while.

But . . . it was really dark. It was so dark she couldn't see so much as a sliver of light, a pinpoint of light, anywhere at all. It smelled . . . musty. Like a basement. Or a freshly dug hole in the woods. And there was something else too, a smell she recognized but couldn't quite place.

She was beginning to feel things physically, as if her body were slowly waking, but it wasn't awake yet. So everything she felt was sort of distant, hazy, uncertain.

She thought she was sitting in a chair. Not a comfortable chair either, not one with padding or cushions. More like a wooden kitchen chair, hard and unyielding.

What she was not, was tied to it.

Or restrained in any way she could feel.

Without trying to move, Nessa considered that almost idly. She'd thought she was tied somehow, because once before, she had nearly woken up, and had been sure she couldn't move.

Now she thought she was a little more awake than she had been before, and she was just as sure she could move. She didn't know how she was sure, because she hadn't tried yet, but she was very sure she could move now.

But . . . move where? Her eyes were open, had been open awhile now, and the dark wasn't getting any lighter the way it normally did after you were in it for a while, and kept your eyes open. It was dark and she had no idea where she was or which direction she should move in so she could escape this place.

Then Nessa heard something. An odd, soft little sound that made a chill skitter up and down her spine.

Somebody else was breathing.

Close.

She wasn't alone here.

SARAH SIGHED. "WE'VE already studied the files on the missings, and even though you're right about that overlap, nothing stands out as something connecting them. I don't want to sound like a defeatist, but I'm afraid we'll find the same load of nothing in these files."

Dante said a bit tentatively, "Once we've cleared—as well as we can—the people closest to the missings, then concentrating on males in our wide age range makes sense. If nothing else, we should be able to get a more complete sense of what's normal, average. That should help us to notice something that *isn't* normal or average, something that might not otherwise stick out."

Robbie was nodding. "Like you said, Sarah, we've gone through the files of the missings, specifically, once already, and nothing stood out. To any of us. We even had all the names run through national databases via Quantico, and everything looks normal, average. No wants, no warrants, nothing unusual. Just your average people in your average small town. So we take a few steps back to look at the larger picture. And that means going through the files on every adult male in the town of Serenity—and in outlying areas. Sarah, your people made a good start, but we'll need them to keep canvassing, especially the outlying areas of town, pretty much at first light."

Sarah nodded, "I'm betting Jonah already has the duty list drawn up. Everybody will be working, especially now that we know reinforcements will be here soon. And, believe me, after what happened to Annie, every officer in the department wants to be the one to find her killer."

Dante looked a little troubled. "No offense, but we don't want lynching parties out there."

"No offense taken. We don't have a huge force, but the officers we do have are well trained, observant, and rational. And Jonah was talking to them when I left to come here with Annie's files. He's not one to stand for hotheads, never has been. He was making it plain that if *anybody* draws their gun, it better be because there was no other choice. You don't have to worry. They'll do their job, and they'll do it well."

Dante nodded, visibly relieved. "It's just that we've seen the mood of small towns change drastically with something like the murder of an officer. Bad gets worse in a hurry."

"I've seen it too. So has Jonah. We won't let that happen here."

"Good enough."

Sarah frowned, her mind shifting to other questions. "We're sure it's a man?"

Dante looked at her steadily. "You, Robbie, and Samantha are the only ones of us we can be sure touched, in some way, the mind of this bastard. What does your gut tell you?"

"Male," Sarah said immediately, while Robbie nodded agreement.

"Not sure why in my case," Robbie added. "There really wasn't a sense of personality. In fact, for most of it I wasn't aware of a presence at all. Just that confusion of memories that didn't mesh."

"Because he was just testing you," Dante guessed. "Unlike with Sarah, he didn't *need* you to remember something that didn't happen. Also why he didn't threaten you, I bet. He didn't, right?"

"No." Robbie frowned. "The first time I was even really aware of him was when I sort of snapped back—and I saw Officer Duncan stagger out onto the sidewalk. I knew her killer was behind her, in that alley, and I knew he was the one who had been rearranging my memories. But it was knowledge, not a sense of him. Maybe just a cop's knowledge that you can't move more than a few steps, if that, with your throat cut." She looked at Dante. "When Sam gets back here, we really need to know everything she saw and felt when she touched Officer Duncan. And I mean everything. She may have the best sense of the killer, even if she didn't see him."

"Because she touched the memories of a dead woman." Sarah shivered visibly. "I thought my gran could be creepy at times with what she knew, but that beats anything I've ever heard."

"It's unsettling to watch. Even to think about," Robbie agreed. "The FBI has a lot of scientific types on the payroll, including a whole slew of medical doctors, and they study us regularly. What Sam can do is, so far as we know, unique. None of our telepaths have been able to do it, and if mediums like Dante see or sense the dead, that's a whole different thing."

"A dead person's brain has energy," Sarah said, almost as if she wanted to listen to how it sounded out loud. It obviously sounded creepy, because she shivered again. "Damn."

Robbie shrugged. "I don't really understand the science of it—except for a physics lesson Bishop has drilled into all of us: Energy can't be destroyed, only transformed."

Sarah looked at her with lifted brows.

"Death doesn't destroy the energy in the brain. That's all our thoughts are, electrical impulses. Synapses firing—or whatever the hell is going on in there. We are creatures of electrical energy, more or less. That electricity doesn't stop because the heart does, because the lungs are no longer drawing in oxygen. That's why true brain death, the complete lack of electrical impulses in the brain, is one of the standards used to declare certain death. From what I've been told, the brain's energy, especially in cases of violent death, lingers from a few moments up to as much as half an hour. I dunno, maybe it takes that long for the brain to realize the body is already dead."

"Oh, jeez, that's even creepier," Sarah told her.

"Stick with us and you'll get creeped out plenty," Dante murmured.

"Something to look forward to," Sarah said. "Or not. I say we get busy with these files. It would be nice to be able to show *some* progress before the others get back."

"I hear that," Robbie said, and opened a file.

THE SOUND OF breathing so close to her in the darkness kept Nessa frozen for a long, long time. She even held her breath, as long as she could, though all that did was convince her that there was more than one person nearby.

Breathing.

Not a sound of movement. Nobody talking. Just the soft, whispery sounds of breathing.

Wait . . . is it the missing people?

And if it is . . . did I get taken too?

That was more terrifying than even the darkness. Because some of the missing people had been missing for weeks, and nobody had been able to find them. Half the town had gone out on searches to help the police, but nobody had been found. Mr. Sully and his dogs had gone out almost every day, until even the dogs looked thin and discouraged, and Chief Riggs had ordered it stopped.

They'd keep looking, he had told them. But it would be the police, and the FBI agents coming to help—

Wait. I know Chief Riggs told Mr. Sully to rest his dogs. And I know he talked to everybody crowded into the school gym that day, just a few days after that man was taken at the theater.

But . . . he didn't say anything about FBI agents then.

Did he?

As scared as she was, Nessa had the notion that getting her memories straight was terribly important. It *mattered* somehow, and not just to her.

There had been that meeting . . . and all the adults had been frightened, holding tight to their children. She'd thought her daddy's grip would turn her fingers white. And the adults had asked what they could do, how they could be safe when even the police didn't know who was taking people away, or even how.

Chief Riggs had told people not to buy more guns, Nessa remembered that. If they had guns and knew how to use them, fine, that was for home protection, but he didn't want people carrying their guns around, and he didn't want anyone getting a gun unless they took the police training course he insisted on before people bought guns. And right now his people were too busy to be teaching those courses.

Besides, having a gun wouldn't have kept anyone from being taken, that was what he'd said. Staying home at night was what they should do. If they had dogs, make sure the dogs were inside with them. Keep their porch lights or other yard lights on all night long, maybe even install some motion-sensor lights so if anybody came into their yards, the lights would come on. Make sure their doors and windows were locked, and an alarm would sound if the glass was broken.

Nobody had said that the people who were taken had not been

taken from their homes. She thought they were afraid to say it. Because they wanted to believe home was safe.

She wanted to believe home was safe.

Nessa knew that her daddy, like so many others, had bought an even better security system than they'd had before. She didn't much like cameras inside the house, and her mama hadn't either, but her daddy had said safety was more important and it wasn't like he was putting cameras in bedrooms or bathrooms.

Yes. Yes, she remembered all that. Was sure of all that.

She was sure that her mama had taken her to school rather than let her take the bus like before. And picked her up. Lots of mamas and daddies had been doing that, and the teachers had made sure who was picking them up and checked their names off on the lists on their clipboards. The teachers had even talked to them about being careful where they should have been safe, about the buddy system and not being alone, not even in school.

Nessa had done just as she'd been told. Because it was scary, people just being taken like that. Even though no kids had been taken, it was scary.

Only . . .

Maybe a kid had been taken now. Maybe she had been taken.

In the awful darkness, alone even though she could hear others breathing, Nessa tried her best to remember being taken. She'd been so *careful*, just like everybody told her to be. Never alone, and safe inside the house her daddy had made safer. Daddy had talked about getting a dog, and she'd been excited about that.

And then . . .

And then . . .

And then she was here in the awful dark. Knowing it wasn't a bad dream. Knowing there were others around her breathing, but knowing they couldn't help her because they couldn't help themselves. Sitting on a chair that felt hard but funny in some place that smelled like dirt and dead leaves and mushrooms and other things her mind shied away from thinking about.

She didn't know how long she had been there, not really. She was hungry and thirsty and felt stiff from sitting for so long. Hours? Days?

Where was she when she'd been taken?

Where was she now?

And most important of all, couldn't she escape?

Nessa knew the others couldn't see her any more than she could see them. She even knew, somehow, that they were in an even deeper, darker place than she was, at least in their minds. It didn't really make sense to her, because she heard breathing and knew they were nearby. And yet . . . they weren't nearby at all. They were far away.

And even though she didn't know where the knowledge came from, Nessa was absolutely certain that if she didn't get away soon, very soon, while he wasn't looking, she never would.

He? Who is he?

That question had barely surfaced in her mind when she became dimly aware of Something Else that was with her.

In her.

Inside her head.

She had a fleeting impression of puzzlement, of dawning uneasiness— and then she closed her eyes and concentrated on her breathing.

Breathing slow and steady, like those around her. Thinking of nothing. Not allowing herself to be scared even though the darkness was heavy and pressing against her and Something Else was like a darker snake in the darkness, slithering around, all around, as it searched for whatever had alerted it.

Nessa breathed evenly and kept her mind still and blank. Because if the snake found her awake and aware, if *he* found her like that, she'd never escape. Never.

The dark, dark snake was slithering closer and closer to her, to her mind, and all Nessa could do was hide her terror and hope it— *he*—passed her by.

THIRTEEN

The owner of the Diner, Clyde Barrow, came himself just before eight A.M. to take breakfast orders from Sarah and the feds. He had already sent them coffee twice during the wee hours of the night, sending it by way of a couple of the cops still roaming—or patrolling— downtown. Clyde refused to be paid, the cops reported; he just wanted to do what he could to help.

The cops themselves, after what had apparently been *some* talking-to by Jonah, were not just polite to the feds; they were pleasant and even friendly.

Clyde was the same, though he hadn't needed a talking-to from Jonah to be that way.

"Breakfast would be great, Clyde, thanks," Sarah said. "We're probably here a few more hours before we're relieved by the others."

"Want your usual, Sarah?"

"Yeah, thanks."

"What about you two agents? Whatever you want, I can cook."

Robbie eyed him, this being the first time she'd actually met him. "Clyde Barrow? Any relation?"

He grinned at her. "Only cops ever ask that."

"Well, we sort of specialize in crime. And study the history of it."

"Yeah, I bet you would." There was only the faintest emphasis on the *you*.

"So?"

"Well, family lore says yes, but I've never done the genealogy thing. And he didn't have any kids, so no way I'm a direct descendant."

"If you really want to know, there's a technical analyst at Quantico that can get you your entire family tree in record time."

Mildly, Dante said, "I doubt the Director would approve."

"Maybe not, but we both know Bishop wouldn't mind." She returned her gaze to Clyde. "Our unit chief."

"Ah. Well, I might take you up on that, Agent. Later. For now, what would you like for breakfast?"

Sarah, who had gone back to studying a file, said absently, "He makes great pancakes. And I don't know what he does to eggs, but they're to die for, no matter how you want them fixed."

"I sing to my hens," Clyde said without a blink.

Robbie believed him. "Someday I'd like to be there for that," she told him. "I think I'll try the pancakes. Butter, maple syrup, bacon crisp on the side."

"Got it. And you, Agent?"

"Scrambled eggs, bacon, toast. And some kind of fruit if you have it. Just whatever you've got. Thanks, Mr. Barrow."

"I'm just Clyde, son. Be back with breakfast in a bit."

Dante stared after him. "I don't think he's enough older than me to call me *son*," he said thoughtfully.

"He's older than he looks," Sarah said, still absently. "He's also the mayor."

Dante blinked. "Well, that was unexpected."

Sarah glanced up with a smile. "In a small town like this, the mayor would have to have another job, or be retired with one paying a good pension, since the pay sucks. Clyde's on his third term."

"I feel like we're on ours," Dante said, surveying the stacks of file folders lined up down the center of the conference table. "I mean, it *looks* like we've been working, and it sure as hell feels like it. But do we have anything to show for it?"

He had joined the other two at the conference table to read through files, saying his eyes were crossing from staring at security video over and over again, especially since he'd found absolutely nothing they didn't already know.

"Well," Robbie said, "we've pretty much eliminated all the relatives and close friends of all the missing people; the only connections they have to each other, if connections exist, are reasonable and not suspicious. So there's that.

"We'll probably have a new batch of files to look over when the first shift gets through their canvass of the outlying areas. Most everything else we have here has been gone through by Sarah and at least one of us, which I think covers just about all the men in the age range we're looking at who live inside the city limits."

Tentative as he usually was when using his learning-stage profiling skills, Dante said, "He abducted six people. We've all been operating under the assumption that those people are still alive, right?"

"Right," Sarah said, looking up from a legal pad of notes she'd been studying.

"Okay. Well, Luke and Sam are the experienced profilers, but if we keep assuming these people are alive, then he has to be holding them somewhere. And it isn't in an apartment or condo here in the downtown area. Or a house. Somebody would have seen or heard something, surely, between his coming and going—and adding to his quota."

"There have been cases of captives held in nice little neighborhoods for years with the neighbors none the wiser," Robbie reminded him.

"Yeah, but most of those cases involved kids or young women being held captive as sex slaves." He shook his head, adding a muttered, "Sick bastards."

"We don't know that isn't happening here," Robbie pointed out.

Sarah made a sort of choked sound. "Even the judge? Look, if it's all the same to you, I'm clinging to the notions that they're still alive, and that he *didn't* take them for any sexual reason."

"Well," Robbie said, "no evidence to the contrary. So I say your notions make as much sense as anything else. The thing is, the aerial and infrared satellite shots Bishop sent didn't show anything unusual. No heat signatures showing a group in an odd place. We were able to identify virtually every structure, and all have been searched and cleared. So where is he keeping them?"

Sarah chewed on her bottom lip. "Six people held captive, some of them for weeks. We don't know why, but we do know this unsub has planned his abductions skillfully, and covered his tracks in different ways, from tinkering with memories to altering security footage. He would have planned just as carefully where and how he keeps his captives."

"If they're alive," Robbie felt duty bound to remind her.

"Yeah. But given that, Dante is right. The satellite shots didn't show any unusual groupings, our searches haven't turned up anything, and I can't think of a place downtown where six people could be held prisoner. *Especially* if their captor couldn't be standing guard all the time. And he hasn't been. Unless he has a partner, his captives have been left unguarded multiple times."

"Luke seemed pretty certain when he checked in last night from the hotel," Dante noted. "One unsub."

"So nobody to guard them when he's gone," Sarah said. "Whatever safeguards he has in place, locks, soundproofing, anything else you can think of, the one thing he definitely needs to hold captives with the best chance of no one finding him out has to be isolation. And any isolated building is going to be in the outlying areas."

"Where there's been nothing but a cursory search," Robbie noted. "Because all the missings disappeared in or near the downtown area. Shit. We may not be even an inch closer to identifying this unsub. And that means we're no closer to finding the missing people than we were when we got here."

"There is another possibility," Dante said.

Robbie looked at him, brows raised.

"Well, Luke hasn't picked up anything from any of them, and you can be sure that at least the teenagers and Nessa would have to be terrified to find themselves captives. All of them, really. So why hasn't Luke felt that?"

"He said he needed time," Robbie said.

"Yeah. But what if it isn't time? What if Luke hasn't been able to pick up anything because the unsub is keeping them drugged? Out cold so they don't need a guard—and too far under to be aware enough to be afraid?"

JONAH SLEPT FITFULLY, which didn't really surprise him. He was almost literally too tired to rest, which always sounded so absurd when other people said it but was so real when it was you. The thing was, Jonah usually had no trouble falling asleep, so he'd never developed any little tricks or method of winding down.

Sarah claimed black-and-white documentaries on any war of the past put her out like a light within five minutes. But that never worked for Jonah, not because he found war fascinating but because he liked documentaries in general and tended to get interested.

Not that interest in anything was his problem. He needed to sleep and wanted to, so he wasn't about to turn on the TV or pick up a book or magazine. He'd drawn his bedroom drapes; since he and Sarah rotated shifts and he occasionally worked a third shift just because, his drapes were blackout and turned his bedroom into a dark cave that mimicked night no matter what time it was.

That wasn't the issue either.

Jonah had never lost anyone under his command before, not even to an accident. The fact that Annie Duncan had been careless in being out, alone and unarmed, on foot in the night when *everyone* knows that was dangerous didn't make him feel any better.

She'd been one of his officers, his responsibility. Telling her devastated parents and younger brother about her murder had been the most difficult thing he'd ever had to do. And dealing with his other officers hadn't been much easier. They were in shock, they were grieving, they were angry, and they wanted someone to blame.

He'd really had to come down hard on them to make damned sure none of them targeted their federal friends. Of course, none of them knew just why these particular FBI agents were so important, so necessary to the location and capture of the monster who had taken six people and killed one more.

The monster who might have killed them all.

They didn't know, and he didn't tell them. That was just the sort of thing a blindly angry cop might, oh, text to a news organization. Not out of malice, but . . .

Jonah thought that if they were lucky, they had maybe another twenty-four hours before national media descended. National media that had been very preoccupied during the last couple of weeks by, among other things, the hunt for a serial killer in the nation's capital, several sensational trials, at least three political scandals, and another senseless mass shooting, this one at a mall on the West Coast.

Even with the Amber Alert on Nessa, the goings-on in little Serenity, Tennessee, hadn't quite surfaced to the attention of the national media.

But they would.

Right now, he had a handle on the strangers in his town, a good sense of them. Once national media arrived, that one area of control would go out the window. And probably make it all that much harder to find this monster, this unsub, and capture or kill him.

He was leaning heavily toward the latter.

Jonah tossed and turned for probably a good two hours before exhaustion finally claimed him. He slept hard, which wasn't all that restful, but then he hadn't expected anything else.

He wouldn't have a peaceful night's sleep until this monster was no longer a threat to his town. And depending on the outcome, he might not have a peaceful night's sleep for a long time afterward.

He had set his alarm, but woke with a start before it could go off at ten A.M. as he'd intended. He turned off the alarm and turned on the lamp on his nightstand, squinting in the abrupt light.

He felt as though he'd slept for years. Or about six minutes.

As usual, it took him some time to extricate himself from the tangled covers, and that hint of normality was strangely reassuring. A hot shower helped; shaving the stubble off his face helped more even if the face in the mirror seemed more gaunt than he'd ever noticed before, and by the time he was dressed and headed for the Diner for breakfast, he felt almost human.

The waitresses were bustling about, but Clyde served him hot coffee without comment, and only a couple of minutes later slid a plate with his usual breakfast order across the counter.

Jonah was about to ask him if something was wrong, then reminded himself that everything was wrong. And when he glanced around the Diner, it was to find it unusually packed for a Thursday morning just before lunchtime.

No wonder the waitresses were bustling.

Packed with citizens of Serenity who were mostly just looking at their chief of police, some trying to be casual about it and some unabashedly staring.

Before Clyde could retreat to the back and turn Willie back up, Jonah summoned him with a slight movement of his head, and Clyde rested an elbow near Jonah's plate and leaned nearer, lifting an eyebrow.

"Clyde, please tell me nothing's changed in some even more horrible way in the last eight or ten hours." He kept his voice low.

"Far as I know, nothing's changed." Clyde's voice was low as well. "Except maybe that those who didn't know about Annie Duncan last night know about her now."

"That's why the stares."

"I imagine so. Somebody goes missing, there's room for hope. Dead is dead. And even with that tent hiding Annie's body, the details have gotten out."

"Goddammit," Jonah muttered.

"Bound to happen, you know that better than anybody. And new details make the old look and feel worse. We had six missing. Now we've got six missing—and one murdered. So maybe some of them have been murdered too. Maybe all of them. Nobody's really talking about it. But it's like the whole town's holding its breath."

"Yeah, I got that."

"They know he's a killer now. So it's natural to wonder . . ."

"If he's killed the people he abducted. Yeah, I don't blame them for wondering. I am too."

"They don't feel safe anymore. It's shaken them."

"I know the feeling."

Clyde half nodded, then said, "I took breakfast to Sarah and the two agents around eight thirty. They all looked tired, and not all that cheerful, even though the gorgeous blonde was curious about my name."

Jonah frowned, and then said, "Oh. The Barrow bit?"

"Yeah. It's only cops that ever ask about it." Clyde shrugged. "There

were files everywhere, but in fairly neat stacks. Sarah said it'd probably be a few hours before they were relieved by you and the other
two agents. Ask me, they need to be relieved now. Even though it's
obvious you should have slept longer."

"I'm fine."

"Yeah, yeah. Eat your eggs, Jonah. Jean asked that you check in at
the station before joining Sarah and the feds. I take it she's fielded some
calls this morning."

"Great."

"She didn't sound too bothered, so maybe the worst hasn't got
out yet."

Jonah nodded, though not with much hope. "Okay. Thanks, Clyde."

Clyde returned to his kitchen, and Jonah concentrated on eating
his breakfast, ignoring the holes being bored into his back. Nobody
approached to question him, though he wasn't at all sure that was a
good thing. Maybe they were afraid to ask.

Maybe they were afraid he wouldn't have an answer.

Or maybe they were afraid he would.

NESSA HAD NO real sense of time passing. She concentrated on keeping her mind still and quiet, so the blacker-than-black snake wouldn't
find her. Somehow, without really being sure how she was able to do it,
she pictured a smooth, dark pond with no ripples at all in the black water,
and made that the quiet, motionless surface of her mind.

And she slipped beneath that. Hid beneath that.

She didn't know how long she'd have to hide, but she knew if she
came out too soon, the black snake would find her. And if it found

her, if *he* found her, she had an awful feeling that he would make sure she could never get away.

She'd be lost forever, unable to ever find her way out of the dark to get back home.

JONAH WALKED INTO their makeshift command center just in time to land in the middle of a conversation.

"I don't see how he'd be able to get his hands on enough drugs to keep them all sedated this long," Robbie was saying. "All the doctors and nurses in Serenity checked out. The pharmacies and drug stores checked out. Hell, even the veterinarians did."

"Okay, then, where do you hide six people who're either tied up and gagged or else making a hell of racket? Could be a basement or cellar," Dante offered.

Sarah pondered, looking at Jonah almost absently, then said, "There aren't many downtown, even under industrial buildings. We aren't close to the New Madrid fault line, but this town was built after some pretty rough earthquakes hit the state a couple hundred years ago, the kind that rip apart structures and create brand-new lakes." She shook her head. "Bad storms, being underground is a good idea. Earthquakes, not so much. The underground structures I know of hold necessary equipment for the buildings. Furnaces, pipelines for water and gas, junction boxes for electricity. Like that."

"What are we talking about?" Jonah asked.

It was Robbie, pacing restlessly back and forth at the opposite end of the table, who answered. "We were trying to come up with possible holding places for six people in the general area of downtown.

Can you think of a place in town where you could do that and be *absolutely* sure no one would discover your hiding place, even with the whole town being searched?"

"No," Jonah replied immediately. He sat down at the table in the chair closest to the door, adding, "Sully took his dogs all over town, did a grid search. That was after Sean Messina disappeared. We checked every building, residential and commercial, from the roof to the foundation."

"Shit," Robbie said.

Sarah frowned at Jonah. "Why didn't you bring us coffee?"

He lifted his own cup in a small salute. "Because you three are about to be relieved; I talked to Luke a little while ago, and he and Samantha will be here shortly. The last thing you need right now is more caffeine. You need sleep, all of you."

"Did you get any?" Sarah demanded.

"I did. I'll admit it wasn't the best sleep I've had, but probably the best I could expect under the circumstances."

"How about Luke and Sam?" Dante asked.

"Luke said Sam always sleeps like the dead after using her abilities that . . . powerfully. Or words to that effect. And he said he slept as well. They had a late breakfast at the hotel. Clyde's a better cook, but the hotel kitchen is pretty good. Just so you know."

"We're full anyway," Robbie told him. "Pancakes for me. Wow."

Dante said, "And I want to hear him sing to his hens. Because those seemingly plain scrambled eggs tasted like manna. Really. Food for the gods."

Jonah shook his head slightly. "Okay, now I *know* you all need sleep. Hours of it."

"That did sound weird, didn't it?" Dante frowned.

"Will it do me any good to ask if you found anything in the files so far?"

Seriously, Robbie said, "We didn't find anything that raised a red flag. And no solid connections between the six missings. I mean, citizens of the same town, and there was some overlap here and there. Two go to the same church. Two others the same school. Three have the same dentist. Three used the same real estate agent to find their apartments or condos. All the adults use the same bank. Small towns are just—not good for victimology."

Sarah pushed a legal pad toward him. "I wrote down some stuff. Us speculating, mostly. A few questions we had. Whatever we really felt was useful or potentially useful is up on the evidence boards, which isn't a lot, mostly just the facts we all knew anyway." She looked at the file box in the chair beside hers, and added, "Sam needs to go through Annie's files and notes. If she had some kind of realization that could help us catch this guy, I couldn't find it in that box. Maybe I just didn't know what to look for."

"Okay. Look, you guys go ahead and take off. Sarah, don't go home alone."

"Tim's waiting at the station. He's supposed to work first shift today, but we didn't think you'd mind."

"I don't. You should all know that, in case you haven't already felt or sensed it, the whole town is beyond tense. Miles beyond tense. They had more hope before. Annie's murder made them face the possibility that all the missings could be dead. Just because we haven't found any bodies doesn't mean they're still alive."

"And if they are still alive," Sarah said, "we can't figure out how he's doing it. It's more than three weeks since the teenagers disappeared; if they're still alive, he must be feeding them, somehow taking care of them, even minimally. One of our questions was the possibility of nutrition through an IV, but that means medical training of some kind, never mind the supplies needed."

"You can get anything online," Dante said. "If you know where to look and what to ask for, you don't have to be a doc, a nurse, or have any medical training at all."

"Yeah, so we should probably be checking with all the delivery drivers who may or may not have noticed an unusual amount of deliveries. On the other hand, if he's been planning this, then I'm guessing whatever he needed, he got a little along, ahead of the abductions, so as not to arouse suspicion."

"Which is where we keep getting stuck," Robbie said. "*If* they're still alive, and *if* he's taking care of them—why? What the hell is the point of it all?"

Jonah was about to respond, then shook his head at her. "Enough for now, at least for you guys. You three go get some sleep. I don't know how much I'll be able to help Luke and Sam with the psychic stuff, but I know how to be a cop, so I'll do that."

Sarah opened her mouth to say something about not leaving even Jonah alone, but then she realized. "Dammit, you've been bopping all over the place alone, all the while telling the rest of us not to be."

"I don't know about bopping," Jonah said gravely. "But I'm not really worried about this guy coming after me."

Lucas and Samantha came in just in time to hear that, and Luke said, "Jonah's probably right that he wouldn't be a target for this unsub. However he views us, it's likely he sees Jonah as the one he's trying to outsmart. And odds are, he won't come after him, at least not directly."

"Outsmart or just drive nuts," Jonah said. He noticed that Sarah was frowning, and gave her a questioning look, to which she replied, "I dunno. Something somebody just said in the last few minutes set off a bell, but I'm too tired to figure out what it was." She shook her head. "Anyway, Jonah, be careful."

"I will. You guys be careful as well."

Lucas frowned slightly, then said to the others, "Okay, our shift. You guys go get some rest. If we catch a break with the case, we'll call. Otherwise, plan to be back here around midnight."

It was Thursday, not long before noon.

FOURTEEN

There was still no sense of time passing for Nessa. It might only have been a few hours, or a few days—or even longer than that—before she thought the black snake, that *he* was not here, at least for now. Not here. Not now. And *he* had not found her for all his searching, she was sure of that. Not yet.

But underneath the smooth, placid surface of her mind, where she hid from the dark snake, a clock was ticking away the minutes she had to try to escape, the minutes before he would surely come back, and she eventually realized that she did have a growing sense of her surroundings.

She kept telling herself that if she could only figure out where she was, or at least which way to go in order to escape, then when the time was right, she could get away. Run.

Go home.

She thought about the others she knew were around her, their breathing soft and even, and a part of her felt horrible that she was even thinking about escaping this prison without them. But a part of her knew that *if* she could escape, *if* she could only get away, then she could go for help. She could tell her parents and Chief Riggs where these other people were. And then they could be rescued.

Even her common sense told her that one little girl couldn't help at least five other people, mostly grown-ups, to get away. All the time she'd been awake and aware, even hiding herself away beneath the surface of her mind, she knew none of the others had stirred.

At all.

That was scary. It was like they were alive enough to breathe, but not alive enough to . . . to really be alive.

Gathering her courage, Nessa opened her eyes and turned her head, trying her best to see something, anything, in the thick darkness around her. But she couldn't. No window, no door, not even the sliver of light somewhere.

She also flexed her feet—she was barefoot, just as she had been when she'd gone downstairs at home to get a drink. Whenever that was. However long ago it had been. Beneath her feet just felt . . . cold and rough, uneven. Maybe ground without any grass. Or maybe something else. She didn't know.

It wasn't until she was slowly and carefully moving her fingers, and then her wrists, and then her arms that she realized there was tape on one arm, and tubing—and a needle stuck in her.

Nessa had been in the hospital once when she'd been thrown from a horse and badly injured. She could remember lying there mostly covered in bandages, but she also remembered getting the blood transfusion that had, the doctors told her, saved her life. She'd been extraordinarily lucky because her blood was rare and it had to be just the right donor.

She remembered that needle in her arm, and also the one in her other arm that had kept her arm from hurting too much.

She didn't think this was that kind of needle. Or the kind that gave blood necessary to live.

When she felt around, she realized that the tubing was taped to her arm and then swung loosely upward, until it connected to a plastic bag attached to a thin metal pole.

Just like hospitals used.

She sat there for a while and thought about that, until another sudden thought, a dawning realization, made her consider what she was sitting on.

It was a chair, but not a normal chair. It had . . . it was . . . someone had changed it. Someone had turned it . . . into a potty chair.

As bad as everything else was, that embarrassed Nessa horribly. Someone had pulled her pajama bottoms down around her ankles, she could feel that now. Someone had pulled down her pajamas and sat her on a potty chair.

And *he* had done the same things to the others, she was sure of that. Because those were the smells she hadn't really wanted to identify all this time. It was people, as helpless as she was, more helpless than she was, going to the bathroom in a pot or bowl beneath a chair like the one she was sitting on.

For some reason, that was the final catalyst Nessa needed. She moved slowly, as quietly as she could, and carefully removed the needle from her arm, pressing a fold of her pajama top against the place that bled when the needle was removed.

Then she sat there for a long time afterward, keeping the surface of her mind quiet, but underneath thinking so fast she could hardly keep up with herself. She shifted around a bit, silently, and then pushed herself to her feet, holding on to the chair a few moments until the dizziness passed. When she was as steady on her feet as she thought she was likely to be, she fumbled for her pajama bottoms and panties and slowly pulled them up.

Then came the scary part. The really scary part. Because she had to find her way out of here. She had to find her way in total darkness, by feel—and she knew only too well that she was bound to feel those other people breathing, to encounter them in the dark.

There was nothing she could do for them except escape and lead rescuers back here to save them.

But for now, she had to move very, very slowly, hands outstretched. She dared not bump into anyone—or anything—with any kind of force. Like those tall, delicate poles holding the IV bags. One of those, if tipped over, would fall with a crash, Nessa knew.

And all it would take to summon her captor was a sound.

Just a sound.

So Nessa held her hands out in the dark, dark place that held smells she could no longer bear, braced herself to touch whatever or whoever she touched without making a sound, and began to slowly, slowly make her way forward.

LUKE AND SAMANTHA were filled in on what the others had found, which was little enough, and what they had speculated, as per the notes Sarah had very neatly written.

Jonah pushed the pad across the table to them, then sipped his coffee and stared at the rather sparse evidence boards.

A picture of each of the victims. An unidentifiable shadow outline of the unsub. Beneath the picture of each victim was a list of their particular info: DOB, height, weight, hair and eye color, clothing when last seen. And below that, the scarce info of when and from where they had been taken, times approximate except for Luna Lang and Nessa, both of whom had appeared on time-stamped video.

"You're frowning," Luke said, sipping his own coffee. "Something bothering you?"

"Yeah . . . but I'm not sure what it is."

"That seems to be going around," Sam muttered.

"Go with it," Luke told the chief. "Speak out loud. Stream of consciousness. Sometimes that's where we find the things hiding from our conscious minds."

Jonah was a little startled. "Hiding?"

Lucas hesitated, exchanged a glance with his silent wife, then said, "This is your town, Jonah. *Your* town. More than any other small town I've ever been in, the center of this place is you. Until this happened, there was no crime to speak of. You tended to stop trouble before it started, stepping in before things could get too tense. You talked, and the people of Serenity listened."

"I'm chief of police, of course they listened," Jonah said, more than a little uncomfortable.

"In most towns, that would be the reason. But not here."

"Why not here?" Jonah asked warily.

Samantha spoke up, asking simply, "Were you aware you're a latent psychic?"

"What? No. Me?"

Luke smiled faintly. "It's not a fully functional ability, at least for now, but you're definitely a latent. If I had to guess, probably an empath."

Jonah had no idea what to do with that.

"You don't sleep well, do you? I mean, you toss and turn even on a peaceful night when nothing disturbing has happened in your town. Even when you're tired. Even when you need to sleep."

"I've always been a restless sleeper," Jonah muttered.

"But it got worse once you became chief of police, didn't it?"

"Well . . . there was more to worry about once I did."

Samantha said, "Don't let it throw you, please. Right now, your latent ability is an asset. You deal well with other people, which is part of your job. You're able to quickly judge the mood if the odd bit of trouble is getting started, and you know who to talk to and what to say to let the tensions ease."

"I'm a trained cop, it *is* a part of my job."

"Like the hunches you get that make you show up at a certain place at a certain time, just as trouble is about to start?"

Jonah frowned at her.

Luke let out a little laugh, rare for him. "Don't be so worried about it. Latent means it isn't a major part of your life. Right now it's hunches and déjà vu and knowing how to talk to people. Chances are, that's the way it'll be for the rest of your life."

"But?" Jonah asked with foreboding.

"But . . . cases like this one, with a powerful psychic playing games and using people as his pawns have a way of . . . ending badly."

"You mean my missing people could all be dead?"

"That's always been a possibility and you know it. But the point is, he took them. Your people are in his hands, stolen away by him, and that's something that demands you use every bit of training and instinct you have in order to see them safe. Your latent abilities could be triggered, go active, for that reason alone."

"Great," Jonah said, hearing the uneasiness in his own voice.

Samantha said, "Our abilities tend to be triggered by trauma, remember? Depending on how you deal with this situation and whatever the outcome is, you could find yourself a functioning psychic when all is said and done."

"But that isn't definite," Jonah said hopefully.

Luke shook his head. "No, not definite. Possible, though. Because even if they're all alive, they're in the hands of a monster. A monster you'll probably have to face eventually. Sooner rather than later."

"Yeah. So?"

"He has an enormous amount of negative energy, Jonah. So far as we know, he's only used it to abduct six people and find a way into the mind and memories of Robbie. He probably tried with Sam, but she has good defenses, and he didn't get in."

Jonah looked at her. "Sure of that?"

"Reasonably. There aren't really any absolutes in all this, but I tend to go out with no warning either because I've used my abilities longer than I should have—or I'm under some kind of psychic attack."

"My life used to be so normal," Jonah muttered.

"Kiss that good-bye," Sam told him.

"She's being dramatic," Luke told him.

"Oh, yeah? Want to tell him about the time I was buried alive?"

"Not really," her husband told her. "Besides, that bastard was out to punish me. Me, deliberately. With very few exceptions, that isn't the kind of case we deal with."

"Wait a minute," Jonah said slowly. Then, almost immediately, "No, it couldn't be that."

"Couldn't be what?" Luke asked politely.

Jonah ran the fingers of both hands through his hair, then rested his elbows on the conference table and stared straight again, frowning. "We've been looking for commonalities. One thing all six of these people have in common."

"Yeah," Sam said. "Have you thought of one?"

Jonah's frowning gaze turned to the evidence boards. "But it's ordinary. I mean, part of my job."

"Want to clue us in?" Lucas asked.

Clearly reluctant, Jonah said, "I . . . saved them. Every person on that board is alive today because of me."

NESSA HAD NEVER been so terrified in her life, and it was getting more and more difficult to keep that terror underneath the placid surface of her mind. One outstretched hand had already touched one person, whose clammy skin had made her stumble backward.

But the breathing, soft and even, remained the same.

All Nessa wanted to do was find a wall. It was weird but an exterminator had come to their house a few weeks back, just to spray for the summer bugs that would be coming. Nessa, ever curious, had asked him how he could be sure he sprayed his bug-off along every baseboard of the entire house.

"I just start following a wall," he'd answered cheerfully. "Start in one direction and keep following a wall. And you end up back where you started."

Nessa didn't want to end up back where she started, but she knew if she could find a wall, then surely it would lead her, sooner or later, to a door.

So that was what she was doing. Hands outstretched, moving slowly, so slowly, so if she touched something or . . . someone . . . she'd be less likely to jerk away and maybe turn over something noisy.

At one point, she reached a section of wood, about up to her waist, and then she felt something that was familiar, but not. It took her several long seconds to realize that it was the lid of a toilet, fashioned from rough wood.

And once she acknowledged that to herself, she could smell the odors rising from a pit far below. This had to be where he dumped the pots or bowls or whatever he kept beneath his prisoners.

Nessa recoiled, only just stopping herself before she could collide with one of the silent, breathing prisoners around her.

She spared a moment to concentrate fiercely, to make the placid surface of her mind even calmer, undisturbed. But it was hard, and getting harder. There was a cry of terror swirling around beneath that placid surface, a scream she kept locked behind gritted teeth.

She had to get out of here. She *had* to.

No matter what their captor planned for them, he had already hurt them in ways Nessa could barely comprehend, ways she couldn't even form words to describe, and she wanted out, wanted them all out, into the normal world again and safe from him.

So she stepped closer to the wooden box with its toilet lid, and reached carefully past it. Wall. It felt like dirt, but Nessa didn't care, she kept one hand on the wall, just her fingertips trailing it, and the other out in front of her in case there were obstacles she still couldn't see in the dark, dark place.

She walked slowly and carefully, vaguely aware that her bare feet were cold, but uncaring. *Just keep walking, just one foot in front of the other, and don't let go of the wall, never let go of the wall . . .*

"IT'S MY JOB," Jonah repeated. "I never thought anything about it before."

"You literally saved these people from death?" Sam asked, her gaze intense. "Never mind modesty, we need the truth. Did you?"

"Yeah. Yeah, I did."

"And you remember them all?" Luke asked.

"I don't think you ever forget saving someone's life," Jonah retorted.

Sam got up and went over to the evidence board. She picked up a marker, and pointed. "Okay. Simon Church. How did you save his life?"

"Before the Jeep, he had a smaller car, a beater, pretty much. I was out patrolling one rainy night when he went past me like a bat out of hell. I called it in, then hit my lights and sirens and took off after him. I didn't know the brakes had failed and he was trying desperately to stop the car. Just outside the town limits, there's a mean curve with a solid drop. Straight down about four hundred feet and into an old granite quarry. There was no guardrail at the time."

"He went over?" Luke asked, intent.

"Yeah. He'd managed to fishtail the car two or three times before he hit the edge, so it both slowed the car and sent him down at a slight angle. I got to the edge to see that part of a dead tree and part of a crumbling ledge were the only things holding that car in place, about thirty feet down. I yelled at him not to move, then went back to my Jeep and got the hook from my winch. I had to move carefully, because it was still raining and I could feel the mud moving underneath every step I took."

He drew a breath. "There was no way in hell to stop that car from falling except for a minute or two. Not long enough to try to attach the hook to the car, to anything solid. So I hooked it around me, and when I got to the car, which thankfully had stopped with the driver's side facing up, I was able to ease the door open.

"Simon hadn't lost his head even though he looked terrified. He'd already unhooked his seat belt. I grabbed his wrist and held on as hard as he did. He started to slide out of the car—and that's when the slope let go. We were both sitting on our asses in the mud, watching that car tumbling all the way to the floor of the quarry. There was barely enough left to put in a wheelbarrow."

"Wow," Sam said.

"It was close," Jonah admitted. "I was just wondering if we were going to try to climb back up holding on to that slippery cable when Sarah got there. We held on, and she operated the winch to pull us slowly back to the top." Jonah shook his head. "No question he'd be dead if I hadn't been able to get down to him."

Sam made a quick note under Simon Church's name, simply SAVED FROM CAR CRASH.

"Okay," she said. "Amy Grimes. What happened?"

Jonah shook his head. "One of those unthinking teenage things. It was about a year ago. Amy had a different boyfriend then, and they decided to have a nice, romantic little picnic. In a pasture. Normally, that time of the year, that pasture is empty because the farmer is about to cut hay.

"On that day, however, I got a frantic call from the farmer, whose place I had left as part of a regular, routine patrol no more than five minutes before. His meanest bull, one that would as soon trample you to death as look at you, had kicked its way out of the stable it was in and had taken off through the pasture. He was just going to let the animal run, burn off his temper, but he caught a glimpse of color at the far end of the pasture and realized somebody was inside the fence. He was too far away to do anything, but he knew I'd been headed in that direction, so he called me."

Jonah paused. "Just as I got there, the boyfriend was bailing out over the fence. Amy was frozen, absolutely couldn't move. And that bull was headed right for her. The farmer had told me to shoot him if I had to. I had to."

"One shot put him down?" Lucas asked matter-of-factly.

"Two. Two quick rounds, which, luckily, I knew where to aim. He was moving so fast that he was dead in midgallop. Flipped over forward. One hoof grazed Amy's arm. That's how close it had been."

Sam let out a low whistle, but all she wrote under Amy's name was BULL ATTACK.

"Keep going," Lucas said. "Judge Carson?"

"Few years back, when I was first appointed, we had something of a meth problem in the area, and that was a problem we definitely didn't need. I didn't want it to take hold, and that meant we had to stop it. My department was aggressive, and I called in outside help, experienced drug enforcement officers to work with my people in locating and taking out the labs. One meth lab blew up before we could get

there, killing the three inside. But we were able to capture the lieutenant of the wannabe drug kingpin of the area."

"And he was willing to talk," Sam guessed.

"That was the plan. We kept him in protective custody right in
the courthouse until Judge Carson could charge him and—Serenity
being a small town with not much on the docket—hear his testimony
at the same time. Judge was fine with it, lawyers were fine with it,
even the dealer was fine with it.

"His boss, however, wasn't. He must have gotten in through one
of the windows, because he didn't go through security downstairs.
Had a silenced automatic and shot two of my officers outside the courtroom doors. Didn't kill them, luckily. His lieutenant wasn't so lucky.
The first shot was to the head, second to the heart. He was rumored
to be a crack shot. The rumors hadn't lied. His next shot would have
been the judge."

"So you stopped him," Lucas said.

Jonah nodded. "It took three shots to bring him down, and he
still managed to wound the judge in the arm. But he didn't kill him."

Silent now, Samantha wrote underneath Judge Carson's name
ARMED DRUG DEALER.

"Next," Lucas said. "Luna Lang."

"She used to own a little cottage, couple of years before she met
Dave. Hired a contractor for some electrical repairs. I honestly don't
know if he screwed it up or it was just an old house and something
sparked the wrong way. I heard the town fire alarm go off, got the
radio call, and I was closer than either the fire trucks or EMS. When
I got there that night, the place was already an inferno. I could hear
the fire engines, but I knew they wouldn't get there in time. I went

in. Luna had managed to make it as far as the downstairs hallway, so I didn't have to go far. But just as I carried her out, the whole roof caved in. The house was a total loss."

Sam stared at him. "I bet it's hell for you to get life insurance."

He managed a faint smile. "Luckily I have no dependents, and my pension would take care of cremation and any bills left."

Sam looked as if she wanted to ask more questions but in the end just shook her head, wrote HOUSE FIRE under Luna's name, and went on. "Sean Messina?"

"He was hiking up in the woods not too far from here. Hunting season, so he had his gun and his dog. Never actually figured out how it happened, but somehow he managed to shoot himself. I was also in the woods, about a quarter mile away, but I was looking for some illegal traps the hunting fairies set each season."

Sam blinked, then smiled. "Ah. You're not sure who's doing it."

"Oh, I'm sure. I just can't catch the bastard. Anyway, I was hunting for traps, and springing and collecting those I found when I heard the shot. Sean's dog deserves some of the credit; he came bursting out of the brush near me barking his head off. Led me back to Sean, who was bleeding like a stuck pig."

"So you saved him," Lucas said.

"Well, I was barely in range to use my radio and have them send our EMS unit. Until they came, I used basic first aid." Jonah shrugged. "They said he would have bled to death if I hadn't known what I was doing."

Silently, Sam wrote HUNTING ACCIDENT under Sean Messina's name.

"Okay," Lucas said. "How did you save Nessa Tyler's life?"

FIFTEEN

Nessa was beginning to think the dirt wall she followed was never going to end. When she paused to rest, which seemed often to her, she could no longer hear the breathing of the other people. She'd thought that was scary enough, but the absence of it, the sheer *aloneness* she felt in that damp, so-dark place, was more terrifying than anything she'd ever known before.

She felt like she'd walked miles. Her feet had gone so cold they were numb, but she had a pretty good idea how scratched up they must be by now, even as careful as she'd been.

But then Nessa realized that the wall she'd been following had been straight for a long time, much longer than any room would need. For the first time, she had a sense of something above her head, as if she could reach up and touch more dirt if only she were a few inches taller. A few more yards, and she could have sworn she could make out a faint light ahead. Very faint, not like daylight exactly—more like dusk.

The final few yards were a climb, or felt like it, though she didn't realize until she at last reached the mouth of the shaft that she had climbed from God only knew how deeply underground.

She stood there, and for a moment closed her eyes to make sure the surface of her mind was still calm and without ripples. Remarkably, it was. She opened her eyes then, looked around to get her bearings—and wanted to burst into tears.

Nothing looked familiar. Absolutely nothing. There was no sign of a cabin, much less a house. No sign of a *shed*. Trails crisscrossed through the woods all around her, but she couldn't see anything wide enough to show that a car had passed this way, or a horse, or a bike.

Even worse, there were evergreen trees all around, filling in for the hardwood trees only now beginning to green out, and because of them, Nessa could only catch glimpses of the sky. The darkening sky.

And, faintly, she could hear thunder rumble.

Damn. She didn't dare say it out loud, and not only because that black snake of a *him* was still back there, and maybe by now knew she was gone.

There was a lot of forest around Serenity. Back when she'd really liked to ride her pony, her father had taken her along a lot of the old trails that wound all through the forest, and Chief Riggs had made sure they were clearly marked, especially for Sunday riders.

But she hadn't ridden in a long time, and nothing she was looking at looked familiar.

Worse, it was getting darker. And if it stormed . . . even if she found some kind of shelter, what if he came after her? What if he found her?

With a choked-back sob, Nessa picked a direction and struck out, trying to listen in case he was behind her, scanning in front of her to see where she was going as long as she *could* see. And wishing she could just stand and scream and scream and scream until somebody heard her and came to save her.

SIXTEEN

"Well?" Sam asked.

"It was nothing heroic," he told them. "Nessa used to ride all the time, first ponies and then the bigger horse her dad, Matt, got for her. She was a really good rider, so more than ready for a well-trained horse. That one was. They don't have pasture, so he boarded the horse at one of the outlying farms. She wasn't allowed to ride alone, none of the kids were, but they'd form groups just about every Sunday and ride most of the day exploring the trails through the woods.

"I got the ranger service out here to clearly mark the trails that were suitable for riding, made sure every rider had a map and a compass in their saddlebags, and put the fear of God into them about not leaving the marked trails. The forest can get dense as hell, and we've lost hikers in years past. I wasn't about to lose any of those kids in those woods."

Sam said, "What happened?"

"The kind of freak thing that can happen whenever you're riding a horse in the woods. They weren't going faster than a trot; that's what the kids swore, and I believed them. Nessa's horse somehow got his hoof wedged in under one of those big roots and fell. Maybe if Nessa had been older or more experienced, she would have had the quick reactions to push herself clear of the horse. But she didn't. And when he fell, he came down on top of her."

"Jesus," Sam muttered.

"Yeah. I counted it lucky she was riding with an English saddle that day and not Western like the others; the saddle horn probably would have killed her. As it was, she had a broken arm and a couple of broken ribs. Worse, she also had internal injuries.

"The oldest boy knew enough first aid that he was able to splint the broken arm, and two of the others set off for town to get help." Jonah shook his head. "She was out cold, and he had sense enough to know both that she shouldn't be jostled and that he needed to at least start heading back for town. So he and one of the other boys fashioned a litter they could carry on foot between them, holding her as level as possible."

"Smart kid."

"The real hero." Jonah smiled. "He's in college now. Pre-med."

Lucas smiled, but his eyes were still intent. "What happened?"

"They managed to get her nearly to the road, where the EMS unit met them. The unit got her to the hospital."

"And?" Luke prompted.

Jonah sighed. "Most people think they know what the rarest blood types are, but scientists are discovering new variations all the time. The rarest blood type, one most people have never heard of, is Rh-null. A patient with that blood type can give to some other Rh patients, but if you've got it, that's what you have to get if you need a transfusion. Nessa has Rh-null blood."

"And so do you," Sam said.

Jonah nodded. "There was none in the clinic's blood bank, and even with a chopper it'd be a good two hours or more getting some here. Doc knew I had it, so he called me. And I came."

After a moment, Jonah said, "I give blood at the clinic as often as Doc will let me. Nessa gives about once a year. With a little luck, we've got enough stockpiled for both of us in case of any future need. Now."

Sam looked at the evidence board, and then under Nessa's name slowly wrote: BLOOD TRANSFUSION.

"Nothing heroic," Jonah repeated. "I happened to have the right blood and I was here. So Nessa survived."

"She would have died without your blood," Luke said, and it wasn't a question.

Jonah half shrugged. "Doc said so later. I asked him to downplay what the risk had been to Nessa, but her dad, Matt, can be a persistent bastard, and he found out. Honestly, I think that's one of the reasons he isn't totally batshit crazy about Nessa missing. He's convinced I can find her and bring her home. Thinks of me as her guardian angel."

Samantha looked at him steadily for a moment, then said, "And can you?"

Jonah gave her a look. "Why, because we have the same blood type? Jesus."

"No. Because you're a latent empath—and you gave her some of your blood."

Lucas said to his wife, "It's a stretch."

"Maybe not. Maybe not if I help."

Jonah could see Lucas stiffen a bit, but the other man's voice was calm. "You've never tried that before. As far as I know, no one has tried that before."

"That's why we practice in the field, according to Bishop. Trying things we've never done before. And the blood type being so rare, plus Jonah's latent abilities, makes this something unique."

Lucas was silent, frowning.

"Have you been able to sense any of them?" Samantha asked, clearly knowing the answer.

"No," Luke replied, still frowning. "I don't know if it's the energy he doesn't really control or what, but every time I've tried, all I've heard in my head was something like static. And I haven't felt anything at all."

"Then we need to try something else." Samantha sighed. "Look, we've still got a day's work or more going through files trying to figure out why these people, indebted to Jonah for their lives, are now targets apparently because of it, since that's the only similarity we've found. We don't have any clues. We don't have *anything* to send us in the right direction, unless we can somehow find out where Nessa's being held."

"The *somehow* meaning me?" Jonah asked warily.

Sam gestured over her shoulder to a table against the wall, where boxes held the personal effects of some of the missing people. "I can touch that. All of it, probably. And maybe, *maybe* I'll catch a glimpse of something useful. But as far as we know, he didn't touch any of the missing people then. Not when and where he abducted them."

"The energy bubbles," Jonah protested.

"Were probably excess energy from when he was initially establishing control over them psychically. That's why there was so much of it, why so much of it was diffused. Even why it seems to be blocking Luke. Whoever this guy is, he's powerful, but I think we're right in believing he isn't in control of his abilities. He's leaving too much around him whenever he uses them. For now, at least. But the more time that passes, the more likely it is that he'll learn better control, better focus. And once that happens, we might end up facing a weapon we can't fight."

"Which makes it even more dangerous, Sam. He's touched Nessa's mind, controlled her. If he senses you're trying to make contact through Jonah, he could try to kill you both."

"Then what, Luke? Spend the day trying to figure out why it's important that *these* particular people whose lives Jonah saved are so important? I'm willing to bet he could add others to that list, other lives he's saved." She looked at Jonah fiercely. "Couldn't you?"

"I guess. Probably. I'm a cop." It was, really, the first time Jonah had seen the intensity lurking beneath Samantha's seemingly quiet, urchinlike exterior, and now he had a fair idea of how these two matched so well.

"Then there are more potential victims, Luke. He abducted Nessa *yesterday*. He murdered Annie Duncan last night. He has five other people he's probably holding captive. I say any shortcut we can try that might lead us to this bastard is worth taking." She looked at Jonah, again fiercely. "How about you?"

"Yeah. Of course." He had no idea what he'd just agreed to but had a hunch it was not going to be pleasant.

Thunder rumbled distantly.

"Shit," Jonah said. "If we get another gully washer, even knowing which way to head in looking for them might leave us with nothing but a simple direction."

"Then we don't have any time to waste." Sam got up and came to stand behind Jonah—who felt profoundly uneasy.

"Uh—"

"Don't worry," Luke said as he got up and stood near his wife, presumably to catch her if she collapsed again. "If this thing works at all, you'll be a conduit. Best case, you might get some idea of where Nessa is being held, and maybe a mild headache."

"And worst case?"

"You'll feel at least some of what she's feeling."

"Oh, great," he muttered.

Sam was briskly matter-of-fact. "Close your eyes, Jonah. And think about Nessa."

"Think about her how?"

"Think of her riding horses, carrying her schoolbooks, standing in that kitchen while some monster took hold of her mind. Make her come alive in *your* mind."

Jonah had no idea if he could do it, but he closed his eyes and thought about Nessa. He had a lot of memories of her, now that he allowed himself to think of them.

Nessa on a pony and then a horse. Nessa grinning at him and waving when he passed by in his Jeep. Lying so still and white and silent in the hospital bed while his blood helped her hold on to life. That chilling video of her in her kitchen, moving like some remote-controlled doll to do the bidding of another.

Nessa . . .

"My feet are cold," Jonah said.

———————

HER FEET WERE cold. She was a little surprised she could feel anything, because she thought they were numb. She'd looked down at them once only to look hastily away, because there were scratches from thorns and sticks, most of them bleeding, and one split toenail where she'd tripped on a root.

A *root*. They always gave her trouble. Always.

She knew the only reason her feet weren't hurting horribly was because they were cold and mostly numb. But the coldness made it harder for her to feel the sharp edge of a stone, or briars, or everything else that could injure the bare feet of a little girl.

It was growing darker as the storm neared, but Nessa was doing her best. She had a sharp stone in her hand, and every few yards, she dug a short scratch in a tree trunk, just barely visible. She did it for two reasons: because she hoped it would keep her from walking in a circle as she'd read lost people often did, and because she hoped it would help Chief Riggs and his people find where the others were being held.

She knew it was a risk. If that snake thing, if *he* followed her and saw the marks, then he could catch up to her. She was sure he could travel faster than she could. So she tried to move faster, but paused to dig into a tree with the rock, her fingers hurting, her feet cold and stinging from the thorns and sticks and hard, cold ground . . .

"WHERE IS SHE, Jonah?" Sam asked calmly. She was holding one hand on each side of his head, a few inches from him, and her eyes were closed.

"Don't know. Woods. Woods all around. My feet are cold. I can hear it thundering, louder now. I'm afraid . . . he might be somewhere behind me . . . but I have to . . . mark the trees. Like Chief Riggs taught us to do. A sharp stone. A slash across the bark. Not deep enough to hurt the tree. Just deep enough to see so we don't get lost."

"Nessa, did you escape?"

"I knew I could." Jonah's voice was oddly his own, and yet there was a musing quality to it. "I don't know why I didn't sleep like the others. They're still back there. In that place that smells of dirt and mushrooms and . . ."

"And what, Nessa?"

". . . and he has needles in their arms, with IV bags. I remember those from the hospital. There was one in my arm too, but I pulled it out. So I could get away. And then . . . I had to be so careful. So *quiet*. Because I knew he would look for me if he knew I was gone. I found the wall, and kept one hand on it, because I knew I could find my way out like that."

"Did you see anything, Nessa?"

"It's dark. It's so dark. I can't see anything. I can hear the others breathing sometimes, but . . . I can't see. I can't help them. Unless I get out. Get away. If I get away, then I can help them. Then I can show people where he kept us."

"Nessa—"

"I'm outside again."

"How did you come out? What did the doorway look like?"

"Not a doorway. Just . . . a hole in the ground. I think I've walked for miles and miles. But I haven't, of course, I know that. Only I'm so tired. And the storm is coming. I still don't see anything that looks familiar. Except . . . there's a rock, taller than I am. And I remember people talking about it. Because it looks like it should fall over and it never does."

"Nessa," Jonah said suddenly. "Can you hear me?"

"I can hear you in my head. Why can I do that, Chief Riggs?"

"We'll talk about it later. Nessa, just beyond the funny rock there are two different paths. Do you see them?"

"Um . . . yeah. One's clearer than the other. I can hardly see the other."

"That's the trail you have to take."

"Are you sure?"

"Just get on that trail and keep walking, Nessa. I'll be there as soon as I can."

"Oh—okay, Chief Riggs."

Lucas had heard only one side of that last bit of conversation, when Jonah spoke. But he watched Sam's lips move whenever Nessa answered.

Sam stepped to one side as Jonah rose, and she seemed more grateful than anything else that Luke's arm was around her.

"Wow," she said. "That was different."

Jonah shook his head the way a man did when he was dismissing something for the moment. "It's not a *mild* headache, just so you know. I have to go after Nessa. If she's where I hope she is, I can get there in less than thirty minutes. I'll grab a couple of my officers who ride; Clyde stables a few horses several blocks back from his diner. You two stay here."

"What about the captor?" Lucas asked.

"Nessa may be able to help us find him. If not, the marks I taught her to make on trees should at least get us near there. No matter how hard it rains, it won't wash away *those* marks."

Luke eased Sam down into the closest chair as Jonah hurried from the building.

"Are you all right?"

"Seem to be. Not even tired, really." She looked at him as Luke sat beside her, and said, "Okay, so I'm a little tired. And I have a mild headache. But that was . . . wild. Luke, you still couldn't sense Nessa, could you? Even after I made contact through Jonah."

"Not so much as a twinge."

"That's what I thought. And I know why. It's not our unsub blocking you. I'm not sure if she learned it on her own or somebody taught her to, but Nessa knows how to overlay a still, calm surface on her mind. Like one of our shields, but completely organic and natural to her. You couldn't sense her fear or pain because it was underneath that surface."

"Jonah could feel it," Luke objected. "He said her feet were cold."

"But he didn't *feel* that. He was just reporting what she was thinking. That was the only thing she would allow out. Just thoughts, not feelings."

"Then how was Jonah—how were you both, I guess—able to home in on her like that?"

"Jonah was the one sensing where she was, and I really think it was that blood connection. Maybe just because it's such an incredibly rare type of blood, and only the two of them have it here. We've always thought of our blood as simply the blood we were born with, nothing more. But now . . . I think maybe Bishop is going to have to add a few new suggestions for the scientists to study."

"But you're sure you're all right?"

"Yeah, I'm fine." She frowned as they heard thunder again. "I'm really hoping we don't get a nasty storm, though. It'll be hard to see even slashes on trees if the rain is falling hard enough."

Luke got up and headed for one of the computer stations. "I'm going to check the weather. And then I'm going to have one of the analysts *really* dig into the backgrounds of these six people. And Jonah's as well."

"Oh, he's not going to like that."

"He will if we can point him to the unsub."

"Especially before dark. What time is it, anyway?"

"A bit after three," Lucas said, glancing at the clock on the computer's toolbar.

"Does it feel to you like we've been here a week?"

"At least. Hmmm. Storm's all around us, but I'm not sure if we'll actually get wet."

"We'll hope it stays away at least until Jonah finds Nessa."

Lucas looked over at her curiously. "You're certain he will."

"Yeah. Those two are connected. I have no idea if either will decide to use the connection, or even explore it. The difference in their ages is going to keep Jonah at more than arm's length, and I'm not sure Nessa wants to be . . . different . . . from her friends. She's at that age."

Luke nodded, then returned his attention to the computer screen. "You covered the camera with tape again, didn't you?"

"Yes. We know hackers can remote-activate those cameras. I don't like not knowing if someone is watching."

Lucas sighed but didn't remove the tape from the computer's camera. Instead, he talked to the technical analyst he could see, rapidly giving him all the names and information he had on the missing people—and on Jonah.

"You want everything I can dig up?" the tech asked.

"Everything. On every one of them."

"Gotcha. I'll be back when I have something."

Luke turned in his chair to find Samantha wandering around the room. Except that the wandering looked like pacing. "What is it?"

"I'm not sure. I just have a bad feeling."

"Nessa?"

"No, actually. I think Jonah is going to find her, and that she'll be in pretty good shape, all things considered."

"Then, what?"

"This thing started long before we got here. And it's pretty obvious that whoever this unsub is, he has a connection to Jonah. Or to one of the people Jonah saved. It just doesn't make sense any other way."

"Okay. So?"

"He tried to get in my head—we think—and failed. He got into Robbie's head and mixed up her memories. He got into Sarah's head and *gave* her new memories."

"Yeah."

"Why?"

"To test us maybe?"

"Well . . . granted we've barely been here twenty-four hours, hard as that is to believe, but a lot has happened. If he's testing anybody, I'd think it was Jonah. Now, maybe he doesn't know Jonah is a latent; you have to be a pretty strong psychic yourself to pick up latents. Maybe he was probing us to find out if he could use any of us to . . . hurt Jonah."

"You think that's the point of this? To hurt Jonah?"

"To destroy him, more like. We've both seen how connected he is to this town. If there's somebody out there who is convinced—

delusional or sane—that Jonah has somehow wronged him, then all this has to be happening for that reason.

"Did Nessa get away because she was able to—or because he let her? If there *is* a trail back to where the others were kept, what will we find? Nessa heard them breathing. You haven't picked up on any fear, so I'm betting he's keeping them sedated. But not so he can control them. I think he's keeping them like that because he knows Jonah's been driving himself into the ground trying to find these people. And when he *does* find them, the others, I think what he finds will be meant to shock and horrify him."

"Torture?"

"No. Jonah *knows* this town. These people. I think the unsub wants to torment Jonah with . . . games. If Jonah finds Nessa, and in finding her is able to find the others, then Jonah wins. But it'll come at a price. The people Jonah cares about are going to be the ones paying the price."

"Then this isn't over," Lucas said.

"I think it's just beginning," Samantha said. "At least as far as the unsub's concerned. And if we don't stop him . . . I think a lot of people are going to get hurt."

DANTE THOUGHT HE might have slept an hour or three. Surely no longer than that, judging by how he felt. He tried to go back to sleep, but things were tickling at the back of his mind, bothering him, and sleep just wouldn't come. Finally, he got up and showered and shaved. Pulled on a sweatshirt and sweatpants, since he wasn't supposed to be back on the clock until midnight.

He was hoping that if he ordered just the right snack from room service, maybe it would help him sleep. Maybe.

Anything was worth a try.

He walked into the common area of the two-bedroom suite, surprised to find Robbie standing at one of the windows, looking out.

"You should be asleep," he said, adding immediately, "Did I hear it thunder a little while ago?"

"Yes, you did."

She turned to face him, wearing a hotel robe, her hair piled on top of her head as though in preparation for a shower.

The gun was . . . extra.

Dante had never had a gun pointed at him like that, not for real, not by somebody he knew whose face was all . . . wrong.

"Robbie—"

"Good-bye, Dante."

The gun went off with an ungodly roar, Dante felt something like a two-by-four slam into his chest, and then everything went dark.

SEVENTEEN

Robbie stumbled back from Dante's doorway, shocked through to her bones. It took her several minutes to get her heart to slow down, but her hands were still shaking when she examined her gun. It didn't smell as if it had been fired. She removed the clip and found it full of ammo. Chamber empty.

She wanted to put the gun back in its holster but held it just in case as she slowly eased open the door of Dante's bedroom.

He was sound asleep. Snoring. Clearly one of those restless sleepers, he was sprawled across the bed diagonally with the covers bunched oddly here and there but decently covering him.

After a long moment of listening to him, alive and breathing, Robbie eased the door shut and went back out into the sitting area of their suite.

She had only slept a few brief hours, but she had the feeling she'd never sleep again. She didn't want to ever sleep again.

A *puppet*, a goddamned puppet, that was what that slimy son of a bitch they were after had turned her into. It didn't matter that he had, apparently, brainwashed her into getting up, getting her gun, and making it as far as Dante's door—but had not been able to force her to do his bidding.

No, that didn't matter. She'd shoot herself before she would shoot a teammate.

But he had *still* gotten into her head, messed with her mind, her memories, making her believe she had shot and killed her partner. And he had done that because he had *not* been able to make her actually do it.

Robbie hesitated only a moment. She took that moment to shore up her shields, trying to make them stronger than they had ever been before. She took a quick shower and got dressed, pulled her still-damp hair back in a hasty ponytail, hesitated for a moment before clipping her gun to the belt of her jeans, then scribbled a quick note to Dante and left the suite.

Their hotel served food twenty-four-seven *and* kept a generous selection of fruit, cheese, and crackers just inside the main floor dining room all afternoon until dinnertime, but she paused only to get coffee in one of the cardboard cups. She had no idea what had been going on at their command center, and didn't pause near the police station even though there seemed to be a lot of activity going on in there.

She thought it seemed dim for midafternoon, and glanced up to see the heavily overcast sky. And hear, faintly, thunder rumble.

Great. A storm. As a general rule, storms weren't kind to psychics.

She walked into the makeshift command center, finding Lucas

and Samantha working. Lucas was at one of the computer stations, and Samantha was studying the evidence boards.

Without so much as a greeting, Robbie slammed the door behind her, and said, "I want this fucker *dead*."

HE WAS GLAD he had found a private place to do his work. No more alleys where passersby could discover him. Besides, it was still daylight—albeit overcast gray daylight. But the storage shed, as close as he had been able to get to the hotel without risking discovery, was sorely lacking in creature comforts, and he found himself lying on a wrinkled, dirty tarp that smelled of turpentine and seemed to have several small chunks of lumber underneath.

His head hurt.

His head hurt *so much*.

It was dim in the shed, but he felt the wetness on his face, under his nose, and knew it wasn't tears. Blood.

He tried to use the tarp to help stop the bleeding, but it was rough and stank and seemed to make him bleed more. Just like he bled more when he tried to move, to sit up.

He could hear it thundering and wished the storm would hurry and get here. They made him feel better, storms. Made him feel . . . stronger. At least since the accident.

The dark usually helped him as well, but not this time. This time, he had pushed too hard, tried too hard.

"Bitch," he whispered. "I'll get you next time. I'll be ready for you next time. Bitch . . ."

—————

BOTH SAMANTHA AND Lucas turned to stare at Robbie after her rather violent entrance, perhaps a bit startled but no more than that. Taking unusual things calmly was one of the requirements to be an SCU agent.

"What's happened, Robbie?" Sam asked.

"I just came out of a waking nightmare." Robbie couldn't be still, so she paced. "It seemed as real as this is. Only in that waking nightmare, I was standing by the window in our sitting room, and when Dante came in, I turned around and shot him. Killed him. You want to take my gun? I wish you'd take my gun."

Sam was frowning slightly. "He already knew he could mess with your mind, change your memories. Why would he give you the memory of killing Dante?"

"Just for jollies?" Robbie was in no mood for speculation but gave it a shot. "I think he tried to make me actually do it. When I came out of it, I was standing outside Dante's bedroom door, in a robe, holding my gun. So he'd gotten me that far. I really think he believed he could make me kill my partner."

"But you didn't," Sam reminded her quietly.

"No, I didn't. Not this time. But when he couldn't make me actually do it, he made me believe I had. He *really* made me believe I had." Robbie wasn't the crying sort of woman, but her eyes glistened with tears she wouldn't shed. "And how can I trust myself now? Around any of you? As long as this son of a bitch is alive, how can I trust myself?"

"Were you asleep or already up?" Luke asked.

Robbie didn't even have to think about that. "I'd been asleep.

Sleeping hard, because I was tired. When I came back to myself, I was standing at his door. I had my gun, but I was still dressed for bed in a sleepshirt, with a hotel robe over it."

"So maybe it was an experiment," Sam said. "To find out if it was easier for him to get into her head, influence her, if she was asleep when he tried. If he's been watching us, he must know we've split shifts. It doesn't seem to be working out very well, since you barely slept and Dante should be here any minute, but the unsub could have seen you two go into the hotel hours ago."

Robbie blinked. "Dante's coming?"

"Yeah. And I wouldn't be surprised if he's nearly as shaken as you are."

"Why? He was asleep."

Sam opened her mouth to reply, but Dante came in just then, not slamming the door as Robbie had, but not exactly calmly. He was dressed in jeans and a sweatshirt, his hair still damp from the shower, and he was rubbing the center of his chest with one hand.

He looked immediately at Robbie. "I had the most vivid fucking nightmare. You shot me. Only it wasn't really you."

Before Robbie could speak, Lucas held up a hand. "What do you mean it wasn't really her?"

"It was . . . her face was like the missing people we watched on the videos. Like the face of a doll. No expression. No life. Creepy as hell, though not as creepy as seeing—and feeling—her shoot me. I mean, I got shot once; it was just a graze, but I remember how it felt. This was like that, only much, much more painful."

"More than a dream," Robbie muttered. "That bastard got into our heads again."

Dante frowned. "First time for me."

"You were asleep," Sam told him. "More vulnerable even with that strong shield. Especially since he can't seem to aim his energy very well."

"Really?" Robbie said. "He aimed it at me pretty well."

It was Lucas who said, "I doubt he meant Dante to know anything at all. It was you he was after, Robbie, you he'd already left . . . bread crumbs to follow. You he wanted to be able to control. What Dante got was . . . spillover."

"Vivid spillover," Dante muttered. "I swear my chest hurts like hell."

Dryly, Sam said to him, "Power of suggestion. Robbie was convinced she'd shot and killed you, and she's a telepath. She doesn't usually broadcast, but in moments of extreme stress . . ."

"I have been known to," Robbie admitted, with an apologetic grimace to her partner. "Sorry." Then she frowned. "I don't like the way this bastard is playing with our minds. My mind. And why's he fixated on me?"

Musing, Luke said, "It could be yours is the only ability he really understands, or believes he does. Close to what he has himself; any kind of true mind control or mind influence has to begin with telepathy. Or it could be he wants to control you for some reason we don't yet know."

"We need to figure that out," Robbie told him. "And I mean soon. I catch him in my head again, I'll give him *more* than a headache or nosebleed."

Dante said, "You can do that?"

"She's not supposed to," Lucas said.

"Oh, tell me Bishop wouldn't approve, destroying a monster like this one. Besides, it'd be self-defense."

"That's a report I'd like to read," Sam murmured.

"I'm still in the dark," Dante complained. "You could destroy him? As in—kill him? With your mind?"

Earnestly, Robbie said, "I'd have to be touching him physically. And I'd have to be *really* pissed off."

"And if you were?"

"Well . . . ever get hold of your daddy's shotgun and shoot a pumpkin or watermelon when you were a kid just to see what would happen?"

"Yeah."

"Something like that." Robbie seemed very calm.

Dante was rather glad she was calm. He looked at Lucas. "When I joined the unit, I was told that psychic abilities couldn't be used as weapons except defensively."

Sam murmured, "Read the fine print. That's *shouldn't* be used as weapons except defensively."

"Sam."

"Well, it's true. Look, we don't have many psychics in the unit either powerful enough or with enough control to actually be able to hurt somebody else. And, like Robbie said, she has to be enraged, completely out of control. That's not only not her normal state, it's almost unheard of."

Reassuringly to her partner, Robbie said, "And Bishop taught me a lot about control. So did Miranda. I've never killed anybody with my mind." She paused, then added, "Blew the hell out of some pump-kins and watermelons, though."

Dante sat down at the conference table. "Nobody ever tells me anything."

Robbie sort of waved the hand not holding her coffee at him, and said to Luke and Sam, "With all due deference to Dante's uneasiness, I'm way more concerned with our unsub and his apparent ability to waltz in and out of my mind whenever he wants."

"It might not be so easy for him," Lucas pointed out.

"I don't know if it was easy for him or hard, but I don't want him in my head again, *ever*," Robbie snapped—if quietly.

"Calm down," Sam said quietly. "There's no way in hell you'd ever deliberately shoot your partner. If this unsub made a try for that, I'm guessing he ended up just as you expected, with a pounding headache and probably a nosebleed. At least. If he's relatively new to his abili-ties, he could have ended up with a lot worse. But whatever he was trying, all he could really do was what he did before. Plant a few memories in your head. Probably quick and brief ones."

HE COULDN'T GET the bleeding stopped for the longest time, and that frightened him, even though he didn't want to admit it.

Only cowards were afraid, and he was no coward.

He finally tore strips from his shirt and stuffed them up inside his nose. The plugs kept the blood from streaming down over his now-torn shirt, but he had to breathe through his mouth, and every time he swallowed he tasted blood.

That was . . . unpleasant.

And he suspected there was something badly wrong with his head. It hurt, of course, maybe worse than it had ever hurt before, but . . . the lumps. They had been there before, of course, but when he put his hands up to feel, he realized there were new bulges. He wondered if that was what happened when a brain grew beyond the capacity of a skull to hold it.

Would the skull crack, eventually? Or would it continue to bulge, as his bulged?

That could be a problem.

Still, he was utterly committed to his plan, and just as utterly convinced it would work. First he would finish punishing Jonah, that was paramount. Because it was all Jonah's *fault*, and he had to pay.

Choices. It was all about choices.

Every choice had a price.

And Jonah would pay. Because when the girl had escaped, all according to plan, she had unknowingly stepped on a pressure plate, and that would set it all in motion.

Jonah would be first through the doorway, if he knew Jonah. And he did. He'd be first through, and he'd see what was waiting for him. The punishment that was worse than being shot or killed; those were too quick.

This . . . this would haunt Jonah Riggs forever.

ROBBIE THOUGHT ABOUT it, then sat down heavily in one of the chairs at the conference table across from Dante, obviously still more shaken than she wanted to admit. "It seemed so real. So unbelievably fucking real." Then she looked around, suddenly realizing. "Where's Jonah? Wasn't he supposed to be working with you guys?"

Sam filled her in on what had been happening, finishing, "He left about an hour ago, so——"

Before she could finish, Jonah came into the command center. He looked windblown, but the relief on his face told them all they really needed to know.

"How is Nessa?" Sam asked anyway.

"In pretty good shape. Cuts and scrapes on her bare feet, and I doubt she'll ever sleep in a dark room again, but Doc says she'll be fine with enough rest and good food."

"He didn't hurt her?"

"No. She doesn't remember him even touching her. Though she was out at first, so . . . still possible, I guess. She wanted a shower, and Doc had a quiet word with her; he doesn't believe she was molested or suffered any kind of sexual attack."

"She didn't see him," Lucas said, and it wasn't a question.

Jonah shook his head. "If I understood her, he was seldom there, and when he was, because she was trying to hide her awareness from him, she visualized a black snake. Although even if she'd opened her eyes, she wouldn't have been able to see him; from what she said, it was darker than dark in that place."

"Was he starving her—the rest of them?"

Jonah shook his head. "Nutrients through an IV as far as Doc could tell from Nessa, and what she could tell him about where and how they were held."

"So the others are alive?"

"They were when Nessa got away. At least, she thinks they were. She could hear them breathing, and in feeling her way out, touched at least a couple of them." He paused, shook his head. "Freaked her out, but she didn't scream. She's a strong little girl. She was certain they were breathing."

"Kept where?"

"I left two of my men with orders not to budge from where we found Nessa, and I didn't backtrack because I wanted to get Nessa to the doc ASAP. But from what she said and where we found her, he's been keeping them in what used to be an old clay mine. Deep underground."

"I didn't know clay was mined," Luke said.

"All kinds of things have been mined in Tennessee," Jonah said. "A couple hundred years back, this state was considered one of the richest in the South for minerals. Anyway, clay was mined for reasons you'd expect: pottery, additives for masonry, that sort of thing. Usually in big open pits, which ended up as lakes once they played out, most of them. But there were a few test shafts bored into the ground here and there; some were successful, and some just . . . ended. It sounds like that's where Nessa and the others have been held. There's a forest there now, but when the shaft was originally dug more than a hundred years ago, the trees were a lot more sparse.

"The shaft, large enough for a man of medium height to stand up straight, was bored down at a slight angle, and at the bottom they found a big cavern. Interesting, but it was unsuitable for removing clay. And there was nothing else interesting there, no other minerals or gems. It was marked on the old map—I have one of my people digging that up now—and notes made that if anyone ever decided to build there, the cavern would have to be blasted first, and fill brought in."

"It's that close to the surface?" Lucas asked intently.

"Safe to walk across, even ride a horse or drive across probably, but not safe to sink any kind of building foundations there. That area was even farther from town than it is now, so they just took simple precautions. The entrance boarded up with timbers, DANGER, DO NOT ENTER painted across them. And people forgot. The paint faded, the timbers rotted, and the forest grew all around it."

"Until the unsub came along."

Jonah nodded. "If he grew up around here, he could have heard about it. There are a few mine shafts scattered closer to the mountains, but the ranger service makes sure the barriers at the mouth of *those* shafts cannot be opened. Dangerous.

"I don't remember any of my friends as kids wanting to explore any caves or shafts, and I haven't had to chase any away in the years I've been chief, but everybody knew it was somewhere in the woods. If he'd been hiking in the woods, he could have found it. Vines had grown up all around there, but they wouldn't have been too difficult to pull away. And it's far enough out that he probably didn't worry much about keeping it hidden while he came and went."

Sam frowned. "Did Nessa say anything about pulling vines away when she was getting out?"

"No. But she was so intent on getting out, I doubt she would have even noticed them."

"We'll need to talk to her," Sam said.

"I know. But right now, the doctors and her family are around her. And we know where to find the others without having to talk to her first. That's our priority, finding the others."

"Agreed," Luke and Sam said in one voice.

Jonah frowned at Robbie. "Aren't you supposed to be asleep?"

"We had a little disturbance."

"Little?" Dante murmured.

Robbie shook her head. "Never mind that for now. I think it's safe to say that both Dante and I are wide awake, *believe* me."

"Okay." Jonah straightened. "I've put Doc on alert at the clinic, and I have my people standing by. Sarah will meet us at the station." When Lucas raised his brows, Jonah added, "My first priority is getting those people out of there. I mean to go in there in force, armed, and wearing vests."

"Do you expect him to be there?" Sam asked neutrally.

"Honestly? No. I expect that by now he knows Nessa's escaped—whether he deliberately let her go or not—and that he'll be watching from a safe distance. My only real concern is whether he has the place booby-trapped. We've never needed a bomb squad."

"I can help you there," Sam said.

Jonah eyed her. "You're sort of handy to have around."

"I have my moments. Our vests are in the SUV. Let's go."

EIGHTEEN

Jonah hadn't known what to expect at the bottom of that long, long shaft into the earth. Nessa had tried to tell him, haltingly, but it was clear there was just something she couldn't manage to tell him, something that horrified her exhausted little soul.

It might have been only the terrors of a little girl lost, but whatever it was, just her expression had made the hair stand up on the back of his neck. So he'd exchanged his service weapon, a Glock .22, for the .44 Magnum he kept more as a showpiece—but also kept clean and oiled. And used at the shooting range whenever he used his service weapon.

The only one of the others to comment had been Samantha, who had said merely, "Looks like that cannon DeMarco carries."

"It kicks like a mule," was all Lucas said.

"I'll say," Sarah agreed, checking the load on her own Glock. "I fired the damned thing once at the range, and it knocked me on my ass. I don't need anything that powerful."

"Probably depends on what you're aiming at," Robbie murmured, envying the other woman her almost preternatural calm.

Sarah looked fairly rested, having logged, probably, a couple hours more sleep than Dante and Robbie, and she was most definitely ready to move, now that Nessa was safe and it seemed at least even odds they were going to find the others as well.

Safe and unharmed, they hoped.

They were all suited up in their body armor and armed, but they didn't ride horses to meet the other two officers. Instead, Jonah's Jeep was joined by four others from the police motor pool, and they loaded up and headed out in those.

Thunder rumbled about the time they turned off a paved road and onto a rutted track, and it was Samantha who asked, "Did anybody check the weather?"

Jonah, who was driving their Jeep in the lead, replied, "The worst of it's supposed to hold off, except for the wind. But sometime after midnight, we're gonna get slammed."

There were still enough dead leaves from the winter past to be blowing across in front of them, and Jonah had the Jeep's running lights on. Which helped more and more as the rutted road disappeared and he appeared to be following no more than a wide space between trees.

"I can see how you wouldn't have to worry about kids coming out here," Samantha said. "Spooky as hell. I know there's a storm rumbling around, but . . . still."

"This used to be fairly good riding on horseback," he told her. "But the undergrowth got out of control and nobody wanted to keep up the trails. Land's owned by a billionaire who also owns four or five mountains in the general area, and to his credit he wants to keep them wild. Hiking or riding is fine, but no lumber and no development."

"Good for him," Sam said.

"Yeah, I more or less agree with him. But a few hundred acres of this wilderness fall within my area of responsibility, so I'm really not keen on hikers or riders out this way."

"Unless you send them," Sam murmured as the headlights illuminated two clearly relieved uniformed police officers, who had their horses tied to trees just off the track. They were holding flashlights, and it was easy to see they'd been waving them around nervously until they saw the lights of vehicles approaching.

Jonah had gone over the plan with everyone, and everyone knew their part. There was no exit from this hole in the ground except the one they were going into.

They waited at the opening for just a couple of minutes, with Jonah and the other feds watching Sam. She swore under her breath, but said to Jonah, "No booby traps. No bombs."

"Sam?"

She looked at her husband and partner briefly, then said to Jonah bleakly, "Go ahead and get EMS out here as quickly as you can. We'll need five stretchers."

"And five coffins?" Jonah asked steadily.

"No. No, they're alive. Let's go."

He gave the order quickly, sending two officers back with one of the Jeeps to guide the EMS truck into the woods.

The first half-dozen people going in, which were Jonah, Sarah, and the agents, all had the big police spotlights that could be carried and gave off an amazing amount of light. They turned them on as soon as they started into the downward-slanting tunnel.

But within a very few steps, one by one they turned the lights off. Because there was light at the bottom of the tunnel.

Bright, bright light.

"It's not a fire," Lucas breathed. "Which means he wants us— you—to see his work."

"Oh, Christ," Jonah murmured.

"It isn't what you think," Sam said. "He didn't physically torture them any more than he physically tortured Nessa."

"Then—"

Jonah broke off as soon as he cleared the tunnel and stepped into the cavern. It wasn't huge, maybe thirty feet from end to end, and about twenty feet across.

The lights had been placed with exquisite care, so that each of the missing people, watering eyes shut tight against the first light any of them had seen since they'd been brought here, weeks for some of them, were the inescapable focus.

Each of them sitting, unrestrained but unmoving, on upright wooden chairs. An IV pole beside each chair, the tubing from the bag snaking down and attached to the needles expertly placed in each victim's arm. Unmoving. Unable to move.

Their pants and shorts, or panties, down around their ankles. And beneath them, fastened to the chairs they could not escape, were pots or bowls or buckets to catch their urine and feces.

"Oh, my God," Jonah said, his voice hardly a whisper.

Lucas leaned over to say something to Sarah, and she immediately turned and began to herd the officers back up the tunnel. "We'll need you later to help carry them," she said, her voice breaking a little. "But not yet. Not just yet."

"People always find new ways to torture each other," Sam said. "Physically is the easy part. But mentally? Emotionally? How do you get over being abandoned in the darkness? Unable to move or speak even to call for help? How do you get over being so helpless that some-one else has to empty— How do you get over that humiliation, that loss of dignity. How do you get over being so alone, and so untouched. For so long. Alone. In the dark."

There was a moment of utter silence, and then they could all hear Amy Grimes mumbling to herself nothing that made sense. Nothing that would ever make sense.

"Let's get some of these lights out," Lucas suggested quietly. "Leave just enough for the medics to work by. And don't break them. All these—all these people have bare feet."

Jonah did his best not to look at them directly, as the level of light gradually diminished, but he eventually realized that none of them were going to open their eyes willingly. Not even Sean Messina, who had been taken barely a week before Nessa had.

None of them wanted to open their eyes even if they could. None of them wanted to believe in the voices they probably thought were imagined. None of them had it in them any longer to believe there could be anything else for them, ever, but the darkness.

WITH BOTH HANDS holding the hot coffee cup on the conference table in front of him, Dante said, "Nessa's the only real survivor." His voice was dull. "She wasn't down there long enough. And she found her way out of the dark, on her own. That will count. That will mean something to her, some day in the future if not now."

Jonah looked across the table at the two most experienced profilers here. They were all here, the feds and Sarah, all with coffee they'd barely touched and eyes that didn't want to meet anyone else's. Every one of them had helped carry the stretchers up that long, dark tunnel, only then accepting the silent, respectful help of the officers waiting outside.

Jonah said, "I know enough about profiling to know it's about damaged people and the reasons people have inside them that give them the ability to damage others. So tell me. How many of the five . . . survivors . . . we brought out of that place are going to have lives worth living?"

Sam was the first to meet his eyes, her own so dark, as dark as they'd been when he'd first met her, dark and unspeakably old in her urchin's pale face.

She drew a breath and said, "Mrs. Lang's baby may help her. The maternal instinct is strong enough to overcome almost anything. Amy Grimes is young, and the young are resilient. It depends on how strong her sense of self is. That's true of all of them. But . . ."

"But?"

"The judge is never going to be the man you once knew, Jonah. He was a man of dignity, and he can never see himself that way again. If he even leaves the clinic, it'll likely be to go to some kind of mental care facility or at least a residential medical care facility. Maybe Sean Messina too. His sense of self seemed to be very wrapped up in being strong, independent, able to handle himself and whatever else came along. But he couldn't handle what happened to him. Even the ones that somehow manage to move on, even Nessa, will be marked forever by what they experienced down in that hole in the ground."

"Because of me."

She shook her head immediately. "No, because of someone with a sick and twisted mind who wanted to make you suffer. And not just by a blow dealt and then over with."

"What do you mean?"

"He knows you, Jonah. He knows how you feel about this town, these people. *Especially* these people. You saved them. Every one of them owed their life to you."

Jonah started to speak, but didn't when she held up a hand.

"This is important. This is why everything has happened the way it has. He wants you to *suffer*. He wants you to spend the rest of your life suffering because of what happened to these people. And even wondering if they would have been better off if you hadn't saved them in the first place. Blaming yourself for what happened to them. For the rest of your life. That's what he wants, Jonah. That's what he needs."

Lucas nodded. "She's right."

Jonah finally took a drink of his coffee, vaguely aware that he had the wrong order, it was too sweet. Not that he cared. "I just . . . I honestly can't think of anyone who could hate me that much."

"That's because he doesn't hate you," Luke said.

"What? All that—and he doesn't hate me?"

"If he hated you," Robbie said slowly, "it would have been you down there." She glanced at Luke, who nodded.

"Exactly. He doesn't want to torture you, he wants to watch you torture yourself."

"I still don't——"

"Think," Samantha urged. "He isn't someone on the periphery of your life the way we originally thought. At least he wasn't always. He looked up to you somehow, admired you. But then something happened. Something happened to *him*, just like it happened to those six other people. Only for whatever reason, you didn't save him. Maybe you couldn't. Or maybe you made a choice, and saved somebody else.

"Think, Jonah. You know who this is. Whatever happened to him was so traumatic it turned a normal man into a monster. And he blames you."

Sarah caught her breath audibly. "Jonah."

"You know who it is?"

She looked at him, white-faced. "You said it yourself. That maybe you shouldn't have gotten him out of there. Because of all the pain. Months and months in the burn ward out in Nashville. Horrible, disfiguring scars. And then . . ."

It was Sam who asked. "What happened then? He survived the burns?"

Sarah was looking at Jonah as if she couldn't look away. "One of the few really bad car crashes we've had here. Five years ago. Bast—— Sebastian Gettys. He was driving too fast and missed a curve. Swerved, hit a culvert, and the car flipped. He'd been on his way home to cut the grass, and he had a can of gasoline in the back, a can with a loose lid. And the car had a faulty wire, one they'd recall the model for just the next year. The fire was . . . God, the fire. It was an inferno.

"We could hear the fire truck coming, but he was screaming." Sarah closed her eyes briefly. "I can still hear that screaming sometimes in my mind. You couldn't stand it. You grabbed a big wrench from your Jeep and somehow pulled the door open. He must have managed to get the seat belt undone, but he was still screaming, beating at the flames."

"You had a blanket ready," Jonah said numbly.

"We covered him, and smothered the flames. I'll never forget that horrible smell of burned flesh. And I'll never forget . . . when the EMS tech looked at him. You just . . . knew . . ."

"That I should have let him die," Jonah said.

"Your hands were bandaged for weeks," Sarah said.

Jonah looked down at strong hands unmarked, and said, "Surface burns. And I never scar. I didn't have a mark on me. But Bast . . ."

Sam waited a moment, then asked, "When did he come back to Serenity?"

"About a year ago," Jonah answered. "I went to see him, but he made it plain he really didn't want company. The car company had settled a fortune on him, took care of all his hospital bills. Set him up in a nice house just on the edge of town, with a great view. And a live-in caretaker."

"Because of the burns?" Sam asked.

"Some of his fingers had . . . fused." Jonah was still looking down at his own hands. "It was difficult for him to do some things. So she cooked and did the housekeeping. Supposed to keep him company, but he didn't want her . . . hovering. He could walk fine even though he limped, and sometimes at night he'd walk around, places he knew he wouldn't run into anybody else. He said he didn't need anybody else. He said he liked the night. He felt normal in the dark."

Lucas knew there was more. "Something else happened, didn't it? To Bast? Something that was . . . unfair? Something recent?"

"A stressor," Samantha said. "A final straw, something that set him off."

"Some people just . . . have the worst luck," Jonah said slowly. "The worst. He fell one day about four months ago. Just lost his balance and fell. So his caretaker called the doctor, over his objections. Within days he was back in Nashville for more tests."

When he fell silent, Sarah said, "We probably wouldn't have known until the end, if Bast had his way, but the doctors here had to know. And his caretaker. It was an inoperable tumor in his brain. They gave him six months. He didn't want anyone feeling sorry for him. And people did tend to avoid him if they could. Because there were changes right away. Small, at first. Losing his temper. Muttering to himself as he walked. We all tried to talk to him, but he'd just walk away. Into the dark."

Jonah drew in a deep breath and let it out slowly. "I saved his life. So he could spend years in a hell of agony, and then die with cancer eating at his brain."

"You couldn't have known," Sarah said.

"I don't think that's much of an excuse," Jonah said.

Samantha leaned forward, elbows on the table. "Jonah. Whatever happened to him, whatever he went through because you pulled him from a burning car, he went through because you weren't prepared to let him die without trying to save him. There's nothing wrong in that. It's one of the best instincts any human being can possess."

"Tell that to the six people he punished for it."

"He didn't punish them for that," Sam said.

Jonah frowned at her.

"You saved those six people, and their lives were just fine. They were alive because of you. He was alive because of you. But then he got cancer." She shook her head. "A doctor would know better, but I'm guessing where the cancer is, its location in his brain, is the reason why it's affected him the way it has. He needed someone to blame. He wanted someone to suffer. And while he was dealing with all that, he discovered that the tumor in his brain had given him something. Something special. A . . . final gift from a mocking fate."

"He was psychic," Jonah said.

BAST HAD THOUGHT it would be enough to watch Jonah suffer. He knew Jonah *had* suffered, was probably still suffering, but . . . that wasn't really what he was thinking about now.

Things kept getting mixed up in his mind. He wasn't even sure why he'd tried to make the telepath kill her partner. Except, maybe . . . he was jealous? No. Beauty and the Beast, that was just a fairy tale. But whenever he touched her mind, he felt . . . so much power. Power he didn't think even she was aware of.

He thought . . .

He *wondered* . . . if maybe she could heal him. If all that power she had could burn away this cancer growing in his brain. Before his skull burst open like an overripe melon.

It felt like that sometimes.

The pressure. The pain. The almost overwhelming urge to find a knife or a chisel and dig it all out of his brain.

Maybe she could do that.

Maybe . . . she was the answer to his prayers.

LUCAS SAID, "BRAIN tumors have been known to trigger psychic abilities. But it isn't a . . . normal trigger, for want of a better word. Instead of concentrating the ability, a tumor can disperse or diffuse it. It's unreliable, even more so than usual with a new psychic. It can be erratic, like a lightbulb getting brighter just before it burns out."

"He was able to control six people," Jonah said.

"*Control* is probably too strong a word. It was more like he . . . sent a jolt of power into each of their minds. The initial jolts allowed him to control them, just for a few minutes. Just long enough. Once he had them down in that cavern, I think he gave them another jolt—and drugs in those IVs. Not just nutrients.

"The doctors will know more once they've run tox screens, but I'm betting that's how he kept them still without having to tie them. There are drugs that do that. Keep the body completely immobile, but the mind alive, aware. And . . . slowly going crazy."

"What about Nessa?"

"I had a look at her chart. Her pediatrician noted that she had an unusually high metabolism. Probably never cause her a health problem in her life, and she'll stay enviably slim no matter what she eats. But she'll also react unpredictably to most medications. Her doctor advised caution and observation whenever she was given anything she'd never taken before. My bet is that her body reacted differently to the drug he used. She realized she could move, just as she told you.

And when she thought the time was right, that he wasn't down there with them anymore, she felt her way out."

There was a long silence, and then Dante said, "We'll have to bring him in. Arrest him. He killed Annie Duncan. Held the others prisoner and most likely destroyed at least a few of those lives."

"Yeah," Jonah said.

"I doubt he'll serve any time," Lucas said. "If he's as sick as I think he is, he'll probably be sent to a critical care hospital. And die there even before charges could be brought against him."

"Or maybe not."

They all nearly jumped out of their skins at the new voice, and yet froze at the same time. Because somehow, he had slipped behind one of the evidence boards—and now he was behind Dante, hauling him up from his chair.

He had a gun pointed at Dante's carotid.

And Bast Gettys was indeed a monster. His face was hideously deformed, one ear gone and the other hardly a twisted lump. His discolored head was bald with ropes of scar tissue, and the lack of eyebrows made him look vaguely surprised. More ropey scarring twisted around his face and neck, and disappeared beneath his shirt. The arm he held across Dante's neck and upper chest was the one with fingers fused. His other hand seemed perfectly comfortable holding the gun at Dante's neck.

"Bast, I'm the one you want." Jonah had managed to turn his chair just a bit, but he didn't want to rise until he had to, since it was impossible to hide the big silver gun he still wore.

"Well, I thought you were," Bast said in a reasonable tone, his head so close to Dante's it would have been difficult to slide a piece of paper between them. "I planned it all out. And it worked. I got the ones I wanted, the other ones you saved. I put them in a dark hole they'll never get out of, even if you carried their bodies out."

"Then you have your revenge, Bast."

"Revenge? It was never about revenge, Jonah. It was about fairness. You saved them, and they were all fine. They were living good lives. You saved me, and I was—I am—a monster. But even that wasn't unfair enough. I had to be something worse. So then I got cancer. I got this horrible black thing eating at my brain. Does that sound fair to you, Jonah?"

Dante spoke suddenly. "It sounds like life to me. Fair, unfair, we all get our share sooner or later. In this life or the next."

"Dante," Robbie said in a warning tone.

"What do you think, Bast?" Dante asked. "Do you think killing my friends will even the score? Do you think that'll make your cancer and your scars disappear?"

"I think *she* can. The telepath. I think she can make the cancer go away. I can see into her mind a little, and I think she can—"

The only thing they could all agree on afterward was that everything happened at once. There was a boom of thunder so loud it shook the building. The lights flickered. They could all see Dante reaching for Bast's gun, all of them knowing he would never make it before that tightening finger pulled the trigger.

All of them were rising from the table, most reaching for their guns. But Robbie held out one hand, stretching it toward the monster who was going to kill Dante.

There was another crash of thunder, this one accompanied by a bright flash of lightning.

That was what everyone said. That Jonah's big silver gun bucked in his hand just a second, a split second, after Bast blew a horribly big hole in Dante's neck. That Dante was falling boneless to the floor, his wide eyes already sightless, as Robbie stretched out her hand even farther and cried out an anguished, "No!"

And no one in the room said it might have been something other than Jonah's shot that took away Bast Getty's cancer for good. His cancer, and his scarred, scarred face and head.

Because it just exploded.

Like an overripe melon.

EPILOGUE

"Just tell me you didn't know it would happen," Robbie said steadily.

The storm continued to rumble around them as though trying to make up its mind whether to make an unutterably bad night even worse. The bodies of Sebastian Gettys and Dante Swann had been taken away by medics whose haunted faces were mute testimony that they had already seen too much for what had been a peaceful life in a small town.

And Bishop and Miranda had arrived.

Robbie was staring at Bishop, and he didn't look away.

"I didn't know it would happen. We didn't know it would happen." He never showed emotion much, Bishop, but the grief and anger in his pale sentry eyes were obvious, and the scar on his left cheek stood out whitely, more obvious than any of them had ever seen before.

Miranda stood beside him. Her fingers twined with his, and she said to Robbie, "We send teams out every time knowing it's possible.

Knowing that maybe our skill won't be good enough—or our luck will just run out." Her free hand lifted briefly, so briefly, to touch her lower abdomen, then fell away. "Even when we get the bad guys, we don't always win, Robbie. There's always a price. A price somebody has to pay. You know that."

"You're both here. I know that. Why weren't you here before? Why weren't you here in time to—to *do* something?"

"Man plans," Bishop said, "and the universe laughs. We should have been here hours ago. But the wind had taken down a huge tree, and there was no other way. Not even a place for a chopper to land. We had to wait for a road crew to clear it away."

Robbie's arms were crossed over her stomach, and her eyes were shiny. "I don't know if I believe you. I want you to know that."

"We do," Bishop said.

"What am I? Can you tell me that? What am I now?"

"You're a telepath, Robbie. You know that."

She drew a breath. "I know it wasn't just Jonah's bullet that took that monster's head off. I know it was mostly me. What I did. What did I do?"

Miranda glanced at her husband, then said steadily, "You wanted to save your partner. And that was enough to focus the energy inside you."

"And turn it into a weapon."

Bishop said, "All of our abilities can be used as weapons one way or another. If we need them to be badly enough. It's why we learn control, Robbie. It's why we test our limits."

Hardly louder than a whisper, Robbie said, "I should have read the fine print."

Sarah glanced at them, and then went to Robbie and took her arm. "I have a bottle of wine and a boyfriend I can kick out for the night," she said. "Come on."

It seemed that Robbie would resist for a moment, but then she allowed herself to be turned and guided, and Sarah took her out of the makeshift command center.

Miranda looked at Jonah, who was sitting at the conference table with his big gun lying on it, gazing at nothing.

"Jonah, there are always monsters," she said. She waited until he looked at her, then said, "Always. You didn't make Bast Gettys a monster any more than we made any one of our many enemies monsters. The world makes them. Fate makes them. Life makes them. All we can do is fight the ones in our paths."

"Do you really believe that?" he asked finally.

"I have to. There have been . . . a lot of monsters in my life. Personally and professionally. Battles I won, and battles I lost. Unbearable prices I had to pay. But I keep fighting, just like Noah fights, like our teams fight, because when we're done, there's usually one less monster in the world. And I can live with that."

"Teach me that, will you?" Jonah requested with a ghost of a smile.

"We were hoping you'd ask," Bishop said.

And Jonah had one of those feelings he'd had before, that everything was going to change.

This time, for the better.

SPECIAL CRIMES UNIT AGENT BIOS

(in order of appearance)

NOAH BISHOP—FBI SPECIAL CRIMES UNIT

Job: Unit chief, profiler, pilot, sharpshooter, and trained in martial arts.

Adept: An exceptionally powerful touch-telepath, he also shares with his wife a strong precognitive ability, the deep emotional link between them making them, together, far exceed the limits of the scale developed by the FBI to measure psychic talents. Also possesses an "ancillary" ability of enhanced senses (hearing, sight, scent), which he has trained other agents to use as well. Whether present in the flesh or not, Bishop always knows what's going on with his agents in the field. Always.

Appearances: *Stealing Shadows, Hiding in the Shadows, Out of the Shadows, Touching Evil, Whisper of Evil, Sense of Evil, Hunting Fear, Chill of Fear, Sleeping with Fear, Blood Dreams, Blood Sins, Blood Ties, Haven, Hostage, Haunted, Fear the Dark*

LUCAS JORDAN—FBI SPECIAL CRIMES UNIT

Job: Special Agent, profiler, weapons expert.

Adept: Neither fully telepathic nor empathic, Luke nevertheless possesses a combination of both abilities, the sum of which enables him to quite often find people who are lost. Lost by accident, the victims of crimes, even sometimes abducted and taken far away. And yet when he is able to use his abilities, Luke can feel the pain and fear of someone in trouble, even home in on their location. It's an ability he's worked very hard to master, and his control has improved steadily since joining the SCU—and since Samantha came back into his life.

Appearances: *Hunting Fear, Fear the Dark*

SAMANTHA JORDAN—FBI SPECIAL CRIMES UNIT

Job: Special Agent, profiler—and excels at a number of esoteric skills picked up in her life growing up in a carnival.

Adept: Seer, clairvoyant. Precognition is not an ability she controls, but she is able, with astonishing power and accuracy, to pick up information by touching objects. And sometimes by touching people. She is also linked in a very real way to her husband, that contact helping him to focus his abilities—and enabling him to pull his wife from whatever distant place or time her abilities take her; each is in a very real sense the anchor for the other.

Appearances: *Hunting Fear, Fear the Dark*

MIRANDA BISHOP—FBI SPECIAL CRIMES UNIT

Job: Special Agent, investigator, profiler, black belt in karate, and a sharpshooter.

Adept: Touch-telepath, seer, remarkably powerful, and possesses unusual control, particularly in a highly developed shield capable of protecting herself psychically, a shield she's able to extend beyond herself to protect others. Shares abilities with her husband, due to their intense emotional connection, and together they far exceed the scale developed by the SCU to measure psychic abilities.

Appearances: *Out of the Shadows, Touching Evil, Whisper of Evil, Sense of Evil, Hunting Fear, Chill of Fear, Blood Dreams, Blood Sins, Blood Ties, Hostage, Haunted, Fear the Dark*

ROBBIE HODGE—FBI SPECIAL CRIMES UNIT

Job: Special Agent, profiler-in-training, proficient with most firearms, and possesses a black belt in judo.

Adept: A born telepath, she's able to read roughly half the people she encounters, and possesses the added ability to telepathically coax some memories from a willing subject. Is also, possibly because of the strength of her shield, the rare psychic able to wear a watch.

Appearances: *Fear the Dark*

DANTE SWANN—FBI SPECIAL CRIMES UNIT

Job: Special Agent, profiler-in-training, and has expert computer skills.

Adept: Reluctant medium, very strong shields. Dante is still coming to terms with his abilities, though he's had them for a number of years. He enjoys the puzzles of investigative work, and though he is not dependent on his own abilities, he deeply appreciates the abilities of the psychics with whom he works.

Appearances: *Fear the Dark*

PSYCHIC TERMS AND ABILITIES

(as Classified/Defined by Bishop's Team and by Haven)

Adept: The general term used to label any functional psychic; the specific ability is much more specialized.

Clairvoyance: The ability to know things, to pick up bits of information, seemingly out of thin air.

Dream-projecting: The ability to enter another's dreams.

Dream-walking: The ability to invite/draw others into one's own dreams.

Empath: A person who experiences the emotions of others, often up to and including physical pain and injuries.

Healing: The ability to heal injuries to self or others, often but not always ancillary to mediumistic abilities.

Healing Empathy: The ability to not only feel but also heal the pain/injury of another.

Latent: The term used to describe unawakened or inactive abilities, as well as to describe a psychic not yet aware of being psychic.

Mediumistic: Having the ability to communicate with the dead.

Precognition: The ability to correctly predict future events.

Psychometric: The term used to describe the ability to pick up impressions or information from touching objects.

Regenerative: The term used to describe the ability to heal one's own injuries/illnesses, even those considered by medical experts to be lethal or fatal. (A classification unique to one SCU operative and considered separate from a healer's abilities.)

Spider Sense: The ability to enhance one's normal senses (sight, hearing, smell, etc.) through concentration and the focusing of one's own mental and physical energy.

Telekinesis: The ability to move objects with the mind.

Telepathic mind control: The ability to influence/control others through mental focus and effort; an extremely rare ability.

Telepathy (touch and non-touch or open): The ability to pick up thoughts from others. Some telepaths only receive, while others have the ability to send thoughts. A few are capable of both, usually due to an emotional connection with the other person.

UNNAMED ABILITIES:

The ability to see into time, to view events in the past, present, and future without being or having been there physically while the events transpired.

The ability to see the aura or another person's energy field.

The ability to channel energy usefully as a defensive or offensive tool or weapon.

BISHOP/SCU STORY TIMELINE

For readers who wish to "place" each of these stories in time, I should explain that—in order to not age my characters too quickly—I have not set these books in real time, but in "story" time. Roughly speaking, each trilogy within the series takes place within the space of a year or a bit less.

In simple terms, if you look at the information offered below, you'll see that from the time the Special Crimes Unit was formally introduced in *Out of the Shadows* until the events in this story, *Fear the Dark*, only about five years have passed *within the series*. (The Special Crimes Unit was being built and developed by Bishop for about three or four years prior to that, but in *Out of the Shadows* the story of the unit, of Bishop and Miranda, and Bishop and his team, really begins.)

Stealing Shadows—February

Hiding in the Shadows—October/November

YEAR ONE:

Out of the Shadows—January (SCU formally introduced)

Touching Evil—November

YEAR TWO:

Whisper of Evil—March

Sense of Evil—June

Hunting Fear—September

YEAR THREE:

Chill of Fear—April

Sleeping with Fear—July

Blood Dreams—October

YEAR FOUR:

Blood Sins—January

Blood Ties—April

Haven—July

Hostage—October

YEAR FIVE:

Haunted—February

Fear the Dark—May